AS D.T. NEAL

THE WOLFSHADOW TRILOGY
Saamaanthaa
The Happening
Norm

Lupinia:
The Selected Poems of Polly Drinkwater, 2007–2015
A Wolfshadow Book

NOVELS
Chosen
Suckage
The Cursed Earth

NOVELLAS
Relict
Summerville
The Day of the Nightfish

COLLECTIONS
The Thing in Yellow
Singularities

AS DAVE NEAL

THE SHUTTERCLIQUE
Brighteyes—Book 1
Inferna—Book 2
Tantrum—Book 3

RETURN TO SUMMERVILLE

D.T. NEAL

RETURN TO SUMMERVILLE

CHICAGO | PITTSBURGH

RETURN TO SUMMERVILLE
© 2024 by D. T. Neal. All Rights Reserved.

ISBN-13: 978-1-944286-84-2

Published by Nosetouch Press
www.nosetouchpress.com

For more information about bulk purchases, please contact Nosetouch Press at info@nosetouchpress.com.

Cataloging-in-Publication Data
Names: Neal, D.T., author.
Title: Return to Summerville / D.T. Neal
Description: Chicago, IL : Nosetouch Press [2024]
Identifiers: ISBN: 9781944286842 (paperback)
Subjects: LCSH: Horror—Fiction. | Ecofiction—Fiction. |
GSAFD: Horror fiction. | BISAC: FICTION / Horror.

Cover & interior designed by
Christine M. Scott, Clever Crow Consulting and Design
www.clevercrow.com

The text for this book was set in Minion Pro.

*For all the sons and daughters of
Madame Summerville, wherever you have landed.*

*And to John Wyndham,
who planted the seeds and let them grow.*

CONTENTS

PART III: DOWNSTREAM

[Editor's Note: What follows is a collection of collateral material related to what happened in the ghost town of Summerville, South Carolina. I collected and curated this content roughly six months after the events documented here took place. I can't speak to the veracity of the claims made here; I can only attest to having come across this by means of some files shared under the names "Summerville Diaries" and such being passed around after *The Seen* indie web studio server was hacked and burned in a tragically suspicious fire.

The Summerville Slaughter referenced herein has been considered a closed case by the local law enforcement. However, upon reviewing this material, I think the reader may find plenty of unanswered questions needing answers.

Where there was need for commentary in this material, I added comments, indicated by brackets and italics. I hope this helps and isn't too intrusive. The truth of what happened will come out eventually, no matter how hard they try to keep it concealed. —Lyle Hawthorne, Editor-At-Large and author of *The Unseen: The Lost Episode*]

0

NO LONGER SLEEPING, Summerville stirred in the hot winds that scoured the South Carolina landscape that formed in the wake of an ever-warming world. The time was right, the harvest was ready. The ripened seeds were spreading, carried forth with zeal borne not on the wings of wasps, but in other ways known only to the whispers of water and wind.

Vines flexed and grasped, and the swaybacked spirit of the dead town flourished, laying claim to the wooded land around it.

Even venerable kudzu could find no purchase where Her vines grew, choking out rivals with a natural malice that formed the heart of an ancient and alien urge. Whether a rogue weed or a hothouse debutante gone wild, Madame Summerville knew and grew, a sense of destiny bound up in every shoot, blossom, branch, and berry.

The others who had come had not quite known their danger, for in that time, She had drowsed through Her days and nights, not accustomed to visitors. Now, however, as wildfires burned and storms regularly tossed the land, something had occurred inside Her, a desire that was inherent to all that lives—a desire to survive.

Accidental acolytes had carried Her green gospel far afield, but She was no longer content with fickle, if fortuitous, happenstance. She wanted more, required more, demanded more. Each seed was sacred, an unspoken promise of propagation. And She had so many seeds to spread, if She was to be Queen to wear the crown that was Hers alone.

It didn't matter how long She had been there; all that mattered was that She *was* there, and in so being, the rest of Her ambition could be sown in fruitful soil, where She might hold sway for eternity.

Her little wasps—Her handmaidens—had guarded Her well, with the mindless, mechanistic ardor of arthropods. But what She had in mind, if "mind" could even describe the way She worked, was something far grander than what might be carried on the translucent wings of willful wasps.

She had no eyes as we might understand them, but could still see what needed to be done, and what needed to be done was a kind of exodus, a journey beyond the close-knit confines of Summerville, where She had first taken root. It would always be a special place, a sacred space, but She had outgrown it.

There would be others—other acolytes, other shrines, other places, where She might thrive. Only when She was in many places would She be satisfied. And for that, She required missionaries and evangelists.

This required a gentler touch, and, as Her blossoms covered the faces of infidels, pumping them with seeds to germinate inside them, to burst and ripen when they were ready. Always when the time was right, venturing far and wide, by day or night.

She held them in Her vines while they slept deeply on beds of Her heart-shaped leaves, the sharpened edges away from them, providing only comfort and succor as She fed them and sustained them, impregnating them with Her sovereign seed. For any who carried Her seeds to term, there was a unique desire that took root within them, an urge to wander. How far they wandered depended on them.

Blossom had traveled far away, but She could still feel Her daughter, so far from home. It was as it should be, and as Her leaves shook, Her vines twitched, Her flowers bobbed, Madame Summerville found that She was content to wait for far more vessels to arrive.

But not *too* long.

PART I

THE NARRATIVES

ONE

[This appears to be a transcription and or dramatization of real events. The people referenced here have been verified as being central to the Summerville Slaughter. As above, it's unclear who wrote this, except that they had access to some of the original source material that has since gone missing. —Ed.]

"ARE WE THERE, YET?" asked Jeph Wales, sitting in the back of the Fawcett Biotech van. The drone jockey was eager to get to flying. The driver, Glen Fields, wasn't inclined to answer. Fawcett Biotech had a problem on their hands in Summerville. Or, more precisely, with something that had gotten out of hand. And Jeph and Glen had been tapped to solve it, without being entirely in the loop as to what senior leadership had in mind.

The two of them couldn't be more different—Jeph was white, short, and blonde, bespectacled, freckle-faced and sharp-tongued, his hair naturally half-assed curly, more so in the balmy Carolinas climate. Baby-faced and sedentary, Jeph did his best work half-slouching in chairs.

Glen was tan, tall, and brown-haired, his hair cropped militarily close. His soldierly face looked carved from mahogany, the product of enough sun-soaked fieldwork effort that gave him an almost priestly demeanor, like someone searching vainly for the Fountain of Youth in unfamiliar places and always failing to find it. Not old by any means, but he was weathered.

"I said—" Wales began.

"I heard you," Fields replied. "We're almost there. Or almost to the almost-there. You should be riding shotgun, you know. I'm not your damned chauffeur."

Wales hopped into the passenger seat, hands raised in cynical surrender and mock-supplication.

"Just getting Charlene ready," Wales said. He always named his drones. For a drone jockey, it only seemed appropriate. Fields was beyond such sentimentality, but didn't judge him for it.

Fields glanced at his coworker, drumming his fingers on the steering wheel as he drove.

"Why 'Charlene' anyway?" he asked.

"Cuz she's nosy," Wales said. "Like my ex."

"Ah," Fields said. They both saw the Circle K at the same time, and Fields pulled them in to get some gasoline. "I'll fuel up while you hit the head."

"Yeah, alright," Wales said, getting out. Fields scanned the Circle K a moment before he got out, a squint of his hazel eyes taking in an out-of-the-way filling station with a lot of old, dead cars on the week-choked side lot. Sun-kissed it wasn't; it was bleached by the daily onslaught of southern sunshine.

This Fawcett job was a simple one, made more complicated by the hush-hush expectations of the team leads.

"We need you and Jeph to survey Summerville," Johnny Wyndham had said, looking hard in Glen's face with his black-rimmed eyeglasses, his balding head and sandy beard carefully pruned and tended. "We have reason to expect some genetic drift from proprietary product in the area. You and Jeph are to conduct the survey."

"Seems like biologist work, Johnny," Fields said.

"Not quite," Wyndham said. "You and Jeph are what we need. Patented Pest Control."

The two of them were on-call troubleshooters at Fawcett. They worked in Fawcett's fields, dealing with pests that might afflict any of Fawcett's prized pet produce. Wales specialized in bugs, while Fields dealt with weeds. Fields assumed that if Fawcett was sending them out to Summerville, it's because they didn't want things getting out. Keeping it internal was most important to the company. The briefing had been circumspect even by Fawcett standards, showing a map of the ghost town, which was encircled by the Black River and hadn't seen ordinary human activity since the 1950s.

"Seems like overkill," Fields said. "What are we looking at, exactly?"

Wyndham looked almost pleased with himself at the secrets he was entrusted to keep.

"Summerville's been a ghost town for decades," Wyndham said. "We have reason to believe that some of our patented super-foods blew downwind and polluted the town. We need you two to inspect it and give us a report on the damage. Early reports have told us that there are active, aggressive wasp communities there. We think maybe Asian Giant Hornets, or some other species that's like them but even more hostile to intruders. That's Jeph's problem. You're to inspect the town and see how much weed activity is there, so we can come up with countermeasures."

So long as the pay was there (and it was), Fields was fine with it. After Iraq and Afghanistan, Fields took the work he was given, without too many questions. He gave Wyndham trouble because he didn't like the man very much. His penchant for micro-managing mixed with plausible deniability made him a frustrating boss.

"You already send somebody else?" Fields asked. "If it's been there for decades, seems like a problem that could've been solved years ago."

Wyndham just raised his eyebrows and clammed up, and Fields doubted he'd get more out of the man.

"This ain't full service, Son," came the voice of an old man, breaking Glen's reverie. He glanced at the Circle K proprietor, who was an old man with a baleful gaze, wearing a well-worn Fawcett Biotech ballcap that had been bleached so forcefully to qualify more as salvage than contraband. Fields glanced at it, and at the man, before stepping out. He was well over a head taller than the old man, who held his gaze a bit defiantly by Glen's estimation.

"Yeah, I gotcha," Fields said, noting his own Fawcett golf shirt, yellow with the logo in blue at his left breast. "Nice cap."

"It'll do until another comes along," the man said.

"Glen Fields, Sir," Glen said, holding out a hand, which the old man shook with his own swollen knuckles, cool to the touch.

"Cooper DeVille," the man said. "Owner and operator of this here Circle K. You Fawcett boys lost or what?"

"Nope," Fields said, circling back to fill up the van.

"Summerville, then," DeVille said. "It's *always* Summerville with you Fawcett people, isn't it?"

"Is it?" Fields asked, letting the pump do its thing.

"People go looking now and then," DeVille said. "On account of the disappearances."

"Oh, yeah?" Fields asked, resisting the urge to light up while the gas pumped.

"Sure as the day is long," DeVille said. "Kids just love the Jut. What's that the shrinks call it? The 'Lure of the Void'—that's what it is. Draws people in. The wasps don't like tourists so much."

"We're not tourists," Fields said.

DeVille watched him a moment, his old, wrinkled face all Up-country-inscrutable.

"No, I suppose you're not," DeVille said. "You military?"

"Ex," Fields said. "Rangers."

"Well, I thank you for your service," DeVille said. "I was Navy, myself."

Fields resisted the urge to ask which war. Likely Vietnam, although he didn't want to be rude by prying. It was the only war that made sense with a man like DeVille.

"We're a long way from the sea, Mr. DeVille," Fields said.

"That we are," DeVille said. "Them hurricanes don't exactly make a fella feel welcome on the coast. More every year. And as for the Navy, I did my time with honor. The sea and me, we reached what you'd call an understanding."

Fields looked around them, at the tinder-dry grassy fields acting as veritable amber waves in the wind. The wind toyed with them with unseen, not entirely playful fingers. There was a frenetic feel to it. A storm was coming, Fields guessed.

"Looks dry enough," Fields said.

DeVille nodded, squinting along with Fields.

"Drought's a four-letter word in these parts," DeVille said. "But I think we'll get some rain yet. What're you two looking for in Summerville, anyway?"

"Company business," Fields said.

"Now *that* sure sounds important," DeVille said. The door to the Circle K opened with a jangle of bells, and Jeph stood there with a couple of gallons of water and some fruit pies in hand, as well as some beers.

"Am I supposed to just walk out with these or what?" he asked. DeVille chuckled, shaking his head as he turned to face Jeph.

"Duty calls," DeVille said. "Nice jawing with you, Ranger."

Fields watched the man shuffle back to his store, while Jeph glanced back at him, grinning. The van had its thirst quenched, the pump switching off. Glen settled up with that and walked away from the pumps, taking a moment to have that smoke.

Stepping away from the blanched brick of the filling station, this oasis of civilization gave Glen a moment to himself to take things in. All those old cars, some with FOR SALE signs, just sitting there. The weeds growing up around them, since many of them had been here for quite some time. None of them had license plates, and Glen wondered where they'd come from.

He could hear crickets in the fields, and the lazy song of cicadas in the breezy trees. Along with the hot and humid wind, the bright blue of the sky and the fluffy cotton clouds up in the sky, it was pretty. One could feel away from it all here. Whatever the concerns of the world were, they weren't in this place. He imagined old DeVille sitting in that rocking chair he had out front and just rocking himself to sleep, soothed by the sounds.

There was a makeshift stand near the cars, a whitewashed clapboard thing with three rows on it, with these pretty little plants in little pots, lined up carefully. The plants were little more than saplings, with fist-sized flowers blooming on them, one to a pot, the blossoms a beautiful red with white and black highlights to them. Fields knew them to be Fawcett flowers by the look of them, reminiscent of what was growing at nearby Facility Seven.

He imagined that Wyndham would blow a gasket to see them growing here.

They seemed to sway of their own volition, and more than a few wasps flew to them. There was a hand-painted sign above the display:

SUMMERVIOLETS, $5

"Summerviolets," Fields said, taking a drag and shaking his head.

"Summerviolets," DeVille said, having appeared again, while Jeph was walking over with two paper bags of groceries in his arms.

"No such thing," Fields said, which made DeVille smile.

"Maybe not, but catchy all the same," DeVille said. "Can I interest you Fawcett boys in one or two?"

Fields held up two fingers, slipping ten dollars to DeVille with his other hand. The old man seemed to like that, as Fields took a couple of choice ones from the stand. If nothing else, it would be worth showing Wyndham that the locals were selling them. He savored the daydream of watching Wyndham lose his mind over it.

"Summerviolet's a robust plant," DeVille said. "As comfortable in sun and shade, and with a powerful thirst. You keep them watered, and they'll grow just fine. They smell nice. Go on, take a sniff, tell me that's not heavenly ambrosia, Ranger."

Glen brought the plant close to his nose and took its scent, and, he had to admit, it smelled good. It had hints of cinnamon and citrus to it, more than a bit of Angostura bitters to the aroma. DeVille's face cracked into a grin as he watched Fields smell the plant. They smelled like the groves of the stuff Fawcett grew. One and the same.

"Ain't nothing in the ever-lovin' world like that," DeVille said. Fields held out one of the plants to Jeph, who shook his head, looking either disgusted or unmanned at the prospect of smelling a flower.

"Trying to quit," Jeph said.

"Summerviolets never let go," DeVille said. "You be good to them, they'll grow on you and hold fast."

Fields looked around them, not seeing any trace of plants like these around.

"Where'd you get these?" Fields asked.

"Summerville, naturally," DeVille said. "Madame Summerville grows thick there."

Glen wasn't going to break it to DeVille, but he was certain these 'summerviolets' were likely part of the genetic drift that Wyndham was fretting about. Made him wish they'd brought along a botanist, made him wonder why they hadn't. Probably cheaper just to have the two of them do the preliminary field-work before they brought in the biotechnicians or plant biologists. Fawcett always tried to cut corners where it could, at least where staff was concerned.

"Madame Summerville," Jeph said. "That sounds real classy, Mr. DeVille."

"She is," DeVille said. "Oh, She sure is. You boys be careful out there, now."

"We will," Fields said, disposing of his cigarette in a weatherworn cement urn at the edge of the station, before getting into the van with Jeph. Fields put the summerviolets in the coffee holders in the back, while Jeph was stowing the feedbags, including pouring bags of ice into their Fawcett-branded cooler, where he had stuffed tallboy cans of Miller High Life.

They waved at DeVille as they drove off, Jeph shaking his head, downing a Thirst energy drink in its fancy blue and orange can, whistling between gulps.

"That old coot was older than old," Jeph said. "I bet he fought the Union back in the day."

"Sure," Fields said. "Let's get where we're going."

"You saw I got us some beers and ice for the cooler, by the way," Jeph said. "You're welcome."

Fields remembered that he forgot to ask DeVille about all the cars on that side lot. Ah, well. He'd ask him when they were done with Summerville.

"I saw," Fields said, glancing back at the Circle K, where DeVille had taken a seat in his rocking chair. "I'll treat on the way back."

TWO

"WHAT AM I LOOKING AT, Ms. Rivers?" Tyler asked, having been called over by the erstwhile hostess of *The Seen*, an indie documentary show that had gotten enough audience to qualify as a job for them and their pals, Justin and Sharon, who handled the filming and sound production.

Holly was ebullient, unveiling the big car from beneath the light blue tarp, revealing a glorious baby blue Cadillac Eldorado convertible with white leather seats.

"This is Ladygirl, Mr. Finn," Holly said. "Won by me at a police auction not three weeks ago."

Holly had black hair she wore short in a pixie-cut that accentuated her big brown eyes and carefree journalistic grin and penchant for preppy white attire that made her look fresh from the country club. She was, in fact, a 29-year-old nepo baby of a family country club dynasty, being the Rivers Glen Country Club near Charleston, having belt-sanded away any trace of a southern accent in her bid to be accessibly coquettish across the country.

Tyler was a 31-year-old black man from DC and had cultivated his own Mid-Atlantic beach goth vibe with carefully selected skull-and-crossbones Hawaiian shirts that accentuated his curly auburn hair that danced just above his shoulders. His blue eyes were carefully screened behind his blue Persol sunglasses, giving him an otherworldly intensity to his gaze that jousted daily with his studiously laconic manner.

The two of them had crossed paths at Georgetown, where they'd first conjured up *The Seen* after some boozy brainstorming that had eventually roped in Sharon Thatcher and Justin Sawyer, who were the audiovisual beating heart of *The Seen*. After a few successfully viral projects, Holly had started calling them "The Fantastic Foursome" and it had stuck.

Sharon Thatcher was a 27-year-old from Paterson, New Jersey, and had a bob of hair almost as black as Holly's, although hers was bottle-fed to the point of outright affectation, with her widow's peak as an emphatic bit of punctuation to whatever statement she was making. She was prone to wearing overlarge sunglasses that gave her a cryptic bearing she accentuated with an almost exclusively black wardrobe. A graduate from Rutgers with a degree in Music Theory, a bad vibraphone-related audition experience had led her to being more comfortable with sound production than performance.

Justin Sawyer hailed from Richmond, Virginia, and at 28 years of age, visually offered a contrast to Sharon's austere Neo-Goth Revival look. He was more inclined to languid beachwear that trended toward pastel button-downs paired with seersucker pants and sandals. His handsomely tanned face and sun-swaddled light brown hair gave him a basic breeziness that played well with any women who saw him. Justin was a graduate of the

Savannah College of Art and Design with emphasis in video production. He had been an avid art filmmaker, with more technical proficiency than artistic ability, although this wasn't something he'd ever accept. Justin had met Sharon at the Folkfire Festival at Chapel Hill, North Carolina, and had formed an erstwhile creative partnership that had led to them running into Holly and Tyler at just the right time.

The Seen was an ongoing web series where they delved into missing persons cold cases and shed light on the disappeared. While not entirely altruistic, *The Seen* had at least earned some indieground notoriety for cracking some of those old, cold cases, offering closure—if not happy endings—in most cases. In America, if someone disappeared, it was usually for a bad reason. *The Seen* team never flinched, even in the face of those dark stories.

"Ladygirl," Tyler said. "And you know this how?"

Holly pointed to the words "Ladygirl" engraved on the expansive dashboard, in what looked to be a nice chrome placard somebody had spent money to get.

"This is the vehicle driven by Ashley Talulah Graham," Holly said, referring to someone Tyler had heard of, because of Holly's research. The story had been that the car had been found abandoned on the Duke campus with the keys in the ignition, and with Ashley Talulah Graham's rucksack in the trunk, and nothing else to identify the owner of the car, save for the registration of one Ethan Allen, a divorce lawyer at Garrett & Barry operating out of Charleston, who had similarly disappeared two years earlier.

The Eldorado had been impounded by the police, where it had been held for a time.

"Why'd you bid on the car?" Tyler asked.

"Because it's part of the mystery of the disappearance of Ashley Talulah Graham, Tyler," Holly said. "There's a story here."

She opened the driver's side of Ladygirl and got in, patting the seat next to her. Tyler knew better than to resist, getting in beside her. It was a big old car, impossibly wide.

Holly keyed the ignition and Ladygirl sprang to life, the ragtop coming down. They backed up, and Tyler admittedly savored the smooth ride of it. Nobody made cars like this anymore. He could only imagine how much gas this monstrosity of steel, chrome, glass, and leather would guzzle.

"She drives like a dream," Holly said. "And speaking of dreams, riddle me this: how does Ashley Talulah Graham's backpack end up in this car, parked at Duke, without a sign of Miss Graham or Mister Ethan Allen? It's a mystery."

"Yeah," Tyler said. "Got it. If you're asking these questions, I'm thinking you already have some answers?"

Holly slipped on her aviator shades and smiled at him.

"I do," she said. "Two years ago, Ethan Allen disappeared, along with Miss Graham, and several of Allen's friends—Kyle Walker, Joshua Kane, and Savannah Greene. All of them disappeared without a trace at roughly the same time."

Tyler didn't even want to inquire how Holly had divined this information. Her methods were integral to her maddening instinct for good stories that played well with podcasting, social media, livestreaming, blogging, and the rest that they did for *The Seen*. She was the host, he was the writer/producer; it was not incumbent on him to sleuth out her sleuthing.

"I know this because their families filed missing persons reports on them," Holly said. "The cluster of them had me looking into it. Walker worked as an accountant at Fawcett Biotech, while Josh Kane was a scuba instructor. Savannah Greene worked as an executive manager at a local realtor. Cell phone records have them together leading up to their disappearances. They crossed paths with Ashley Graham at a Piggly-Wiggly off of Route 521."

"The cops would have investigated this," Tyler said. "Yes?"

"Of course," Holly said. "They looked into it. But get this: the cell records for everybody else drop out at this old ghost town—Summerville—not a half hour from a Circle K. Only Ashley Graham's tracks from there to Duke."

"Meaning?" Tyler asked.

Holly enjoyed cruising in Ladygirl, he could tell by the way she smilingly eyed the Charleston locals who stared at them as they drove by with looks of wonder and envy. Ty tried not to be self-conscious as a black man being driven around town by a white woman, but he could feel the eyes on them all the same. There was something slyly ostentatious about such a willfully luxurious car, and the convertible qualities it possessed made it even more apparent.

"I don't know," Holly said. "But I think *The Seen* needs to look into this, Tyler. I've been laying the groundwork for weeks."

Tyler was already scrolling through his phone, the keywords like incantations:

> Ashley Talulah Graham
> Ethan Allen
> Kyle Walker
> Joshua Kane
> Savannah Greene
> Summerville
> Duke University

"There's two Summervilles," Tyler said.

"The dead one," Holly said. "The ghost town."

"Okay," Tyler said, seeing shots of a yellow STOP sign and vines. Someplace called "The Jut."

"The area police checked it out," Holly said. "No signs of foul play. Just an old, dead town, overgrown with kudzu or whatever. And lots of wasps."

Tyler didn't like that. He hated wasps. Their aggression put him off.

"I don't want to get stung," Tyler said.

"Oh, Tyler, come on," Holly said. "We'll bring beekeeper suits and bug spray. We'll take precautions. The key is the story."

Holly was rabid in her pursuit of stories for *The Seen*. It was that determination that helped make them relevant in the hoary world of indie media. Not that this was any guarantee of success; their audience fluctuated depending on the story, which caused Ty no end of worry. What they needed was a steadily upward trajectory, versus the hit-or-miss that plagued their line of business. Yesterday's darlings became tomorrow's pariahs.

"What are you proposing, then?" Tyler asked.

"Field trip for *The Seen*," Holly said. "We get Sharon and Justin on-board, we trek out to that ghost town, we explore it. If nothing else, if there's zilch worth filming there, we'll sell the *mystery* of it. People love that. They can write their own endings. Speaking of that, when I bid on Ladygirl, you would not believe it: Ethan Allen's sister, Isabella Allen, bid for it, too. You should have seen the look on her face when I landed the final bid."

Tyler could only imagine, but he knew Holly well enough to know that it would've only been an enticement. Holly relished any challenges that appeared.

"Seems harsh," Tyler said. "She wanted her brother's car back."

Holly had money, had always grown up with it, so for her, an auction was like bouncing on a trampoline—it was just a petty amusement. Tyler felt bad for anyone getting in Holly's way.

"She confronted me after the auction," Holly said. "Pretty woman, in a *very* ordinary sort of way—straw-colored hair, like in her 30s. 'That's my brother's car,' she said. 'He's gone missing. He loved Ladygirl more than life itself. He would have died before abandoning her like that.' And you know I told her about what I did with *The Seen*, how I was going to find out what happened to Ethan. Didn't make her any less miffed at me for outbidding her. I told her I'd get her closure on what happened to her brother, but it didn't mollify her."

Tyler wasn't going to debate it with Holly. There was no point. The deed was done. The car was hers.

"Where are we going, anyway?" Tyler asked, looking around them.

"We're just driving, Ty," Holly said. "Driving and discussing."

As they made their way through Charleston's pretty streets, Tyler was already forming plans for how *The Seen* would get to Summerville, even as clouds clotted overhead, blocking the sun, making it seem like rain would fall at some point soon.

Driving in a convertible made one more weather-aware than normal. He chose not to see it as an omen.

THREE

GLEN AND JEPH reached Summerville by midday, and the two of them parked the van on the broken road that ended in the Jut, opting for a leisurely air-conditioned lunch before they got to work. One of the things Glen enjoyed about fieldwork was not having bosses breathing down his neck. Still, he called in to Fawcett on their radio.

"Dispatch, this is Fields and Wales at the Summerville site," he said. "We've just arrived. We'll call in once the work's done."

"Copy that, Glen," Dispatch said. "Be careful out there."

Fields sat back and cracked one of those cooler beers that Jeph had bought, while eating a ham sandwich. The dead end of the Jut was just that—a spar of broken road that led to the tree-choked ghost down, which, despite the drought, was green and well-shaded.

Somebody had slapdashedly spraypainted "THE JUT" on the road, using yellow paint. There was a kind of scarecrow somebody had tethered to the STOP sign with some rope. It was wearing a well-weathered Fawcett Biotech Hazmat suit, the Fawcett lozenge on its chest, and somebody had done target practice on it with yellow-and-black–feathered arrows, a trio of them clustered at the logo, right over the heart. The scarecrow wore a dusty gas mask and was wearing a crown of dried vines around its head.

"Nice welcome," Jeph said, eating a chicken breast sandwich. "You think there's somebody in that suit?"

Glen shrugged. "Damned if I know. The cops were here. They'd probably have taken that down if they'd seen it. Likely folks with strong opinions about Fawcett."

"Did Fawcett send other people out here ahead of us?" Jeph asked. Fields sighed.

"Like I just said—damned if I know," Fields replied. Although he was sure others had been here before. Redundancy was one of Fawcett's baselines—the right hand might not know what the left hand was doing, but both were damned sure doing something.

The way the scarecrow just hung there on the sign, Glen didn't think there could be somebody in there. Those Hazmat suits were like jumpsuits—one-piece numbers you zipped up into. He'd worn his share at Facility Seven, tending the crops there, back when there was worry about weeds encroaching on the varietals.

"You think that's someone we know?" Jeph asked.

"You're the drone pilot," Glen said. "Why don't you send Charlene over there to check it out while I eat my lunch?"

Jeph looked almost defensive. Of course he could take the drone.

"You know what? I will, like, as a warmup," he said, stepping into the back of the van to get Charlene prepped.

"You do that," Fields said, taking a welcome swig of cold beer. "I'll watch from here."

Charlene was a bugbuster drone, equipped with a mint soapy-spray solution that was considered safer than more conventional insecticides. Fawcett had been making use of them in their experimental fields more routinely over the past few years. The other nozzle—one that Jeph was particularly proud of—was a flamethrower connected to an incendiary homebrew of Jeph's own design.

Jeph got outside and set up his drone rig, sending Charlene up, holding her position while he went back into the welcoming cool of the van.

Glen half-watched, glancing at Jeph in the rearview mirror as he stumbled around in there. He had a chair where he could sit and pilot the drone from a comfortable position.

"Alright," Jeph said, flipping on some monitor screens that tracked what Charlene was seeing. The whir of the drone could be heard through the closed windows of the van, and Glen watched its shadow move over the Jut, nimbly arcing to level with the scarecrow. "Can't see through the mask goggles. I could probably cut the ropes on it."

"Yeah, maybe do that," Glen said. "Set the sucker free."

"You got it," Jeph said, carefully moving Charlene toward the rope binding the figure, pivoting it to reveal a set of shears on an armature that grasped the rope.

"I thought you were going to use the rotor blades," Glen said.

"And ruin Charlene? Not a chance," Jeph said, pushing a button that caused the shears to clip the rope, making the effigy list to one side. He then made it clip the other ropes, and the thing pitched forward in a pile.

"Cool toy," Glen said, taking his beer and hopping out to check out the fallen scarecrow, which was at the edge of the Jut. The old STOP sign bore silent witness.

Fields didn't think there'd be anybody inside of it, but effigies were creepy enough on their own, and he'd take some comfort knowing it wasn't holding a body.

Outside, there was only the heat and humidity, the calling of the crickets, and the whirring of Charlene overhead. At the edge of the Jut, he could see the emerald tangle of the ghost town in the shadows, overgrown with leafy vines and big-ass versions of the summerviolet flowers he'd picked up at the Circle K. He'd meant to ask why he called them "summerviolets" at all, given that they were red, and not violet at all. At Fawcett, they were called "Varietal V"—any other names for it were closely guarded by the company.

"What do you see, Glen?" Jeph asked from their walkie talkie link.

Glen ignored him, walking up to the mangled scarecrow, giving it a soft kick. The thing rolled over easily and was clearly empty. He tugged off the mask and saw just a knot of dried vine in the suit. Despite the arrows sticking out of it, there was nobody inside of the suit. Glen didn't know whether to be relieved or disappointed by the revelation.

"Nothing here," Glen said into his walkie talkie. "Just dust and dried vine. No bones or body. All clear."

Charlene hovered overhead, looking this way and that, expertly flown by Jeph. Glen tugged at the arrows sticking out of the chest of the effigy, then knelt and took out his pocket knife and cut them loose.

"Broadheads," Glen said, holding them up. "Also, these look like crossbow bolts, not arrows."

"I wouldn't know the difference," Jeph said. Glen looked around them, seeing only the sun-saturated trees growing close to the banks of the Black River. Much like the invariably bullet-riddled signs one saw out in the hinterland, the prospect of some yokels lurking around with crossbows made him uneasy.

A wasp flew past him, near his face, startling him from his thoughts. The wasp turned around and seemed to be watching him. Glen wasn't about to be cowed by a wasp, looked around them. Then he saw it, the mass of a wasp's nest nestled in some big old tree just off the Jut. Up and out of reach, but massive—big as a boulder, boiling out of hollowed-out tree trunk. It was like a paper tumor growing out of the dead tree.

"Found a wasp's nest," Glen said. "About 11 o'clock off the Jut."

Charlene spun on her axis, Jeph turning her camera's eye on it. Jeph whistled over the radio.

"Damn," Jeph said. "That's a big one."

Glen surveyed its location relative to the river below.

"How about you kill that thing," he said. "No way am I crossing the river with that nasty sucker looming like that."

"Sure," Jeph said. "Fire or water. Call it."

Glen was inwardly irked by that, since Jeph was making it his call, so whatever downstream ramifications arose from it, it was on him, since he'd made the call. It was a very Fawcett move to make, which is why it bugged him.

"Water," Glen said. He didn't want to be the one responsible for a wildfire out there in the drought-impacted landscape. Fawcett would hang him out to dry if anything untoward happened.

"Water it is," Jeph said, making Charlene pivot again. "You might want to come back to the van. It's likely to get festive here in a few."

"I'll head over if I have to," Glen said, taking a lengthy pull from his beer. "Right now, I just want to watch."

"Alright," Jeph said. "Consider yourself forewarned."

Charlene whirred over to the mammoth nest, which was this grey mass of paper and bark around that long-dead tree that hung like a leprous specter over the tangle of the town. Big red flowers danced in the distance on stalks amid the sea of green that enveloped Summerville.

"You know what? I think I changed my mind," Glen said. "Torch that thing."

"I *knew* you were going to say that," Jeph said, pivoting Charlene again. A couple of wasps ventured too near her rotors, and were shredded, the sound calling to mind a weed whacker hitting something.

Charlene spat fire at the nest, the nozzle spewing its sticky flammable spray on the nest, igniting it at once. Jeph flew Charlene around the main visible part of the nest, the fire solution lighting it up like a torch. Even from where Glen stood on the Jut, he could see the wasps frenzying at the application of fire, trying to emerge from the nest to attack Charlene, but being caught in the spreading fire or splattered by the spinning rotors. A few even flew after Glen, only for him to swat them away.

"Damn, Jeph," Glen said. "That's impressive as hell."

Jeph had Charlene drop lower and spray some other parts of the dead tree, hoping to ignite the whole thing.

"How much firejuice have you got in there?" Glen asked.

"Charlene can carry a gallon of that and of the water solution," Jeph said. I've got more in the back of the van."

"What the heck is that stuff?" Glen asked, finishing off his beer, wishing he'd brought another. The wasps that hadn't been caught in the nest conflagration were zipping about, trying to hit Charlene, who would slice them apart with her rotors upon approach, and did. There was a popping sound Glen could hear along with the crackle of the fire, as bug bodies burst apart from the heat. However many wasp larvae were in that burning tree were finding it an oven in the wake of Charlene's assault.

"My own kind of napalm," Jeph said, having Charlene travel up and down in key spots, immolating any openings where wasps might be emerging. "Hopefully the tree is dry enough to just go up."

It seemed like the god of hellfire was there for Jeph that day, because the dead tree did catch fire properly, once Charlene had run out of firejuice to spray. She flew back, and Glen could smell the scent of gasoline and woodsmoke mixing with the intoxicating aroma of the flowers growing across the banks of the Black River. That, and the acrid stink of carbonizing chitin.

Charlene flew back to the van, landing carefully on her launcher, while Jeph emerged with a satisfied grunt, opening the solar panels on the launcher so Charlene could recharge.

"She's nowhere near depleted, but I figure a little sunbathing can't hurt," Jeph said, taking out a rag to wipe the bug guts off her rotor blades. His motions were loving and careful caresses, carrying the pleasingly astringent smell of cleaning solution.

"I'm impressed," Glen said, walking back. "How many gallons of that firejuice did you bring?"

"Four," Jeph said, nodding to the van.

"That's not regulation, you know," Glen said. Jeph met Glen's gaze and smiled.

"Out here, it's just between you, me, the bees, and the trees," Jeph said.

"Wasps," Glen said. "I'd feel bad if it was bees. Wasps? Not so much. Wasps have a malice to them."

Poking in the back of the van, Glen could see the containers of firejuice. Jeph grabbed one of them and a funnel off the tool rack and went about refilling the empty container. Once done with that, he capped it and set it off to one side.

"The key to a good civilian napalm is you want it to be viscous but not so sticky that you can't spray it through a nozzle," he said, mopping off the nozzle while he was talking. Glen grabbed another can of beer from the cooler, and even got one for Jeph. They cracked theirs and drank, heading over to watch the tree burn while they drank.

"Little suckers didn't know what hit them," Glen said, watching the dead tree crackle and burn. Thankfully, the overhanging canopy of trees helped disperse the smoke, so they weren't sending a smoke line skyward for everyone to see. The last thing they needed was a volunteer fire department or county sheriff's deputies turning up to put an end to the party.

Jeph looked around the area, grinning as he drank.

"The undergrowth around the tree looks damp enough that it shouldn't spread," he said. His eyes went to the gas mask of the effigy, which caught the reflection of the fire.

"Fire purifies," Glen said.

"It sure as hell does," Jeph said.

They watched the corpse of the tree eventually crack and fall toward Summerville, landing with a terminal crash that caught some of the decrepit buildings there. The sound of breaking glass, cracking wood, and breaking brick was somehow rewarding, even as the fire failed to catch on the carpet of heart-shaped leaves of green that surrounded the ghost town. The fire just burned on the tree's hollow trunk, and on the frantic bodies of the wasps that sought to flee the destruction of their home.

"What now?" Jeph said.

"My turn," Glen said, finishing his beer and crunching his can.

FOUR

[As noted already, I'm unsure who authored this, although Tyler Finn is my primary suspect, since he would have been present at the time, and was the writer of the *Seen* team. Why he sought to render this fictionalized third-person account instead of a nonfiction narrative is mysterious. —Ed.]

SHARON AND JUSTIN were less enthusiastic about Holly's idea for this particularly *The Seen* documentary. In fact, when she and Tyler had pulled up, they were already saying "No!" from the side porch of their rental house, running out to confront them as Holly slid Ladygirl up.

"Where did you get this thing?" Justin asked, running a hand through his newly-made boy band bleach-blonde hair, while Sharon crossed her arms and shook her head. Sharon wore an all-black romper with combat boots, while Justin was chilling in a red and white floral short-sleeved button down and ivory slacks with flip-flops.

"Police auction," Holly said, hopping out and giving the sturdy door a lengthy caress. "This is Ladygirl. Ladygirl, this is the rest of the team."

"Ladygirl," Sharon said, ogling the Cadillac. "She's fuckin' monstrous, Holly."

"She's perfect," Holly said. "She's our mystery mobile, Sharon. Circa 1975."

Justin looked at Tyler for explanation, who only shrugged.

"This is tied to those missing people Holly's obsessing about, am I right?" Justin asked.

"The very ones," Holly said. "Let's have some sweet tea on your porch and I'll talk y'all through it."

Despite (or maybe because of) her stridently neo-gothic bearing, Sharon was more careful about blending in locally, so she always brewed up sweet tea at their place, which she and Justin had rented for the summer while Holly and Tyler had worked out some haunted house stories set in Charleston.

Once they'd gotten situated with a pitcher of sweet tea and were sitting on wicker furniture on the side porch, Holly went about her pitch. Not that she needed to, but she preferred buy-in from the whole team before any escapade.

"Here's what we know," Holly said, recounting what she knew so far. Tyler took notes while she talked. "Ethan Allen and his passengers vanished somewhere near *this* Circle K."

She held up her tablet and let them look at it.

"There's a ghost town about thirty minutes away from the Circle K," Holly said. "I think that's where they were headed. Ashley Graham stole Ladygirl around there and drove her to Duke's campus, where she subsequently disappeared."

"*That's* the mystery?" Sharon asked. She toyed with her sweet tea, giving it a surly swirl, the ice clinking against the glass as she did so.

"Yes," Holly said. "That's the mystery."

"Not at Duke, though?" Justin asked. "Where Graham vanished."

"Ashley Graham's only part of the mystery, guys," Holly said. "I want to see what happened at the Circle K. Where they parted ways. *Something* happened out there. We can always go to Duke any time we like."

"But the cops looked into it," Sharon said.

Holly scoffed, while the others shifted nervously in their seats.

"They didn't find any bodies," Holly said. "Here's the thing: people disappear around that area all the time."

Her fingers danced on her tablet, as she produced a map for them to review. It showed clusters of disappearances along the banks of the Black River.

"Over the past several decades, there have been scores of disappearances in the area," Holly said. "North of Summerville, south of it, and so on."

"Serial killer," Sharon said, sipping her sweet tea. "Gotta be."

"The legendary Black River Butcher?" Holly said, referring to a machete-wielding maniac rumored to be operating in the area for years. He'd never been caught, qualified as an urban legend, or at least a rural one. "Could be. But say that it *is* the Black River Butcher—that doesn't account for the Ladygirl Five."

It was Justin's turn to scoff.

"The 'Ladygirl Five'—that's what you're calling them, Holly?" Justin asked.

"Why not?" Holly said, a bit defensively. "It has a ring to it."

Sharon set down her iced tea and shifted on her wicker seat with a creak. She toyed with the laces of her shiny combat boots.

"If foul play is suspected, isn't it ghoulish for us to be driving around in that car?" Sharon asked. "We don't want to skeeve out our audience."

Holly and Sharon went back to their early days with *The Seen,* where they first became best frenemies, the four of them meeting up at Alligator Andy's in Chapel Hill when Holly and Ty had first propositioned them about forming their indie film crew. Their creative clashing was what made for a powerful cocktail on *The Seen.*

"Ladygirl is *precisely* the hook for the story," Holly said. "You know how people talk about walking a mile in someone else's shoes? Here, we're driving hundreds of miles in their car. We'll get a feel for it, maybe soak up the vibe. People will be interested in it because it makes the mystery real. I'll talk about what I've discovered, what Tyler's learned, what we've researched. All you two have to do is make us look good and sound good. You know, production. Let *us* worry about the story mechanics."

"Driving in a ghost car to a ghost town in hopes of finding out what happened to the Ladygirl Five," Justin said. "What could go wrong?"

"Exactly," Holly said. "If we find out what happened to them, the episode will slay. *The Seen* will break big for us. And we need that badly."

"For you, maybe, Holly Hobby," Sharon said. "The rest of us? Not so much."

Holly pointed to Ladygirl, who just sat silent in the myriad shadows made by the trees, minding her own business.

"That big, blue boat over there will raise us all," Holly said. Tyler looked up from his tablet, where he'd been taking notes. Ty was always one to listen and reflect before speaking up. While he was not a writer-writer (like a novelist), it was his writerly way that Holly found charming.

"Holly's done a ton of background on it already," he said. "We just need you two to come with us. We'll hit that Circle K, shoot some travel B-roll along the way, and shoot the town. Since nobody knows what happened to the Ladygirl Five, we can write our own ending. What we're doing is offering up a mystery for our audience. It's on *them* to solve it, not us."

Sharon and Justin exchanged looks, while Holly nursed her iced tea, waiting for them to agree to it. They were production; it was Holly and Tyler who set up the episodes and the parameters of their projects.

"How many shows have we done, guys?" Holly asked. "Thirty shows over the past four years. What's the problem?"

Sharon squared up with Holly, telegraphing her concerns—like Godzilla versus the Smog Monster—which one was which was up for debate, since both of them would've wanted to be Godzilla.

"It just feels weird using *their* car," Sharon said. "Ghoulish, like I already said."

"It's not *their* car anymore," Holly said, imitating Sharon's emphasis. "It's mine. I won it at the auction, fair and square. And since when did you *not* dig ghoulish, Share?"

Holly wasn't going to bring up again the indignation of Isabella Allen, the look on her face. It wasn't something they needed to know. Besides, what was Ms. Allen going to do? Holly outbid her. Breaks of the game. She glanced at Tyler, who kept mum. He knew how to do that better than anybody in the tri-state.

"It's a great hook, like *I* said," Holly said. "It'll immediately get our audience excited about the story. Ladygirl's a beautiful car. Totally old-school, proper vintage. How about this? We go driving around town in her, maybe hit Cannibal's Kitchen for an early dinner. My treat."

At the mention of the locally infamous eatery ("All the Meat You Dare to Eat"), the others were more amenable. Cannibal's specialized in Carolina barbecue and southern seafood, served up with a wink and a nod by the saucy staff.

"Okay," Sharon said. "But you're seriously buying."

"Yeah, totally," Justin said.

"Fine, fine," Holly said. "Now, let's get rolling before nightfall, just so we can enjoy all the gawking from people watching us cruise around town. Tyler, get us a table for four, would you? A booth with a view."

FIVE

[I think this part was more or less tied to some lost Fawcett audiovisual footage. Who transcribed it? Was it Tyler Finn ghostwriting it yet again? The verdict is out on the authorship of this. —Ed.]

GLEN HAD SUITED UP, which meant wearing a blue and yellow Fawcett jumpsuit, a machete tied to his hip. He also wore a bright yellow Fawcett hardhat with a light on it, just because down near the town, it was likely to get dark before sunset.

"How're you going to ford the river?" Jeph asked, fiddling with Charlene.

"Inflatable," Glen said, pointing to the Fawcett-branded inflatable raft, which he was filling up using a battery-powered pump he'd pulled from the van. He put on his work gloves while the raft was inflating.

Beyond the Jut, the fallen tree was still burning and throwing off smoke. What wasps remained were scattered and bewildered by the remainder of the blaze. But as they had hoped, the dampness near the riverbank had kept the fire from spreading, which brought them relief that they weren't going to get busted by Wyndham or anybody else from Fawcett.

"What are you doing, exactly?" Jeph asked, while Glen disconnected the pump from the raft.

"I need to take samples from the site," Glen said. "They might be what that old man was selling at the Circle K, but they might be something else, too. If I can gather a half-dozen samples or so, we should be all set. We get them back to the labs and they can determine if they're the property of Fawcett or not."

"Still think it's weird they sent you instead of some of the plant biologists," Jeph said.

Glen finished another beer and laughed into it as he did so.

"Fieldwork is what I do," Glen said, stowing the empty can, wiping his face with a sleeve. "The plant biologists at Fawcett, well, they have more important things to do than gather weeds out here in no man's land. Just keep that drone out of my hair."

"I'll keep watch from above," Jeph said. "Charlene's good for around ninety minutes with the power packs I have on her."

"Shouldn't take me that long," Glen said. "Just don't light *me* on fire."

"Promise," Jeph said.

Glen hefted the life raft on his shoulder, made his way to the edge of the Jut, took a look down. There was a steepish descent on the one side, mostly mud, roots, and leaves that led to the riverbank. It appeared by be manageable, especially since he was wearing work boots. Others had made that trek before, he could tell.

"Testing," Glen said into his walkie talkie.

"Copy that," Jeph said. "I'll send Charlene down once you've crossed the river."

"Fine by me," Glen said, working his way carefully down the slope, which was awkward with the inflatable boat. Out of the sunlight, in the shade of the trees, it was markedly cooler, with only the scent of mud, water, woodsmoke, and that sweet-n-spicy floral scent in his nose.

Across the river, he could see those red flowers shuddering on their vines, like they were watching him. No wasps, at least, which made him happy. Weedwork was way worse with wasps. What wasps remained had scattered to the winds, punch-drunk on smoke and the annihilation of their hive.

Glen got the raft to the river, tying it to a fallen tree branch while he pried off the paddle which was affixed to it with a clamp. He settled into the raft, untying the line, letting the current take him. He was fit and outdoorsy, used to things like this, so it didn't take him too many strokes of the paddle to cross the river, just a bit downstream from where he'd first descended.

The river lived up to its name, being almost black, no doubt from all the tannins in it. The woods around here was quiet, which kept Glen on edge. The natural noise that had been up at the Jut wasn't here. This place was way too quiet. Smothering that thought, he reached the other side of the bank, and secured his raft, aware of all of the heart-shaped leaves festooning the hill, and the big flowers that seemed to be tracking his progress.

He took out his walkie talkie.

"I'm on the other side," Glen said. "Just keep the drone out of my mix."

"Got it," Jeph said. Glen checked the raft to make sure the bowline he'd tied was secure, knowing already that it was. He carried that sample collection kit on his backpack and drew his machete because it felt good to have it handy.

Behind him, up at the Jut, he saw Charlene hovering, her camera eye on him. It did a little pirouette overhead, letting Glen know that Jeph saw him eyeing the drone.

Glen turned his gaze on the leaves, which were shiny, almost waxy, and took off his backpack, taking out some shears after stabbing his machete into the rich earth.

"Guess we'll start with you," Glen said, reaching down to snag a trio of the leaves. They were sharp-edged, and if not for his work gloves, they might have cut him. He could see the white streaks on the yellowy leather where the leaves had hit his hands. Smiling to himself, Glen nipped three of the leaves with his shears, noting the way the leaf carpet seemed to tremble when he did so, catching a breeze he couldn't feel in his jumpsuit.

Glen took out a black Sharpie and wrote "Summerville Leaf Sample #1: Riverbank" and sealed up the bottle, which he put in the pack. Then he took out some paper towels and dampened them in the river, laying them out in a clear plastic bag. He fished out a trowel from his backpack, and carefully dug around another of the leaf clusters, mindful of the way the leaves seemed to flick on the vines that carried them.

He dug and gingerly uprooted the cluster, nipping it clear of the vine. He let the clipping bathe in the river a bit, clearing the soil from the roots, before he carefully wrapped it in the paper towel, sealing it in the bag, writing "Summerville Root System Sample: Riverbank" on it, before setting it in the raft, in the plentiful shade. He didn't want the samples to be damaged before they could get them back to Fawcett's facilities.

Charlene hovered overhead, Jeph moving her carefully through the branches. Glen gritted his teeth and went up

[FILE CORRUPTED]

[This portion of the narrative stops due to corrupted files, and the third-person fictional dramatization does not reappear in the recovered collateral. I'm not certain why but will speak more on it in the following section. Online searches for these lost files have proven fruitless, despite repeated efforts to discover what happened to Glen Fields and Jeph Wales leading up to their reappearance later in the documents. —Ed.]

PART II:

THE
BLOG
ENTRIES

[Perhaps confusingly, the remainder of the accounts relies on blog (unfortunately, not vlog) entries by *The Seen* staff, specifically Holly Rivers and Tyler Finn, without reference to the third-person dramatized content you've already read. These blog entries emerged as a result of Tyler Finn's own uploads to *The Seen's* servers, which at least showed an effort to record the goings on in a manner that might afford others to learn what exactly happened, at least from the perspectives of some of the participants. Some of the entries are short; some are lengthier. I hope they're illuminating, and if you have your own theories about them, please upload them to the Seenster Wiki.—Ed.]

BLOG ENTRY 1
(Holly Rivers)

Ghost Towns & Otherwise

Hey, all, this is Holly, and you know why I'm here. I wanted to talk to you about a ghost town. You know what I like about ghost towns? Everything. There's always a story there, something more than meets the eye.

Summerville is like that. And I have to offer a point of clarity here: I'm not talking about the Summerville incorporated in 1847 in Dorchester County, also known as "Flowertown" and host of an annual Flower Festival. Not that one, but you're forgiven for thinking that.

I'm talking about the other Summerville—originally Summersville, named after farmer Josiah Summers, who'd founded the little town in 1854, on the banks of the Black River. It had been a resupply waystation during the Civil War and was the site of the sinking of a Confederate blockade runner called the *Cottonmouth.*

Summersville was a geographic afterthought after the Civil War, and the townsfolk went about their business content to be disregarded by the rest of the world. With only three streets: Main Street, First Street, and Temple Street, Summersville never got very big.

Sometime between its founding to its eventual doom a century later, Summersville lost its way. Some even thought maybe it lost its mind.

Summers Versus Summer

By all accounts, the Waynesville Earthquake of 1916 was a major one in North Carolina, being somewhere around 5.2–5.5 on the Richter Scale. Its effects were felt across several states, and it shook Summersville to its roots, in that it caused a deviation of the Black River, which ended up cutting off the town and drowning it in time.

The original river route had made Summersville an attractive stopover for stateside travelers. After that earthquake, the shift in the river had acted like a hangman's noose around the neck of the town, beginning a slow decline from 1916–1954, as the town had become badly affected by seasonally disruptive flooding, which, coupled with new highway patterns undertaken during the Eisenhower Administration, had transformed the town from the quaint antebellum stopover to a desolate Old South revenant.

Sometime in that era of decline, the town tossed away its second "s" and went by "Summerville" even though its sister town to the south already had that name. Maybe it was tied to the passing of Josiah Summers II, and the end of the family dynasty that had kept the town going. There is an urban legend that with the death of the last Summers heir, the town had ceased to be theirs anymore.

Others theorize that the post-quake town performed better in summer, when the Black River was less flood-prone. The drier summer months were more accommodating to it, whereas the other seasons were less welcoming.

Whatever the cause, people moved out and moved on, and year-to-year, there were fewer left willing to put up with the loss in consumer traffic and the flooding. Kud-zu commandeered the periphery of the town, and something else. Something else. The disappearances.

BLOG ENTRY 3
(Holly Rivers)

The Black River Butcher

Information about the Black River Butcher is at best apocryphal, the result of lackadaisical police work and perhaps an overemphasis on the importance of tourist dollars in the region.

Nobody wanted to hear about a possible serial killer, and if the Butcher was operating in the area, he was more of a bogeyman than someone desiring newspaper ink, exposure, infamy, and capture. If the Butcher was killing people, he was being very careful not to leave bodies behind for the authorities to discover.

The eyewitness accounts (revealed through strictly anonymous sources by their own insistence) indicated a hooded figure (dusty black or grey overcoat being the most common descriptor), wearing dark work gloves and wielding a machete. Those accounts involved some couples making out along the Black River, where they were accosted by the Butcher, who attacked their cars with his machete, leaving scratches on the vehicles, and the ruination of at least one convertible. The photos show damage to the cars in 1972 and 1974, conveying a sense of the rage and violence of the Butcher.

I have to stress that nobody has linked the Butcher definitively to any murders, and the Butcher never claimed any. The sensational name arose from those two attacks on couples in the region.

> [There is a map of Summerville included in the Appendix of this book, for your consideration. —Ed.]

The disappearances are a greater concern, which is why we are looking into it. Along the Black River, there have been dozens of disappearances from 1950 through 1978. These have occurred primarily in the tourist season.

We are not going to document all of the disappearances, but from our investigation, we've found that around a hundred people have vanished along the winding Black River, which remains a popular location for kayak and canoe enthusiasts, allowing for a scenic pass through the ghost town of Summerville.

The Ladygirl Five are to be the focus of our documentary.

The Ladygirl Five

I've taken to calling them the Ladygirl Five as a way of accounting for the disappearance of five young people at roughly the same time, including:

- Ethan Allen (33 years old)

- Kyle Walker (32 years old)

- Joshua Kane (34 years old)

- Savannah Greene (29 years old)

- Ashley Talulah Graham (25 years old)

As far as I'm concerned, the mystery of the Ladygirl Five begins and ends with Ashley Talulah Graham and Ethan Allen. They are braided together because the 1975 Cadillac Eldorado convertible was the prized possession of Mr. Allen, although it was believed to have been driven to the Duke University campus by Ms. Graham, who had left the keys in the ignition and had left her backpack in the trunk. This had been corroborated by campus security cameras that indicated when Ms. Graham arrived with the car by herself and parked it, before walking alone across the campus. Other cameras show Ms. Graham meandering around the campus, clutching her stomach in some of the footage and seeming to talk to someone who couldn't be seen, before eventually disappearing.

After sitting untended for a week, Ladygirl had been ticketed and removed by campus police and later relegated to the sheriff's office, where the vehicle was impounded for over a year, only to be auctioned off.

Full confession: I participated in the police auction for the vintage car, beating out other participants, including Mr. Allen's younger sister, Isabella Allen, who was leading a private effort to locate her missing brother.

At the time, security cameras at the area Piggly Wiggly had identified the Ladygirl Five a day before their disappearance, and a security camera at a local Circle K had showed all of them there, including Ms. Graham, until the others had left her behind, ditching her at the filling station, owned and operated by Mr. Cooper DeVille.

Mr. DeVille can be seen on the security footage giving directions to Ms. Graham, who sets off on foot. This is the last time she's seen on-camera before reappearing on the Duke campus.

Indeed, that Circle K stop was the last time any of the rest of the Ladygirl Five were seen. From my perspective, that Circle K seems like a good place to investigate, don't you?

BLOG ENTRY 5

(Holly Rivers)

The Old Man & the Circle K

Seemingly a sanctuary out here away from civilization, the Circle K of interest looks like something perhaps built in the 1980s that has never quite been renovated, beyond some digital fuel pumps that take credit cards (thankfully, since Ladygirl has a powerful thirst).

Mr. Cooper DeVille was almost jubilant at the sight of us, or, more specifically, the return of Ladygirl. His wizened features split into a false toothy grin as he looked on it with glee.

"Why, that looks like an old friend returning," Cooper said, reaching out and petting the car with knobby knuckles. Tyler was refueling her, while Sharon and Justin went into the store to use the restrooms and buy stuff.

"You've seen this car before?" I asked.

"Sure did," DeVille said, eyeing me with bleached blue eyes. "The police asked a question or two. Where'd you find her?"

"Duke University," I said. "On campus. Abandoned."

"Abandoned," DeVille said. "You don't say."

"I just did, yeah," I replied.

I'll admit that I was pleased that this old man had remembered seeing the Ladygirl Five. I made conversation with him to see what I might cadge out of him.

"You saw the Ladygirl Five?" I asked.

"Huh?"

"The five people who were in this car a couple of years ago," I said. Of course he knew.

"Yeah," DeVille said. "Why do *you* care?"

"We're part of a documentary series," I said. "We're looking for missing people."

DeVille's manner was curious. Not rude, but quietly evasive. I could feel it. It was a sense more than it was a vibe or an aura. Just a hint of it, which, naturally, had my full attention.

"Documentary? Like television?" he asked.

"The Internet," I said, fearing that I'd have to explain that to him as well.

"About *them?*" he asked, as if he couldn't believe it.

"Yes," I said. "Five people disappeared at one time. One of them reappeared hundreds of miles away, before she vanished as well. There's a mystery here. We're hoping to solve it."

DeVille just looked at us, shaking his head, while Sharon and Justin were examining some plants on a display at one side of the station.

"All filled up," Tyler said. "That is one big-ass gas tank."

"Okay," I said. "See what they have in there. We'll leave in like ten minutes."

Tyler nodded and went on in, while the others looked at those beautiful red flowers on display. DeVille followed my gaze.

"Those are summerviolets," he said. "I came up with that name for them."

"Are they local?" I asked. DeVille smiled and nodded, walking me to them, like he was a proud grandfather. They had a nice scent, something spicy and floral, almost edible-feeling. Butterscotch laced with cinnamon and honey, maybe. Hard to define, but certainly a pleasing scent.

"They sure are," DeVille said. "Not native, perhaps, but local."

"They're pretty," Sharon said, holding one up and taking a sniff of it, the little red blossom. She had Justin take a whiff, too, and they agreed that the flowers were nice, decided to buy two of them, which set them back ten dollars.

"Summerviolets grow anywhere there's water," DeVille said. "They'll take root in anything—sand, gravel, dirt, rock. Anywhere it can sink its roots is good enough."

The side lot of the Circle K was full of derelict cars and vans, sitting like phantoms, most of them in some liminal space between dusty and rusty, with weeds growing between them, like the vehicles had been planted there long ago.

"Are all of these cars yours?" I asked.

"They are, now," DeVille said. "You'd be amazed what people abandon on the roadside."

"Seems like that's the work of the highway patrol," I said.

DeVille scoffed at that.

"No fancy highways out there. Besides, wreckers' got more important things to do than go after abandoned vehicles in the upcountry," DeVille said. "Leastways, they know where to find 'em when I run across 'em."

This might seem uncharitable, but out of the blue, I wondered if this man might have been the Black River Butcher. Isn't that weird?

"How old are you, Mr. DeVille?" I asked.

"Not a day over eighty," he said. "Do I look my age?"

"Been here all your life?" I asked.

His eyes raked over me, his expression wrinkled, non-committal.

"So far, yeah," he replied. Sharon and Justin were watching me, playing with their newly-purchased flowers.

"You ever heard about the Black River Butcher?" I asked. "Didn't he operate out here? You'd have been maybe in your thirties back when he was active?"

DeVille smiled at me, shaking his head as he did so.

"You ask me, there never was a Black River Butcher," he said. "He's a myth. Like Bigfoot or the River Rascals."

"You think so?" I asked. He nodded, meeting my gaze.

"I do," DeVille said. "People just say things; they don't know what they're talking about."

A vintage VW van rolled up, itself a surreal vehicle painted psychedelically with flowers of all sorts and colors with "The Flower Children" painted on its sides with crazy letters. A cluster of young people exited, looking like caricatures of hippies from people who'd never been born yet when there had been actual hippies hitchhiking their way across the world.

"Hey, Mr. DeVille," one of them said, a young man with pale eyes that looked like younger versions of DeVille's. His brown hair danced around his shoulders, and his plentiful beard carried a biblical gravitas. He looked us over. "These folks giving you trouble?"

"Nothing I can't handle, Tanner," DeVille said, watching the others tumble out of the VW van, some of them eyeing Ladygirl covetously. The group were a sea of batiked linen, patched denim, beads, bangles, and tattoos. I counted two guys and eight women. They smelled of patchouli, pot, and that flowery scent I'd gotten from the summerviolets.

Tanner smiled at us.

"Sweet ride. Y'all headed to Summerville?" he asked.

"We are," I said. "We're doing a documentary on it."

Two women walked up, flanking Tanner. One had cinnamon-colored hair that went half-down her back. She wore a striped orange and brown tube top with well-frayed cutoff jean shorts. The other wore a pink bikini top with a black vest and some cargo shorts and flip-flops. Her hair was shoulder-length and mousy brown. Both had hard eyes, like a couple of dolls. Whether black or brown, their gaze was intense.

"This is Tressa and Tonya," Tanner said, indicating that Tressa was the one with the longer hair. "They're my sisters. Not by blood, but, you know, by..."

"By choice," Tressa said. "You're Holly Rivers, yeah?"

"You heard of me?" I asked, admittedly flattered. In the world of social media, being known was its own kind of wonder. There was so much demanding attention from people. To even be noticed was its own rare blessing.

"Yeah," Tressa said. "Your show, *The Unseen*."

"*The Seen,* actually," I said.

"I get it," Tonya said. "Clever. It's, what, wordplay, am I right?"

Tanner and Tressa laughed, and Tanner pointed out there others, who were flocking to DeVille's store.

"That's Evan at the pump, and the others are Joanna, Dara, Layna, Sabrina, Lia, and Ruth," Tanner said. "Like the van says, we're The Flower Children."

Tyler walked up beside me, arms folded. Tanner was taller than he was.

"Are you a band or what?" Tyler asked.

"A band," Tanner said, laughing with Tressa and Tonya. "Nothing so, I don't know, ordinary as that."

Tyler and I looked at each other a moment, while DeVille shuffled into his store, dealing with the rush of visitors, which looked like more business than he'd typically see in a week.

"What *are* you, then?" Tyler asked. I let Tyler take the lead on it, while I studied them.

"Ever heard of Johnny Appleseed?" Tressa asked.

"Sure," I said. "Who hasn't?"

"We're like him," Tanner said. "Only with flowers. Those summerviolets you see over yonder? Ours. We pick some for Old Man DeVille, so he can sell them. Others we just plant wherever they'll grow. We've been real busy the past few months, propagating them."

"And they grow *anywhere*," Tonya said, smiling at Tyler in a way that I didn't like. Tyler and I weren't exactly a couple, but we were very, very close. There was a partnership there, a sense of mutual understanding and respect.

"We're planning to send a bunch to the Flower Festival in Summerville next year—only seems right."

"We can guide you to Summerville," Tanner said. "The dead one, I mean. The ghost town."

I wasn't about to say no to that.

Listen to the Flower Children

The drive to Summerville wasn't long after the Circle K. I felt like Mr. DeVille was sorry to see us go, or sorry to see Ladygirl go, at any rate. The way his eyes dragged in our wake as we passed was something I won't forget.

Sharon and Justin were content to sit in the back with their flowers, while Tyler and I were more on-task, with Tyler even taking some shots with his phone to capture some B-roll that he thought Justin might be able to use in post-production.

It was fun driving Ladygirl along the winding road, trailing the VW van, which was venting glossy bubbles that someone in the van had seen to putting to the wind, the dayglo wands of pink and green emerging sporadically from windows on the van, the bubbles catching the sun in rainbow colors, flying after the van in the most charming, playful manner.

The Flower Children were a mixed bag of youthfulness, being all races and temperaments. They were of the sort I imagined would have difficulty with local law enforcement, strictly for existing.

"We don't even know who these people are," Tyler said.

"They seem harmless enough," Sharon said, snuffing on her summerviolet.

"Totally," Justin said. "Harmless."

I glanced at them in the rearview mirror, and they both looked pretty chill, playing with their pet plants. Looking ahead, I could see those big, puffy clouds thickening and darkening in the distance, that periwinkle and grey prominence in the sky that portended thunderstorms.

"Looks like a storm is coming," I said.

"Should we put the top up?" Tyler asked.

"Once we get to Summerville," I replied.

The VW van took a turn off the main road, coming to a stop near a chained barrier. Evan from the van got out and undid the chain and moved it out of the way. I could glimpse the ROAD CLOSED sign that hung from the chain, rusty from disuse.

The Flower Children rolled on through, and we followed. I could see Evan, who was black with auburn-hued curls and was wearing a white Cuban *guayabera* shirt with some green cargo shorts, replaced the chain on the road barricade, the caution sign shook in the breeze, while Evan waved at us while running back to the VW van.

Tyler glanced behind us, frowning as he did so.

"Great, we're locked in here," he said.

"It's just a chain, Ty," I said. "Are you worried?"

He grimaced a bit as he formulated a reply.

"I *always* worry," he replied. "That's sort of my job, Holly."

Sharon sniffed the air, clutching Justin's arm.

"Do you smell that?" she asked.

"Smoke," I said. "Maybe it's a campfire."

"No, something else," Sharon said. "Flowers."

We drove along this dusty, barely-used road until we saw the van stopped to one side. There was another van there, too, a Fawcett Biotech van. The road ended in a jagged spar marked with "The Jut" and the Flower Children got out of their van. Someone had added a white- and red-striped barrier at the Jut, what amounted to the road barriers you'd see on a highway, with a sign that said DANGER! ROAD CLOSED! I could see there were white reflectors on the upright posts that marked the dropoff point, so if you came up here in the dark, it would be hard to miss.

Hanging over the Jut like some strange scarecrow was a figure in a Fawcett Biotech hazmat suit, wearing a gas mask and a crown of dried vines. It had been shot three times in the chest with arrows, and was hanging from a noose.

"What the hell is that?" I said. "Justin, get out your camera, record this."

"Got it," Justin said.

We parked and got out, Tanner and the others greeting us with smiles, carrying garlands of braided vines and those strange red flowers.

"Aloha, Seensters," Tanner said, watching some of the others give us garlands.

"We're pretty far from Hawai'i," I said, noting the unmistakably fragrant flowers of the summerviolets like the ones DeVille had sold to Sharon and Justin. The scent was pleasingly powerful, but not overpowering.

"And yet the Aloha spirit prevails even here," Tonya said. I pointed to the effigy hanging over the Jut, which was swaying this way and that, while some of the Flower Children were setting up the VW van as a kind of camper.

"What the hell is that?" I asked, pointing to the figure.

"That's the Swinging Man," Tanner said. "The Swinging Man symbolizes the everyman made captive to conventional societal norms, suspended in the air, unable to find firm footing, at the mercy of the winds and whims of the world. It's kind of a scarecrow to protect this sacred space from intruders."

My eyes went to the Fawcett van, which looked to be untended.

"There are Fawcett people here?" I asked. Fawcett Biotech was a big regional employer, specializing in patented GMO superfoods and bioengineered crops. It wasn't lost to me that the missing Kyle Walker had been an employee at Fawcett. Coincidence? Time would tell.

Sharon and Justin had gone to the edge of the Jut, standing at the road barrier, with Justin filming the vine-choked town, which was a strange sight, being the lopsided shapes of midcentury southern buildings covered in mantles of green with big scarlet flowers growing everywhere, dancing on unseen breezes.

The blackened remains of a burned and fallen tree marred the otherwise idyllic emerald landscape. We could see smoke rising from it and embers glowing within the hollows of its trunk. I thought maybe the tree had been recently hit by lightning. Something devastating had befallen it.

"It's beautiful," Sharon said.

"Yeah, it is," Tressa said. "It's great for swimming, too. The river."

Several of the Flower Children were already capering down the slope to the riverbank, taking off their clothes and diving into the water, laughing and splashing as they went.

Tyler and I joined Sharon and the others at the Jut.

"Where are the Fawcett people?" I asked.

Tanner shrugged. "Damned if I know. We just rolled up and they were there. The van, I mean. Official Swinging Man business, is my guess."

I peeked into the van, which didn't look like it had been there a long time. I wondered what Fawcett might be doing here. Trying the door, I saw that it was locked. The whole van was locked up.

"Company killjoys," Tanner said, hovering nearby. "Wherever they are."

"Have you heard of the Ladygirl Five?" I asked. Tanner and Tressa both shook their heads.

"Is that a band?" Tanner asked.

"They're five people who disappeared in this area a couple of years ago," I said.

"Ancient history, Ms. Rivers," Tressa said. "Two years ago might as well be an eternity around here. We live and breathe in the miraculous moments here."

The look they shared didn't convince me. I think Tanner and Tressa knew *exactly* who I was talking about. I directed Justin and Sharon to set something up with cameras, so we could start recording. I wanted to capture some of this vibe before I really started interrogating them.

"Is this where you collect the flowers?" I asked.

"Yes," Tanner said. "There are tons of them. Little shoots. You don't mess with the big flowers. But the little ones *want* to be taken."

"No?"

"Madame Summerville isn't keen on that," Tressa said. Tonya had ventured down to the riverbank and was swimming with the others. "She's willing to share, but only on Her terms."

"Who is Madame Summerville?" I asked. Both Tanner and Tressa pointed to the ruin of Summerville.

"We can show you tomorrow," Tanner said. "It's gonna rain, and we don't want to be down there in the rain. It gets too sloppy in the rain. Not that I mind a little slop, but with your cameras, you want it to be tidy, I'll bet."

Tyler looked at me with a knowing kind of satisfaction, compounded when some thunder sounded somewhere.

"Let's get the top up on Ladygirl, Tyler," I said, and we battened down the Cadillac while the wind started kicking up. Some of the Flower Children were setting up a grill and some folding chairs and festive flower lights of red and white.

"You're welcome to hang with us," Tanner said. It was hard to say no, with the heady scent of the garlands around our necks making everything seem alright. "We've got stuff to eat and drink."

I hadn't exactly planned for us to camp out here, hadn't expected to have to, but as the rain started to fall, I decided maybe it was the right play, after all. Sharon, Justin, Tyler, and I sheltered under the VW van canopy with Tanner, Tressa, and some of the others. Evan was carefully working the grill, getting a fire going, while the rain hammered down around us.

There was a sense of bliss here, being dry while the rain poured around us, with the scent of a warming grill burning, throwing off welcoming heat. The smiles of the Flower Children didn't waver in the driving rain and wicked wind, and the VW canopy seemed sturdy enough to shelter us. Shelter mattered.

"What about the rest of your group?" I asked. The thunder and force of falling rain was loud and made it necessary to raise my voice. Tanner just laughed.

"They're already wet," he said. "The rain's not gonna make them any wetter. We Flower Children love playing in the rain."

I wondered if the Fawcett people would show up, wherever they were. The Swinging Man simply rocked in the rain, water dripping off his boots, splattering the ground. He did a slow spin as lightning flashed, which gave a haunting feel to him.

"You've heard of the disappearances around here?" I asked, Justin filming my asking Tanner these questions. Justin's eyes were focused on his small flip-up monitor screen that let him track the shots while remaining aware of his environment. Sharon kept her boom mic out of the shots, capturing the sound while looking half-stoned in the process. I wanted to check if she was alright, but didn't want to break up the rhythm of our shooting, even in the storm.

"Sure," Tanner said. "Who hasn't?"

"Are you from around here?" I asked. Tanner shook his head.

"We're from all over," he said. "Tonya, Tressa, and I are from California. Evan's from New Jersey. Joanna and Dara are from Georgia. Sabrina's from North Carolina. Lia's local, and Ruth's from Nebraska."

His voice was calm and casual, relaxed, even. Something about Tanner's nature gave off that vibe, even though his eyes were flat. The flat friendliness of the Flower Children was unlike anything I'd ever seen before.

"How'd you all meet up?" I asked, which made Tanner and Tressa laugh, as if I'd said something funny, which I hadn't.

"Gosh, a number of us were part of a canoe trip down the Black River. Lia had been our guide, took us here. We enjoyed ourselves so much, we just stayed on. Joanna and Dara had arrived with Sabrina and Ruth, having met up in Charleston. We all just came together. Some saw our social media posts about this place, before we decided to keep quiet about it. When it's right, it's right. There's just something about this place."

"It's a *sacred* space," Tressa said, a trifle emphatically, to my ear. Of course, I latched onto it.

"Sacred how?" I asked. Tressa looked around, pointing to the falling rain, which lent its lovely scent to the air that blended with the grill and the ever-present aroma of those flowers.

"It just is," Tressa said. "You can't feel it?"

Evan was putting meat on the grill—steaks, franks, burgers. I would have thought the Flower Children would have been vegetarian, but from the look of it, they weren't. Or at least most weren't.

"They're from Charleston, Tress," Tanner said. "They wouldn't know sacred if it stung them."

Tressa and Evan chuckled at this, while we felt a little defensive.

"We're from DC," I said. "*The Seen* is, that is. That's where we're based. Close to the grant money sources, you know?"

"That explains it," Tanner said to his peers, and they laughed, showing brightly whitened teeth. "Nothing is sacred in DC, am I right?"

"Just democracy," Ty said, more than half to himself.

I looked at Tanner and Tressa, pictures of particular privilege that I couldn't entirely relate to. Yes, I came from my own privilege, but these two and their peers, with the luxury of living out of their vintage van, seemingly selling flowers, it put me off. There was proper, patrician privilege and there was slumming it because one could afford to do so. Like a child of privilege who decided they wanted to become a fine artist—their journey could hardly be considered arduous, coming with access to lodging and supplies and even exposure that street-level artists could seldom gain.

Tanner and Tressa seemed like they came from money but didn't do much of anything with it, and maybe thought it made them more down to earth. For all of my failings, at least I'd started *The Seen*.

"We're hardly heathens, here," I said. Never mind that nobody on *The Seen* was encumbered by faith in anything less tangible than bounce rates, heat maps, and viewership stats. There was lightning and thunder in the skies, and I felt exposed, despite our protection from the rain.

"Too bad," Tanner said. "We're *all* heathens here, aren't we, Tress?"

"We sure are," Tressa said, drinking from a bottle of beer, more of which Tanner was handing out.

"Heathen is the new orthodoxy, as I see it," Tanner said, cracking his own beer. "Christianity's just so played out. Even the loudmouth Christians aren't very Christian, you know what I mean? We're past all of that. We're all about Madame Summerville here."

At the mention of this Madame, the other Flower Children raised their bottles in a toast and drank, muttering something like "If it Bleeds, it Seeds." Tyler and I shared looks.

"Who's Madame Summerville?" I asked again. "You pointed to the town, but is she a person here or what?"

"This is Her land," Tanner said. "She's like Mother Nature's bastard child, and we're all Her stepchildren."

"Meaning what, exactly?" I asked.

"Lia's going to show you," Tanner said. "She's swimming in the rain right now, but once it stops, we'll show you. *She'll* show you."

Justin kept filming, Tyler was photographing, and Sharon was minding the audio with a hard-eyed determination. I'll admit that the beer had gone to my head more than I anticipated. I wasn't tipsy, but I was feeling it.

Tanner watched us with alpha male amusement as we helped ourselves to the grilled meet Evan was cooking up, and it felt good to eat and drink, safe from the rain, even with the Flower Children. The others appeared at the Jut, having wrapped up their river swim.

Evan kept the fire going, plating all of the food he'd grilled up in meaty mounds on the foldout table—rows of scalded corn, zucchini, hot dogs, burgers, chicken breasts, portobello mushrooms, halved peaches seared with savory sauces of uncertain origin.

The river swimmers looked invigorated, at ease with themselves in their own state of nature. Tonya led them, while Joanna, Dara, Layna, Sabrina, Ruth, and Lia followed. They were drenched and laughing in the rain, and every time lightning split the sky and thunder rumbled, they cheered. Their frayed clothes were wet and hanging over their shoulders, and I realized they were all otherwise naked, their bodies forming a moving tapestry of tattoos and piercings as they strode barefoot into the camp.

Justin pivoted to capture the spectacle, while Tyler chuckled to himself, and Sharon just worked the mic, trying to take it all in.

Tanner watched me watching them and laughed again.

"We're *free* here, Ms. Rivers," Tanner said. "Free as the wind and rain. There's two types of people in this world—those who try to hide from nature, and those who embrace it. Guess which ones we are...."

He got up and tossed off his shirt, stepping out into the rain with arms outstretched, the beer in one hand, looking up at the sky and cackling while the others from the river encircled him, and he spun around with them until he reached Lia, who was pale and beautiful in this rusting steel magnolia way.

I hadn't really noticed her before, compared with all of the others. She was mousy, with dripping bangs and big brown eyes, and a cheerleader sort of nose that looked like it might wrinkle in mean girl disapproval at the slightest provocation. She had a southern kind of beauty, which is to say it was a traditional attractiveness that might turn the eye, if not the head. She clutched her stomach and gave a wounded smile to Tanner that spoke of a shared vulnerability.

Tanner held out his unencumbered hand and a red-flowered crown was put in it, tied with a red and black ribbon. He placed it on Lia's head, to the exultation of the other Flower Children, who began chanting her name: "Lia! Lia! Lia! Lia!"

The other Flower Children, the ones who were with us at the VW, joined their peers in the rain, and they danced around Lia, who was now in the center of the circle, where even Tanner had abdicated, and around and around they went.

"Tell me you're catching this," I said.

"Oh, yes," Justin said.

"Me, too," Tyler said.

"Same," Sharon said.

Even the Swinging Man circled as if in unison with the Flower Children, privy to the secrets of what was transpiring in front of us. The Flower Children danced for hours in the rain, while we filmed them until we got exhausted just watching them and went about eating some more of what Evan had cooked.

"How very *Golden Bough* this all is," Tyler said, between measured burger bites.

"They seem happy enough," Sharon said.

I was trying to frame it, how I'd speak to it when we put the episode together. Things like this, when experienced, rarely lent themselves to words in the moment. It took time to sort everything out.

"We don't even know if this has anything to do with the disappearances," Tyler said.

"True," I said. "But maybe there's something here. Neo-pagans in South Carolina? That's something. I need to dig deeper on this. We're not so far into the hinterlands or even near the upcountry. Let's get to Ladygirl and have a team meeting."

We ran across the road to Ladygirl, giggling in the rain as we did so, Justin and Sharon cursing as they sought to protect their equipment from the storm, while Tyler and I concentrated on getting Ladygirl open for them to access easily.

Once we were inside, there was a sense of security as it helped cut off some of the sound. If the Flower Children were paying attention to us, it wasn't apparent. They were so wrapped up in their crazy whirling dance and chanting.

"They're a cult," Tyler said. "Obviously."

"We have to see what they're up to," I replied. "This is good stuff, guys."

"We should get out of here," Tyler said. "Like now, while they're busy having their thunderstorm rave. We captured a bunch of footage."

"I *have* to see Madame Summerville," I said. "Maybe it's a Voodoo thing, like a spirit."

Sharon toyed with her little summerviolet in its pot, letting the plant drink down some of the rainwater that was dripping off her. Her eyes were glassy, and the garland hung heavy around her neck, the rain-touched red blossoms sprightly in their own storm-saturation.

"I agree with Holly," she said. "We have to see Madame Summerville."

Justin nodded. "I agree. I want to see it, film it."

"Whatever IT exactly is," Tyler said.

Tyler was the worrier of our team. I understood and appreciated that about him. He offered the contrary voice. I tried to reassure him.

"That's why we're here," I said. "Why we're *The Seen*. It's on us to bear witness, Ty."

"Okay, but I swear, once we film Madame Summerville, we're out, yeah?" Tyler asked. I put my hand on his forearm, intending to reassure, not sure if I succeeded in that.

"Promise," I said.

Looking In & Looking On

The storm passed quickly, and the Flower Children had stopped their dancing when it had moved on. By now, it was nearing sunset, and there was some discussion between Tanner and his flock (?) as to what to do. Everything dripped and steam rose as the prevailing heat and humidity clashed with the squall that had passed through.

We had exited Ladygirl when the rain had ceased, and Justin and Sharon were working their audiovisual alchemy while Tyler was taking more photos. Everything smelled of rainwater and wet soil. There were rivulets traveling down the Jut, while the Swinging Man turned this way and that, the rainwater rolling off his waterproof suit.

From what I observed, there were two factions debating among the Flower Children, with Tanner and Tressa advocating for a sunset ceremony, while Tonya and Evan arguing for a sunrise ceremony. It was like they didn't even know we were there and hearing them hash this out was fascinating.

"The storm was a sign," Tanner said. "The waning of the day and the hearkening of a new beginning."

"Exactly why it should be sunrise," Tonya said, baring her teeth. "A new day rising."

"Let Lia decide," Tressa said. That seemed to persuade, and the Flower Children began chanting her name again, and Lia blushed, her hands across her belly, caressing it. She didn't look pregnant to me. The veins in her arms looked ropy, standing out against her alabaster skin. Given how tan the others were, it was strange to see Lia look so pale in the evening light.

"Sunrise," Lia said, softly. "Let it be sunrise, y'all."

Tanner put an arm around her shoulders.

"Can you make it?" he asked. Lia nodded.

"I will," she said. "Let it be a golden dawn."

That seemed to satisfy the others, and even Tanner and Tressa accepted it. The momentary discord was banished as if it had never been. Only then did Tanner and Tressa acknowledge us again, as we'd been unobtrusively filming. The rain dancers and river swimmers had gone to the VW to devour the rest of the food, and there was laughter again in their ranks.

"Sorry you had to see that," Tanner said. "We're a very passionate group."

His already handsome face was only further ennobled by his chastened, almost boyish bearing in his Californian contrition. Tressa watched me watching him and I could sense a hint of jealousy in the hardness of her jet-black eyes.

"Lia gets the final say," Tress said. "That's the only way. It's *her* day. That's most important."

Tyler piped up the way I always knew he would, because his journalism-adjacent degree made it a required next step.

"Why Lia?" he asked. Tanner was unfazed by the inquiry. In fact, even after whirling around in the rain, he seemed entirely at ease with us.

"Lia's local," Tanner said. "She's from Summerville. I mean, the other Summerville. Flowertown. She helped get our group together, honestly. She's the first of us."

Tyler seized on that, innocently inquiring in a way that was anything but. Nobody sleuthed things out the way Tyler did.

"She's the founder of your cult?" Tyler asked.

"No," Tanner said, sharing a laugh with Tressa. "She's more like a prophet. Is that fair, Tressa?"

"*Very* fair," Tressa said, noshing on some of the grilled corn. I could smell the chili powder and butter on it as it slicked up her chin, catching in the festive light from their van. "Lia first encountered Madame Summerville and led us all to Her."

"When?" Tyler asked.

"Months ago," Tanner said. "Honestly, time—old time, like what *you* know—it becomes less important when you're on Madame Summerville time, if that makes sense. There are no clocks and watches here. No phones anymore, either. We live in and for the eternity of the moments we experience here. We are fully present."

I wasn't going to engage Tanner in a debate about whether modern conceptions of time could really be framed as "old time"—given that modernity itself was grounded in the capture of time by means of timekeeping and was a relatively recent phenomenon in the history of humankind. Another debate for another time, one might say.

"You don't mind us filming all of this?" I asked. We normally gathered signed permissions forms, and I counted on Tyler to do so at the end of it all, but this group didn't seem like they'd be overly concerned about it.

Tanner and Tress laughed, both of them shaking their heads.

"Not at all," Tanner said. "Hell, we *want* you to film it. Let it, you know, go viral. We'll get people making pilgrimages to this place."

"Why?" Tyler asked.

"To experience Madame Summerville," Tressa said. "You'll see tomorrow at sunrise. We all commune with Her. Our time comes."

I glanced at Lia, who was in a place of honor at the VW camper, her flowery crown on her head, her pale face smiling uncertainly as she feasted on grilled chicken and zucchini. She looked to be in her mid-20s by my estimation. I'd never appeared so carefree. I wanted to interview her, but didn't want to do so with all the Flower Children lurking around her.

"What does that mean, Tressa?" I asked. Tressa seemed bemused by my inquiry, like I distracted her for a moment with my question. God knows what she was thinking.

"Madame Summerville chooses us," Tressa said. "Not everyone passes Her tests. It's hard to explain, but She knows worthy from unworthy. The vessels that bear Her, the ones that meet Her standards."

All at once, the fragrant garlands we wore felt heavier.

"Are we worthy?" I asked.

Tanner laughed, and Tressa giggled—the difference between their expressions of amusement making me uneasy—Tanner's was too garrulous, and Tressa's was too guarded. It left me in the middle, feeling like I was the punch line of an inside joke.

"We shall see," Tanner said. "We gave you garlands so you'd feel welcome, so you'd feel a part of things. That's how we are."

I looked back at the Fawcett van, which was still unattended.

"What about the Fawcett people?" I asked. "Were *they* welcome?"

There was a trace of a frown, just a shadow of it that might have gone unseen in the waning light, but I caught it.

"They're *not* friends to Madame Summerville," Tressa said, before Tanner could chime in. "They burned down a tree that was *very* important to Her. It was a desecration."

That sounded juicy, so I pursued it, while my team caught it all.

"I saw the fallen tree," I replied.

"We all saw it," Tyler said.

"That tree contained a colony of wasps," Tressa said. "Protectors of the town, the way we saw it. A big nest. Those Fawcett men burned it down."

Fawcett men. Tressa was the mouthier of the two of them, so I thought I'd be able to provoke her into saying more.

"Company men," Tanner said. "You know how Fawcett Biotech is, Ms. Rivers. They see the world as *theirs* to conquer. No respect for Nature, except as something to increase their own market share. Patent pirates is what they are. Patently piratical."

"Where are they?" I asked. "These company men?"

"We ran them off," Tanner said.

Tyler looked around us, warily, glancing at the Swinging Man a moment, and at me.

"You ran them off?" Tyler asked. "Are the cops coming, then?"

Tanner put a hand on Tyler's shoulder, giving him a squeeze.

"County's got bigger fish to fry than us," Tanner said. "And it's a long walk to civilization from here. Those Fawcett fellas have a ways to go before they can get any-where to do anything about it."

"And spotty cellphone reception," Tressa said. "In case you hadn't noticed."

Of course, at mention of that, Tyler and I slipped out our phones and checked. Sure enough, we barely had a bar between us.

"That's unfortunate," I said. "And portentous, yeah?"

"You tell me," Tressa said, smirking.

"Be nice, Tress," Tanner said, cuffing her with an arm while she played with her long locks. "Ms. Rivers is here to help us. She's trying to put together a story."

Tressa shrugged off his arm and just looked us up and down.

"We'll see what they say at sunrise," Tressa said.

BLOG ENTRY 8

(Holly Rivers)

Droning On

The night wasn't the most comfortable for us, cooped up as we were in Ladygirl. The storm had made things briefly cooler, but the heat and humidity hit the roof as night set in, and we opened the top and tried to chill.

Tanner had kindly lent us a couple of citronella candle buckets what we set up around the Eldorado, to help keep the mosquitoes at bay. The scent of the candles mixed with the summerviolet aroma, and made it nice, despite our relative discomfort.

Ladygirl was a massive car, and it made for a comfortable drive, but sleeping in it wasn't entirely ideal. The flickering glow of the citronella was mesmerizing, however, and helped set a mood.

The team was used to field work, and we'd done what we could. One wonderful thing was the night sky, which was incredibly vivid, a diamond-decked tapestry of inky black. Even Tyler was impressed by it, and he tried to affect a jaded vibe most of the time.

Meanwhile, the Flower Children were quietly singing and dancing, feasting at their camper van. Sharon and Justin joined them, which amounted to passing around bottles and cups for drinking, while they chatted with one another. Lia was still at the center of it all, looking high as a kite, her flower crown still on her head, the ribbons jerking as she moved.

Tyler looked on from where he was in the back seat, shaking his head.

"What do you think is going to happen?" he asked. I looked back at him, could only see a hint of his face, illuminated by the camper lights.

"Something terribly neo-ritualistic," I said, feeling stupid the moment I said it. *No duh, Holly.* The Fawcett van was a shadow in the dark distance, raising questions I hadn't gotten around to asking. I slipped out of the convertible and crept over to the van, while Tyler looked on from the shadows, whispering to me.

"What are you doing?" he asked.

"Snooping," I said. From where I was, Ladygirl offered some cover against the VW camper, and would let me poke around without being obvious about it. I reached into the wheel wells and hoped to find a spare set of keys, which took me about ten minutes to do.

My efforts were rewarded, as I found a magnetic box on the inside of the front bumper, seeing the Fawcett logo on it, and saw that it contained a spare set of keys. Tyler was watching, his head silhouetted by the light from the camper. The Flower Children were singing, with someone playing a banjo and someone else playing some bongos and a guitar.

I crept around to the far side of the Fawcett van and quietly keyed into the passenger side. Beyond me, in the woods, I could hear tree frogs and crickets mixing in with the psychedelic songs of the Flower Children.

The door to the van opened easily and I slipped in as quietly as I could, quickly turning off the interior light that went on when I opened it.

Inside the Fawcett van, there wasn't anything that seemed out of place, beyond the intoxicating scent of summer-violets. Inside the back of the van was an interesting setup—a broken industrial drone, as well as some control equipment. No blood or anything too weird.

I turned on my phone flashlight and looked it over. The broken drone had a camera on it, as well as two bottles connected to spray nozzles. One smelled minty, while the other smelled flammable, that sort of oily scent that felt downright incendiary.

Of principal interest for me was the camera, which had a USB cable port on it as well as a removable SD card. I quickly took out my multitool and unscrewed the camera, moving as quietly and carefully as I could.

Whoever flew this drone had taken good care of it, and it came out cleanly. Tyler texted me, and I was thankful it came to me, even though it moved slowly.

TYLER: WHAT RU DOING?

HOLLY: Snoopin. Shhhh. Keep watch.

T: K.

H: Ping me if anyone's around.

As I removed the camera, I could see "CHARLENE" was printed on the drone with embossed stickers. Turning off my phone light, I pocketed my phone and kept the drone camera close at hand. I was dying to see what was on it.

Justin was our prime videographer, but this drone's camera looked layperson-friendly, and I was more than a novice with audiovisual gear. I moved my way back through the van, careful not to trip over anything.

Tyler: Someone's coming.

Holly: K. Back in a sec.

I slipped out of the van, closing it as quietly as I could. I decided I'd keep that key box handy, just in case.

"Hey, Tyler," Tonya said. "Where's Holly?"

I could overhear her.

"Nature called," Tyler said, which made Tonya chuckle.

"Yeah, Nature calls 24/7 out here," she said. "Hope she didn't stray too far. There are some more drops beside the Jut out there. In the dark, anything can happen. Especially if you're not used to it."

I judged my approach based on where I heard her voice, and when her back was turned, I crept up on the shadowy side of Ladygirl and set the drone camera near the right rear wheel, bathed in shadow, before standing up.

Tonya turned her head after I'd risen, and her face broke into a challenging sort of smile as she saw me.

"Hey, Ms. Rivers," Tonya said. "You and Tyler want to join the rest of us at the van? We're going to be up late. Nobody sleeps much ahead of Evanescence."

"No, thanks," I said. "Evanescence, eh?"

I knew what evanescence meant—it was the state of fading from existence. And since we were covering disappearances in the area, that felt almost painfully on the nose. Was Tonya testing me?

"Yeah," Tonya said. "Lia's evanescing at dawn. She's going places. You'll see. We're all going that way, eventually. She's just first in line."

Her way of saying it was casual, even breezy. There was resignation in it, but no weariness. Not the kind of fervent exultation one might have expected.

"Is this your first, uh, Evanescence?" I asked.

"Oh, no," Tonya said. "It's hard to explain. Lia's the first in line among *us*. But we've experienced others evanescing. People just come by, and Madame Summerville wants them. You know it when you see it."

I couldn't believe how open they were about their fanaticism. Cults always seemed to me to be secretive about their rituals, but the openness of the Flower Children was bizarre.

Without asking, I knew that Ty was recording it. He was marvelously sneaky about that. We were great partners that way, each understanding the other, working together.

"What does Madame Summerville look like?" I asked. Tonya scoffed.

"She's beautiful," Tonya said. "You'll see at dawn. We'll trek into town. Summerville proper. We have a raft we use to ford the river. Swimming's the best, of course, but for tourists, you know, we're accommodating. Get you over the river and into town. To the Madame's Chapel. It's on Temple Street. That's where She lives. It's hard to really pin Her down to one spot, because She *is* the town."

Tonya didn't strike me as the most loquacious of the Flower Children, so I wondered why she was telling us all of this. Maybe she was just piquing our curiosity, saying things she knew would get us more curious.

"Summerviolets never stop growing," Tonya said. "They start out small, but you let them be, they'll grow bigger. There are big blossoms in Summerville. Big as pie plates. Big as manhole covers. You'll see. That's how you know you've got a strong colony—the size of the flowers tells the tale."

"Madame Summerville is what, then? A plant?" I asked.

Tonya looked back at me like I was a fool.

"Of course She is," Tonya said. "She's got plans for you, Ms. Rivers. And for the rest of your crew."

"What sort of plans?" I asked. Tonya had said it as mildly as she could, but I felt some threat buried in the heart of her words.

"Not evanescence, if you were worried about that," Tonya said. "It comes to all of us eventually, but not for you. Not yet. She needs *The Seen* to be seen."

There it was. The casual way she spoke of it triggered me, and I had to fight to keep my cool. Everything in me was screaming to jump into Ladygirl and get out of there, but the voyeuristic drive to get some audience-engaging scoop was overriding my survival instinct.

I imagined it's how those tornado chasers must feel, seeing the storm tearing a hole in the sky and the ground and still wanting to get as close to it as possible for the sake of some killer footage.

"How can you know?" I asked.

Tonya laughed, a hollow kind of thing, devoid of mirth, packed with something else entirely.

"We know," Tonya said. "Madame Summerville provides—not just flowers, but fruit, seeds, pollen, oil, fabric. Even a cut vine can grow back if the conditions are right. That's how it is with Her. She is generous."

I could feel Ty wanting to ask questions, but knew he was being unobtrusive, recording quietly. That was his way.

"Fruit?" I asked.

"Berries," Tonya said. "Sweet berries. Not poisonous. They're delicious."

She fished something from a pocket, holding out some dried berries that looked orange and blue by the camper's lights toying with the shadows.

"No, thanks," I said.

"Good high from them, for real," Tonya said, popping a few in her mouth. "The seeds are like cherries, only they're shaped differently. Like little footballs. We call them 'hearts' of course."

She chewed on the dried fruit and spat out the seeds, which were visible in her palms. Rather than tossing them away, she pocketed them reverently.

"Every part of the summerviolet can be used," Tonya said. "She is so giving of Herself. The leaves can be used to brew a tea. We've got some over at the camper, if you like. *Strong* tea. The berries you can eat fresh or dried. You can make jam or preserves out of them. You could even make a pie. I can't bake, but, you know, that's what I've heard. You can make rope from the vines, if you know what you're doing. Paper, too, even. Paper that lasts. And cloth that doesn't wear out. A ton of products. It's how we Flower Children keep ourselves going. She provides."

I wasn't about to try a dried berry that came from Tonya's pocket, but she seemed to be enjoying herself. Glancing at the camper, I could see that Sharon and Justin were downing some of that summerviolet tea by the look of it. Their laughter wasn't quite infectious, but there was an aura there.

Tonya rocked a little from where she was standing at the front of Ladygirl, and I wondered if it was the influence of the berries or something else.

"Too bad you won't join us," Tonya said, shaking her head as she rejoined the others. Ty and I watched her go.

"Tell me you caught all of that," I said, softly.

"You know I did," Ty said. "Did you find anything in the van?"

"You know I did," I replied, my eyes on the revelers.

Good Mourning, Sunshine

Sleep came whether we wanted it to or not. I had secured the drone cam under the driver's seat of Ladygirl, since Ty and I didn't quite have time to review it without drawing attention to ourselves. I figured I'd just check it out when we got out of there. That was the plan between us, whispered in the shadows, while the Flower Children and half our team danced in the dark.

I hadn't even realized I'd dozed off until morning came and the Flower Children were calling to us, with Tanner, Tressa, and Tonya shaking tasseled tambourines and urging us up.

Squinting blearily, I could see that Justin and Sharon were already geared up, Sharon wielding her boom mic like some totemistic staff, while Justin carried his camera gear on him like a soldier. Both of them were jarringly glassy-eyed, while Tyler and I were muzzy-headed and slow to rise.

The Flower Children were bearing Lia on their shoulders, and were wearing red, yellow, ochre, and amber batik summer dresses and gowns, with the men among them wearing open white shirts. All of them bore garlands of summerviolets but only Lia wore a crown.

Ty and I got up and out of Ladygirl, trying to unobtrusively observe and record. I wanted to interview Lia, but judging from the look in her eyes and the fervency of the Flower Children, I didn't think I'd be able to get in there.

"Lia! Lia! Lia!" the Flower Children cried, while the tambourines beat out a cadence as they made their way to the Jut, while the Swinging Man did a mindless pirouette borne of breezes we couldn't feel at ground level. The Sun was showing its face somewhere to the east, while the trees stood as sentinels and protectors from the beams of light.

We followed behind them, filming, while I half-narrated, as I often did when we filmed one of our documentaries.

"They call themselves 'The Flower Children' and beyond quaint associations with the counterculture of yester-year, this group represents something else entirely," I said. "Peace and love? I'm not so sure they know what that even means."

The Flower Children, following Tanner, Tressa, and Ton-ya, had worked their way down the steep slope that led to a swollen Black River, which was flowing stronger in the wake of the storm that had passed through.

I could see that they'd conjured up a kind of floating raft made up of Fawcett-branded blue and yellow bar-rels and boards carefully lashed with rope. I hadn't been down to the riverbank before, so I was unsure if this was something they'd had there openly, or whether it was concealed.

"Your team can set up here, Ms. Rivers," Tanner said. "We'll come back for you."

"Fine," I said, not having to tell Justin to capture it all. He worked his camera well, shooting for coverage the way he always did, while Sharon sucked down the sound with her recording equipment. They worked flawlessly together.

"Here on the banks of the Black River, we find ourselves far away from the everyday world," I said. Sometimes I would speak these lines knowing that we'd re-record them as overdubs in post-production. It helped to foot-note the moment, felt more natural this way.

The Flower Children carefully boarded their raft and Tanner and Evan used poles to get them across the river, while others banged their tambourines, and Lia held her arms across her middle, her face a smile-grimace, tears running down her cheeks. It looked like joyous rapture fused with an ineffable terror. That eerily ecstatic expression won't ever leave me.

I directed Justin and Tyler to film and photograph Lia, while Sharon looked on, keeping her boom microphone on me as I narrated.

"Lia looks captivated by the as-yet-unclear ritual, and yet I see something else in her wide-eyed gaze," I said. "What is it? Transcendence? Uncertainty? Ecstasy? Grief? Maybe all of them combined. We came here to Summerville to find out the fates of some missing people, and instead have discovered something else entirely. What have we found?"

"Evanescence," Sharon said, through gritted teeth, her eyes like buttons as she gazed longingly across the Black River, her summerviolet garland as fresh as it had been the day before, the red blossoms seeming to writhe against her chest. My eyes dragged to Justin, who wore his own garland.

Ty and I had left ours back with Ladygirl, but the fragrance of the flowers was as strong as ever. Maybe stronger, given our proximity to the town itself. The air sparkled with pollen, or the pollen made us see sparkles. I was willing to concede both possibilities as equally real.

"Evanescence," I said, mindful of Sharon's slow, solemn nod. The Flower Children had crossed the river, and there was a joyful ritual underway as they disembarked, with the ceaseless banging of tambourines lending a crisp, staccato sound of cymbals to the sonorous chanting of Lia's name. Evan and Tanner poled the raft back to us in slow, confident strokes, their forearms rippling with each motion.

"We should get out of here," Ty said.

"Come on, Ty," I said. "There's something here we need to capture."

Ty shook his head, wincing at me. He snapped some more pictures with his tablet, then stowed it in his messenger bag.

"Not me," Ty said. "I'm going back to the car. Hell, I'm going to snoop around up there. You don't need me for the shoot, and I don't want to be there."

I loved Tyler as much as Sharon and Justin. We were a team and had worked so many shoots together. I'm not going to say it was a betrayal, but it kind of felt that way somewhere in the backrooms of my heart.

"Come on, Ty," Sharon said. "Don't be a coward. *This* is what we do."

"I'm *not* being a coward," Tyler said. "I just think it's better if I hang back. Something about this is way messed up. We don't know what these people are really about. And I think I can do more back at the vehicles."

"Like what?" Justin asked, turning his camera on Tyler, who hated being filmed. I could see him squirming both inside and out.

"I'll know it when I see it," Ty said. "Look, you three are the production team. I'm pre- and post-production. I'll see what you shoot and we'll work it out."

"Okay," I said. Everybody had agency in our team, and I respected Ty's decision. We had history, and that history counted. And Sharon and Justin would go where I went. It was like when we went into some Appalachian caves in search of a secret shrine we'd heard about a few years back, where some kids had disappeared. It's what we did.

> [This is referring to *The Seen* Episode 16, "Happy Valley & the Ambrose Grotto"—which was tied to a cryptic series of disappearances in the area tied to an enigmatic cave shrine. Great episode! —Ed.]

"Be careful over there," Ty said, scrambling up the slope while Evan and Tanner reached us on the riverbank.

Tanner watched Ty work his way up the leafy, muddy incline, cocked an eyebrow, while Sharon and Justin stepped carefully aboard the raft.

"Problem?" Tanner asked.

"Ty didn't sleep well last night," I said, covering for him. "He's going to try to take a nap while we're shooting."

Tanner nodded and shook his head almost at the same time.

"Writers are sensitive, yeah?" he said.

"Very," I said, taking Tanner's offered hand to step onto the raft. We were careful to maintain our balance on it, while Evan and Tanner poled us back across the river, toward Summerville. The heavy rain had made the river flow faster, but nothing they couldn't navigate, it seemed.

"It's beautiful," I said, as we worked our way beneath the canopy of green from the trees interlaced overhead.

"It sure is," Tanner said. "There's nothing else in the world like this place. At least for now."

"Meaning?" I asked.

"We're just out there spreading the good news is all," Tanner said.

Evan smiled to himself as he and Tanner poled us over to the other side of the riverbank. I stole a backward glance at Tyler, who'd reached the top, and was taking photos of us with his tablet. Seeing me seeing him, he gave a wave, which I returned. He watched us until we got off the raft, setting foot on the leaf-covered ground of Summerville.

When I looked back again, he was gone.

Dancing With Myself

[From this point on, we start getting blog entries from Tyler Finn, as you can see. They follow the same stylistic format as the Holly Rivers ones, which makes me think this was a standard practice for the production team for *The Seen*. Tyler was far more attentive about uploading files to *The Seen* servers than Ms. Rivers, for which we're all thankful. —Ed.]

Holly and the others went along with whatever the Flower Children were up to, but did you think I'd do that? Fat chance. I don't trust hippies—nothing personal against them, but the Flower Children gave off some weird cultish vibe that I couldn't quite put my finger on.

Not to geeksplain or anything, but I remembered that old episode of *Star Trek* (The Original Series: Season 1, Episode 24, "This Side of Paradise") where the crew gets hit with these spores by these flowers which bliss everybody out—even Spock. A Lotus-Eaters kind of narrative which likely hit hard in 1967, when that episode aired, while the 60s counterculture was surging.

Not going to lie: when the Flower Children gave us those summerviolet garlands, I was immediately skeeved out. We're in South Carolina. Who does that? I wore mine to be polite, but I was seriously creeped out by it and took mine off as soon as I could.

I didn't want Holly or the others to tease me about it, but there was something very off about the flowers—they smelled wonderful, but they tripped me out, too. I'm one of those people who likes to hold onto my edge, whether through caffeine or whatever, and I could feel those flowers making me feel off. Kind of high.

What's more, and this might just be a side effect or something, but I swear I felt them move, just a little bit. First chance I got, like without being rude, and I hung my garland on the rearview mirror of Ladygirl, before thinking twice about it and tossing it away when nobody was looking. I didn't want the plants anywhere near me.

This might make me seem paranoid, but I've known Sharon and Justin for years, and they were acting weird. Weird is weird, man. I know it when I see it, and they were being *weird*. Holly was still Holly, but there was no way I was going to bring it up with her.

That's the burden of being a writer; we just *see* things. And I was seeing things up on the Jut. First off, where were the Fawcett Biotech employees? I don't see why or how a company might send some people out here to do whatever they wanted them to do and them just to disappear?

No way. They vanish, and these Flower Children just happen to turn up. I grew up in DC, and if there's anything I understand, it's that there's a reason everything happens.

Something happened to those Fawcett employees. I can't say exactly what happened to them, but all I knew was they weren't here. While Holly and the others were busy documenting whatever ritual insanity the Flower Children were going to perpetrate on Lia, I figured I'd review the drone footage and see what had occurred. Maybe it was nothing.

I know that if I had done something to somebody and it was recorded on a drone, there's no way I'd have simply left behind the SD card and camera. On the other hand, I wasn't some drugged up neo-cultist like Tanner and the others, either. Maybe they didn't think to cover that up, or, perhaps more frighteningly, maybe they didn't care.

All I knew was that I had to see what had taken place. Justin was the ace audiovisual tech, but I knew my way around camcorders and cameras, and with the right USB cables in Ladygirl's trunk, I was able to slot into the Charlene drone camera and download the files to my tablet.

It looked like the Fawcett guy had YouTube-compatible tech on his drone, which was sort of curious to me. I just assumed folks at Fawcett might use proprietary software. It was also possible that they hired out this Jeph Wales as a private contractor to save money, which gave him more latitude in his dronework. They probably had him sign some nondisclosure agreements as a precondition for employment.

The files loaded readily on my tablet, and I grimaced at the memory hogging they represented. Then again, I'd rigged out my tablet for *The Seen,* which meant it had as much memory as I could get away with, and my tablet could deal with it, despite my concern.

I started from the last shots taken, since those were most important to me, and glanced around before I rolled on it. Everything was basically weird-normal (I know that seems counterintuitive, but that vibe is all over the South if you look for it)—birds and crickets, tree frogs, wind, stuff like that. The Flower Children were all in the ghost town, and it was just me there by myself.

The final shot was the drone crashing to the ground before the camera blanked out. That made for a jarring blast of blur and tree shapes, ending in a terminal bounce on the weed-cracked asphalt of the Jut. I went backward before that and could see the drone had been hovering over the road, above the van. I could see the Flower Children van parked behind it, could make out Tanner, Evan, Tonya, and Tressa and the others circling the van, rapping on it with their hands.

Those first four were carrying crossbows on bandoliers across their backs. Their faces were bizarre, because they didn't exactly look angry; rather, they were just smiling oddly, talking to someone in the van. Had to be Jeph Wales in there, piloting the drone.

Rolling back earlier, Jeph was cautiously navigating the drone through the trees, overlooking Summerville. It took me a minute to understand what I was looking at, but I could see that the drone had been following Jeph's partner, who was this lanky guy with a boonie hat and a machete who was working his way to the ghost town. The man was hacking this way and that with his machete, trying to clear a path.

From my borrowed perspective, it looked like he was having a rough go of it, since the vines and leaves were thick and appeared difficult to cut. I watched his progress until something had distracted Jeph—which had to have been the Flower Children, since he'd turned the drone around and buzzed back toward the van, and I could see the crazily-painted VW van there.

I went back earlier and could see Jeph filming his partner as they torched the largest wasp nest I'd ever seen, growing in an old, dead tree. The thing burned like a torch, and wasps raged about it. Going still further backwards, I could see that Jeph had sicced the drone on the nest, with wasps flying at the drone, only to be dispatched by a flamethrower. The timestamp on it had this taking place two days before we'd gotten there.

Then I heard a truck pull up, and I quickly stopped my playback and shut my tablet, turning to see who'd showed up. It was an old red tow truck. Two guys got out—one was that Circle K guy, Cooper DeVille, and the other was a younger, broad-chested young man with a reckless brown beard and squinty eyes. Both wore ballcaps, with DeVille's being that old Fawcett one, and the other being one which had an alternately smug or peevish wasp on it.

"Hey, there," said DeVille. "There she is. Ladygirl. That's the one I was telling you about, Noah."

They walked up to Ladygirl and pawed at her, which had me stepping out and feeling more than a bit uneasy, being a lone black man confronting two white southern guys in South Carolina. DeVille chuckled a little, while Noah looked me over.

"You find what you're looking for here, Son?" DeVille asked. His rheumy eyes flitted over the VW van as well as the Fawcett one, before dragging back to Ladygirl and me.

"We're shooting now," I said, which made DeVille laugh, at least until he sniffed the air.

"Something burned?" he asked.

"Ehh, the wasp nest, I think," I said. "We only just got here."

DeVille walked slowly, deliberately to the Jut and shaded his eyes, tsking. He took off his hat and held it to his chest.

"They burned it, Noah," DeVille said. "Torched the whole damned thing."

"We didn't," I said. The caliber of their displeasure motivated me to distance myself from the act. "Maybe the Flower Children did it."

DeVille and Noah both turned and looked at me as if I'd said something simultaneously awful, incomprehensible, and insane.

"They'd do no such thing," DeVille said. "Those hippie kids know better than that. They're good kids."

"All I know is that *we* didn't do it," I said.

"It's Fawcett," DeVille said, pointing up at the Swinging Man. "Them's the ones what did it. We're here to take their van, anyway. Got to tow it."

Noah nodded. He reeked of fresh wintergreen and old sweat.

"Got to tow it," Noah said. "Plain as day."

"I think the Fawcett guys might have a thing or two to say about that," I replied. DeVille laughed, a dry kind of rasp.

"They have something to say about it, they can find it at the Circle K," DeVille said. All at once, I thought of all the other vehicles in his half-assed impound lot.

"Along with all those others you've got?" I asked.

The balance I was trying to achieve was somewhere between sass and sarcasm, conveying my disbelief without exactly confronting these two men. DeVille might have been an old man, but Noah was young and burly, looked like he could hurt me.

The other thing that struck me was that this old man was clearly involved with something or other going on here. Each of those cars at the Circle K had to be tied to disappearances in the area. It was just something that came to me as I watched them. Maybe Cooper DeVille was the Black River Butcher.

"Along with all the others," DeVille said, grinning at me like some yellow-toothed Jack-o'-Lantern. Noah went back to the tow truck and drove it around, back up behind the van. While he did that, DeVille looked me over. "You're the quiet one of your bunch. I seen you the other day, bein' all quiet and such."

"Yeah," I said. "I suppose I am."

"Gotta watch the quiet ones," DeVille said, caressing Ladygirl, wiping off some dust. "They're the secret keepers."

"That so?" I asked.

He nodded, while Noah worked to hook up the van. DeVille whistled, tossing a metal shim to Noah, who caught it one-handed. The younger man walked over to the driver's side and slid the shim down between the door and window, jimmying it a bit until he unlocked the van and entered it.

"I sure can't wait to take this lovely lady home with me," DeVille said, stroking Ladygirl's flanks with arthritic hands.

"Oh, I don't think Holly would part with her," I said.

"You never know," DeVille said. "Never know what people might leave behind in a place like this."

The old man looked me right in the eye as he said this, and I just held my own gaze. It seemed important to do so.

"Are you the Black River Butcher?" I asked.

"Haw! I never butchered nobody," DeVille said, while Noah emerged from the van. "I just keep this place clean is all. I'm what you'd call a steward of the land."

Noah went back and checked the chains before he worked the levers to hoist up the van. The machinery whined as it did so, and I watched the van rise up. This felt very wrong to me, but I wasn't about to say anything. DeVille just watched me, smiling more than half to himself.

"Clean of what?" I asked.

"Abandoned vehicles," DeVille said. "People litter them all over the place. So careless."

I knew he was hiding something. But seeing how un-fazed he'd been by my suggesting he might be a serial killer, I was a little wary. Noah had finished lifting the van, lit a cigarette and watched us both a moment.

"We're all set, Coop," Noah said.

"Great," DeVille said. "We'd have come yesterday, but the storm that blew through, no way we were going to do it then."

He glanced around, grimacing.

"Looking for something?" I asked.

"Where's the rest of your crew?" DeVille asked.

"They went down to Summerville with the Flower Children," I said. That hit DeVille's funny bone, as the old man slapped his thigh with a freckle-tanned hand and guffawed.

"Did they, now?" DeVille said. "But not you?"

"Nope," I said. "I hung back."

"Why?" DeVille asked, glancing at the garland on the ground. "You don't like flowers?"

"Too many mosquitoes for my liking down there," I said. DeVille chuckled again, gesturing for Noah to pick up the garland. The young man did it without question and put it around his neck, beaming at me with the cigarette on his lip. DeVille smiled back at us both.

"Ain't no mosquitoes," DeVille said. "Not down there, leastways. Madame Summerville don't like 'em none."

The offhand way he said it bothered me, and I wanted to record him, but with Noah nursing his smoke and DeVille right beside me, I couldn't do it without being obvious. Holly might have been able to talk her way through it, but not me.

"Who is Madame Summerville?" I asked.

DeVille nodded in the direction of the town, which reminded me of what Tanner and Tressa had done.

"She's over yonder," DeVille said. "Your friends'll meet Her soon enough."

"That so?" I asked.

"Mmm hmm," DeVille said. "You about done there, Noah?"

Noah nodded, walking over to the tow truck.

"I *been* done, Coop," Noah said, toying with the flowers on the garland.

"You take care, Son," DeVille said. "Don't be a stranger, now."

I saw him look Ladygirl over one more time before he shambled over to the truck, taking his time to get in and drive off. I watched them go, could feel DeVille's old eyes upon me through the side mirror as they went.

There wasn't a moment that passed when I wasn't glad that I'd opted out of the Summerville sightseeing the others had done. Had I not been up there, who knows what DeVille and his sidekick might have done.

Once they were out of sight, where I couldn't hear them anymore, I ran over to the VW van, determined to see what the hell was going on.

BLOG ENTRY 11
(Holly Rivers)

Ah, Lia

My first impressions of landfall at Summerville was the carpet of leaves, which looked like a sea of glossy green aces coquettishly pointing our way into the ghost town. We followed the Flower Children, while Tanner narrated.

"Be careful of those leaves, Ms. Rivers," Tanner said. "They're pretty, but they'll cut you if you're not paying attention to where you're going."

Most of the Flower Children were either barefoot or wearing sandals, a sea of tanned, bare skin. I could see a few cuts on their ankles, but they didn't seem affected by them, chanting Lia's name as they moved. Lia was singing, too, her own words more like wailing to my ears. Apparently being involved in an arcane ritual didn't lend one the ability to carry a tune.

The approach to the remains of the town wasn't as steep as the area near the Jut, and I'm not sure whether that's a result of the earthquake-shifted land or some peculiarity of the area. The old photos of the town indicated that there had been a bridge along Main Street, something that had connected the town to the road, but whatever it had been, there were no traces of the bridge beyond the spar of the Jut. Scrap metal salvagers likely came for the remnants of the bridge after the town had been drowned in the floods.

Whatever the case, the landscape was covered with the green leaves that grew from tangles of vines that were like arteries and veins and making our way to Main Street in the wake of the Flower Children, the red trumpetlike flowers proliferated in that space, always seeming to be facing us like onlookers. They seemed to watch us the way sunflowers tracked the progress of the Sun.

The broken remains of old businesses, garbed in green, hung like sentinels around us, like lost gods and titans of another time—a simpler time if not a better one. I directed Justin to cover the approach, and he didn't hesitate in capturing it all.

With the rhythmic music of the Flower Children ahead of us, coupled with the dizzying aroma of the flowers, it was hard to think clearly. I felt like I was floating.

"Where are we going, Tanner?" I asked. Tanner smiled reassuringly at me.

"Temple Street," he replied. "Naturally."

"Naturally," I said. There had only been Main, First, and Temple Street in the town, even before the disasters had laid claim to it. I had wondered why Temple Street wasn't Church Street but couldn't find anything that might have clarified that. "What's at Temple Street?"

"We made a temple," Tanner said.

"You made it?" I asked. Tanner nodded as we kept walking. The vibe here was very strange, as everything was covered by the flowery vine, and the manifold animal sounds one could hear on the periphery were absent, here. What we heard within Summerville (besides the murmuring music of the Flower Children and Lia's swoony caterwauling) was the breeze and the rustling of the vines. The scent of the flowers was so very strong. It was musky and intoxicating. Am I being too dramatic? I felt it.

If Ty had been here, he'd have asked questions, bless his heart.

"What pollinates those big flowers?" I asked. I couldn't imagine what even would, given their size, which ranged from dinner plates to pizza pans to manhole covers, just like Tonya had said the night before.

"We do," Tanner said. "We distribute the pollen any time we come through here. Madame Summerville doesn't mind. She likes it."

I could see that some of the vines had been cut here and there, relatively new cuts that had hints of sap on them like amber-hued blood.

The Flower Children continued their procession, and I was acutely aware of the ace-shaped leaves guiding us along. I snapped shots with my phone, as the view was incredible, and the green leaves and red flowers formed a sort of pattern that called to mind painterly works like Vincent van Gogh. When the breeze hit them, they swayed and bobbed, creating fascinating patterns in their florid florality that I found I had to blink away, finding them gone when I looked again.

Justin and Sharon were entirely mesmerized by the plant phantasmagoria around us, with Justin slowly whirling to take it in, while Sharon followed in his wake like an ardent disciple.

Within this cool canopy of vines clutching tightly to trees, where dappled light danced in a sea of drowsing shadow, there was a strong sense of enclosure, and, strangely, peace. Maybe it was the heavenly aroma of the pollen, or just the languorous aura around us, but I felt it.

The "temple" was a broken-down church, reduced by decades of exposure to the elements to four corners of broken brick and a promenade that ended in the spiderweb remnants of stained glass framing, with only the broken feet of a forgotten saint on a cracked plinth visible in the sea of vines and flowers.

I need to take some time with this description to adequately convey what I saw, because it was like being at the heart of something unforgettable. The vines were thickest here—far thicker than my arms, thicker even than those of the men. And they twisted snake-like (wormlike?) throughout the structure of the dead church-turned-temple, where there were no pews. The colors were a blend of brown, red, green, tan, and grey, as well as our human tones, like we were in the middle of a monstrous mosaic or a chaotic kaleidoscope. The euphoric pollen probably colored my perception of the moment, weaving lilting transcendence out of latent (if not blatant) intoxication.

Instead, there was the long-lost remains of a bonfire that stood as a mound of rain-drowned ash. Beyond it were the largest flowers I'd yet seen, being larger than truck tires, and blood-red, with black accents and twitching anthers of white. *Were* they twitching? Or was that my inebriated imagination? I'd have to consult Justin's footage to be sure.

"Justin, are you getting this?" I asked.

"Yes," Justin said, filming this gigantic plant growing throughout the temple, with the Flower Children ambling up, having ended their pilgrimage. They reverently stepped to the mass of ash and jabbed their fingers into it—their index and middle fingers—and each running a two-fingered stripe from their foreheads to their chins, their eyes closed in reverie. It was clearly a deeply meaningful gesture for them.

They clasped hands with each other and made three circles around the ash pile, while the flowers seemed to dance with them, moving this way and that. At first,

I thought it was maybe a breeze that did it, but I was convinced that the flowers moved of their own accord in this hypnotic kind of dance. We were at ground zero of a mass hallucination, I was certain.

If they'd been aware of us, the Flower Children in the presence of the massive flowering plant at the altar of the sundered cathedral didn't seem interested in us at all. Instead, their eyes were fixed on Lia, who broke from their circle to scale the ash pile, moving fitfully, straining as she climbed. She wept as she did so, while they chanted her name with a ritualistic cardiac fervor that beat stronger as she made her way to the top.

Lia reached the summit of the mound of ash and threw her arms skyward, while the largest of the red blooms hovered out of reach, floating like something out of a daylit nightmare. I couldn't shake that feeling, that sense of foreboding as I watched all of this. I'd wanted to say something to Justin and Sharon, but they had moved closer, eager to catch it all, the flowers on their garlands dancing around their necks in miniature emulation of the larger specimens.

All the time this was going on, I was thinking this would be our best-ever episode of *The Seen,* and that might make me sound shallow, but I felt that even as I watched ash-covered Lia bring her arms down and rip off her clothes and split apart in a burst of blood that made me want to scream, but I couldn't find the breath to do it. Even if I had, I wouldn't have been able to be heard, as Lia shrieked as she blew apart, splashing the whirling Flower Children with her blood.

You can see Justin's footage of it for yourself and hear Sharon's recording of it if you don't believe me, but Lia exploded. In her moment of holy evanescence, Lia Larkin ended in a cracking of bone and rending of flesh and an outpouring of blood that drained into the ash.

Playing it back slowly, you can see the moment when Lia ceased to be, her young human form detonating into something unrecognizable, and, in her place, three young summerviolet saplings—drenched in blood and bodily fluids—stretched their fresh leaves and vines, their unopened blossoms bending to catch the bits of sunlight.

"Ohmigod," I said, taking pictures with my phone with enervated fingers. My knees were weak, and I wanted to pass out. How I didn't is something I'll never know; maybe it was my professional desire to observe and report on this that kept me going. Maybe I was too stoned to fully feel what I was seeing.

The young vines and shoots of the plants, not brown, but tender green and blood-bathed, flailed about to find purchase in the ash. At the sight of this, Tanner, Tressa, and Tonya climbed the ash pile and grasped the summerviolet saplings, placing them in pots that they'd recovered from some shadowy alcove at the front of the temple, packing them with ash.

While they did this, the Flower Children chanted Lia's name and continued their circular dancing, while the bloody plants were brought down. They held them overhead reverently, and the Flower Children broke their circles to bow before them at the waist, hands outstretched, the ones bearing tambourines shaking them vigorously. It would have felt sacred if it weren't so profane.

You'll wonder why I didn't run away at that moment, but I was transfixed by what I was seeing, and I was strangely confident that this would be seen by thousands of our viewers in our media channel. The viewership would be stratospheric. Are those damning thoughts? I'll leave it for you to decide. Suffice to say that I was there, and it was incredible. Horrible, yes. Terrible, absolutely. But it was awesome as well, in the oldest understanding of the word.

Tanner, Tressa, and Tonya walked up to the biggest of the blooms and bowed low, placing the little pots at the base of the thickest clutch of vines.

"Madame Summerville," Tanner said in unison with Tressa and Tonya. "We live for you. We live with you. We give Lia to you, in Blessed Evanescence."

The plant—Madame Summerville, okay—did not seem to speak to them. But I felt something in the manner of its bearing that it was pleased by the sacrifice of Lia, by the hideous birth of the saplings. It made me think of the little seedlings at the Circle K—were they spawned like this? Was this how this horrid plant reproduced itself? How could such a thing even be?

Ordinarily, Sharon would have been among the first to flee the scene. Justin had a tougher stomach and un-flinching eye, but Sharon would have run away. Instead, she just stood there, recording the sound of it all, with those flat eyes, her flowery garland seeming to shudder against her chest.

We should not have been here, recording this abomina-tion. My bleary eyes dragged to the ash pile, where the remains of Lia were already vanished into the ash, gone as if she'd never been.

"Sharon, Justin," I said, loudly whispering, for the cele-bratory noise of the Flower Children brought no sense of peace to me. My audiovisual team looked at me, looked through me. They looked drunk or drugged. "We need to get out of here."

They just looked at me without comprehension before returning to gape at the spectacle in front of us, roboti-cally recording it all.

Belatedly, I remembered that I wasn't wearing the garlands they were and thought maybe that offered me some protection from the soporific pollen thrown off by Madame Summerville. Even then, what pollen I had inhaled had made me lightheaded. On impulse, I made to back my way out of the temple, only to feel a jab at my ankle as I was cut by one of the points of the leaves.

Seeing how they had been ace-shaped upon entrance, I understood at once that they were now heart-shaped from this angle. I quickly adopted a stomping stride to attempt to make my way through them. To my increasing dismay, however, I saw that the leaves were cutting at my ankles, making them bleed, despite my efforts to traverse them.

I quickly dialed up Tyler but could get no signal from my phone. Glancing back at Sharon and Justin, I could see those two filming me, their eyes as lifeless as before. What's more, Tanner and the others were watching me, smiles on their faces.

"You wanted to see, Ms. Rivers," Tanner said. "Did you like what you saw?"

"Lia's dead," I said, feeling idiotic for saying what everyone in that horrid place already knew.

"She's reborn," Tressa said. "She lives on in evanescence. We'll all experience it in time. So will you."

Like the ant sliding down the dewy maw of the pitcher plant, it's hard to know when my point of no return was. Turning up in Summerville at all? Running into the Flower Children? Taking the raft to the ghost town? Following the Flower Children into their hellish eco-shrine?

When was the right time to turn back? Maybe Ty had picked the right moment. Maybe he'd known. All the same, some part of me—and it's honestly hard to tell if that was the sane and rational part of me, or the idealistic and naïve part—it argued against this turn of events.

"You can't kill us," I said. "We're here to tell your story."

Tanner laughed, his ash-streaked face all smiles.

"Nobody dies here, Ms. Rivers," Tanner said. "We all live forever. And you'll tell the story all the same. So that others know what's coming, and who. Madame Summerville *wanted* you to see this."

Without hesitating, I took off running, even as the leaves hacked at my ankles, my blood spilling as I went. I had to get out of that place…if it was the last thing I ever did.

Fortunately, or unfortunately, it was not, as great big dangling vines that hung overhead whipped down and took hold of me, pinioning me with rough-barked ease, and lifted me off my feet.

Finding my voice at last, I screamed, unable to believe what was happening. The strength of the vines was incredible. I felt like a toy in their grip, saw my sandals fall from my feet as I struggled.

All the while, Justin and Sharon were filming this, their faces rapt. I hated them in this moment, for their weakness and voyeuristic complicity, documenting my capture.

The plant held me tight in its nightmarish embrace, one of the big red blossoms moving like a cobra into my sight line. That moment, that last moment, everything was so richly embroidered in my memory—the Flower Children gazing up in religious wonder, Sharon and Justin in stupefied amazement, and that red flower closing in on me, eclipsing the world, the anthers quivering as they doused me with the fragrant pollen in a puff, and I found myself passing out in fits and starts, mouth agape, all rage and terror gone as I—tranquilized—succumbed to the ministrations of the monster in front of me.

Anesthetized as I was, I hardly felt the plant as it latched onto my face, the sugary nectar in my throat as it went down, down, down, until sweet oblivion took me at last.

Better late than never was my last thought entirely of my own.

Vantage Point

The Flower Children hadn't locked their VW van. Whether this was an oversight or a deliberate omission was anybody's guess. All I knew is that it allowed me to see what they were up to.

And they were up to things.

Inside that trunk, I found four gaily-painted psychedelic crossbows, each with a half-dozen bolts that had hunter tips on them, those nasty broadheads that meant that once they went in, they weren't coming out easily.

They also had some zip-ties, duct tape, and rope, as well as work gloves. This was one of those proverbial serial killer kits that police sometimes talked about. For all of their smiles and easy-breezy bearing, the Flower Children were up to something sinister.

Whatever it exactly was, I wasn't going to give them the satisfaction of leaving their toys here. I took their trippy crossbows and moved three of them to Ladygirl's trunk. If nothing else, they wouldn't have those. I kept a quiver of bolts, hanging it from my belt, and put a bolt in the crossbow I kept. Fuck it. Fuck them.

I tried to text Holly, but the phone signal was crap, and I wasn't able to reach her or any of the others.

Instead, I poked around the VW van, finding only racks of little summerviolets in tiny pots, dancing and swaying in their weird way. There were other products, too, carefully labeled—hand-labeled summerviolet tea in mason jars, as well as summerviolet berries, jams, preserves, lotions, incense, and poultices. There was soap, too. The scent of the flowers was almost overpowering, made me feel high just being there. I would have felt more comfortable if there'd been bricks of weed back there, instead of the summerviolet stash.

Sneaking out of the van, I felt self-conscious about having snooped at all, so I closed things up and walked over to the Jut, peering down to Summerville. But with all of the foliage there, I couldn't see anything.

What the hell was I supposed to do? I wasn't some action hero, and I wasn't entirely prepared to shoot anyone with a crossbow. I remembered shooting bows in summer camp, but shooting at targets was one thing; shooting down people was another matter.

Still, from the Jut, even I could understand that I had the advantage of the high ground. Even fit guys like Tanner and Evan would have to work to scale the slop to reach the Jut. In that time, I could do all sorts of things if I needed to.

Pacing at the Jut, I tried to make a plan of action, without precisely knowing what I should do. Holly had the keys to Ladygirl, so I couldn't drive off. And, despite them leaving the VW van unlocked, the Flower Children had the keys to it. I might have been able to walk to the Circle K. I thought there could have been a payphone there, amid the other ancient items Mr. DeVille kept in stock.

I rehearsed what I might say to the sheriff, how that would play out. After all, I was the one toting the crossbow. What might a southern county sheriff think about that? Some black writer guy from DC wandering around with a crossbow, impugning the actions of some hippies in a VW van? Hell, maybe they'd make me mayor. Or throw me in jail to sleep off whatever I'd imbibed along the way. Glancing up at the Swinging Man, I thought there could be even worse fates.

At the very least, I could show them the drone footage, which pointed to something off about the Flower Children, and perhaps the complicity of Cooper DeVille, if he wasn't cousin to the sheriff, which was always possible.

No, that decided it for me. I'd take the drone camera, my tablet, my backpack, and the crossbow, and I'd trek on foot back to the Circle K. What I wasn't going to do was linger and wait for the Flower Children to show back up. That would've been stupid, since I only had one shot with the crossbow, and there were too many of them. They could just rush me.

If I simply ghosted them, Holly might be peevish, but that was about the worst of it. I didn't want to abandon her or the others, but something was very wrong about the Flower Children, and I would have felt better about it if there were some police here.

Glancing at the mid-morning skies, that seemed like the best course of action, so I took it.

Borne Again

> [This is a very intriguing part of the Holly Rivers blog entries, as she's been exposed, and we get a glimpse into the mindset of someone infected by the supposed plant creature. I say "supposed" here because of the hallucinatory effect of the pollen and the astounding video footage to corroborate it making it questionable as to whether what Ms. Rivers had experienced actually took place. —Ed.]

Hours or days later, dazed, I came to laying on a bed of leaves, with the Flower Children around me in a circle, lending me their thoughts and prayers, the ash still bisecting their faces.

"Wake up, Ms. Rivers," Tanner said. I could see Sharon and Justin recording it, their faces glazed with shiny pollen the way mine was.

My throat was sore, but not overwhelmingly so, and one of the Flower Children—Tressa, I think—held out a wine skin for me. I took a drink of it, the summerviolet wine making my throat tingle, but taking away the soreness.

"What happened?" I asked. What had happened? The memories were more like snapshots, and while I could remember something happening to me, the jumble required some unpacking.

"You're one of us, now," Tonya said. "You and yours."

I looked at Sharon and Justin, both of whom nodded. Sitting up, I shooed everyone away from me. It came back to me, the memory of the flower. The puff of the pollen, the dreadful sense of intimate invasion.

"What the hell," I said, shaking it off. I was still in the temple, the flowers crowded around, always spectating. I found them intrusive, unwanted. Not days; hours.

"Madame Summerville *likes* you, Ms. Rivers," Tanner said. "She's taken a liking to you. You'd know if She didn't."

The Flower Children laughed at this, a trifle too enthusiastically, emphatically. The memory of Lia splitting open jolted me.

"Lia died," I said, but Tressa was quick to correct me.

"Lia *evanesced,*" Tressa said. "We told you about that. We're all taking that journey eventually. It's a rite of passage."

The part of me that was still me was trying to make out facts and figures.

"How long do I have?" I asked.

"Madame Summerville works in mysterious ways," Tonya said. "The fastest we've ever seen has been a matter of days. The stronger you are, the longer it takes. Most of us have weeks left to us."

The Flower Children all seemed fine with that fate, laughing nervously to each other and sharing knowing looks. I wasn't happy about this, got to my bloodied feet, which were crisscrossed with gashes that had my browned blood upon them.

The sense of violation was absolute. I couldn't entirely pinpoint it, but it hung in the back of my head. Looking down, I could see that the green leaves had shifted their position, were now pointing away again, and in my mind, I thought something like "aces good, hearts bad" without precisely knowing why. It was intuitive, like that sense of whether you were alone somewhere or not, or whether someone was watching you. The sensation nagged at me.

"Doesn't that bother you?" I asked. I took out some wet naps and mopped off my face, eager to get the pollen off of me. I could see the glittery amber stain of it on the naps, mocking my failure to escape. I had been colonized.

"Why should it?" Tanner asked. "Madame Summerville's given us purpose. Do you know how many people wander around adrift, without purpose? We have purpose, now. So do you."

I wasn't going to debate Tanner on this. Instead, I walked over to Madame Summerville, the heart of all of this, the mother plant. She was implacable, being just an assemblage of thick vines and big leaves, with those massive flowers. How could She communicate with Her thralls? How was Her will made manifest?

> [You'll notice that Rivers capitalizes "She" and "Her" here (and henceforth in the Rivers blogs). Even at first exposure, some aspect of perception of Madame Summerville changes in the victims. Whether this is some side effect of infection or a psycho-emotive response remains to be seen. I had originally thought it was tied to cult members, but it's clearly not, since at this time, Rivers was not consciously part of any Summerville cult. —Ed.]

"What are you? Where did you come from?" I asked. I'd never interviewed a plant before, but, hell, there was a first time for everything.

The visions came unbidden, a sense of a botanist whose name I didn't know, would never know. Someone long ago. A white woman, pale-complected, with short brown hair held at bay by a bone white hairband.

She had big blue eyes and wore glasses and had been working on splicing various plant breeds with the intention of creating robust varietals that would make for both nutritive feed for livestock and aggressive enough to overcome invasive species such as kudzu, cogongrass, and numerous introduced and invasive privet species.

This woman had found something in the cornfields of her home, an unusual plant growing in the heart of a small crater, the meteorite like a broken egg. She had gathered up the meteorite bits and the strange plant and taken it to her botanical workspace, where she planted it in a row box, observing it.

> [Again, this detail is, at best, highly speculative, given the altered mental state of Ms. Rivers. Did the plant parasite truly come from outer space? The botanist in this vision is most likely Dr. Rosemary Forster, who was listed among the missing and/or dead in the terminal flooding disasters that led to the abandonment of the town. Dr. Forster had been active in plant research for decades. —Ed.]

I could see the first strains of Madame Summerville strangling the rival plants, Her vines showing hints of thorny spikes that could pierce the shoots of Her competitors, killing them off. Even trees had no chance of resisting Her, although it was more a case of Her growing all over them and eventually toppling them. Her ambition was fierce and uncompromising.

How people factored into Her propagation was a mystery even the visions couldn't entirely decipher. Perhaps a lab accident, or something more deliberate on the part of Her caretaker, Madame Summerville grew in Her caretaker's greenhouse when Summerville still lived, before the earthquake and seasonal flooding ended the town's life. Her caretaker had died in one of those deluges, drowned in the darkness of the Black River, one of the many lost souls in the disaster. She'd carried seeds of Madame Summerville with her, but whether they had sprouted anywhere is unknown.

> [As part of my own explorations on this topic, I've canoed along the Black River past the burned ruins of Summerville—which are already growing with native plants, incidentally—and I've not found traces of the summerviolets growing wild along the riverbank. The distinctive red blossoms are fairly easy to spot, and yet I haven't seen them despite several trips down the river. I have a theory about that which I may share later. —Ed.]

When the people had fled, Madame Summerville had been left behind, forgotten. In the shadows, She had waited until the others were gone. Her vines let Her slip free of the cracked and broken greenhouse that had birthed Her, and She had spread. There was no one left behind to stop Her. Her first victims had been squatters who'd sought to make their homes in the ghost town, unseen by the world, shielded from prying eyes.

She had made short work of them, when the men—there had been three of them—had brewed a liquor from Her berries. They had drunk themselves senseless from Her intoxicating fruit, and She had fed upon the men while they drowsed, had grown daughters from their rotting bodies, had found them to be excellent fertilizer.

Her caretaker had helped make Her potent and edible. She was a practical plant, with manifold uses. Her adaptability and robust character made Her ideal for the landscape in which She'd been spawned. And yet, the flood that had allowed Her to thrive amid the bones of the dead town also served to keep Her contained.

The others came, and She laid claim to them with Her traps. The wasps had been easy to bring to Her bosom. Her little protectors, She could not be said to love them. But She valued them all the same. Her enemies were their enemies, and they never hesitated to come to Her defense.

It was what some would call a symbiotic relationship, although Madame Summerville was, as ever, Queen. And still, She found them wanting. They were servants of the status quo, and Madame Summerville wanted something more. There was land to take, and when the Old Man had come, he had been young.

How different he had been then, with his machete and his wild eyes. She had watched him work along the river, the baneful barrier that had kept Her prisoner.

They had an understanding, something borne of proximity and habit, and he had given Her sacrifices without comprehending what She truly needed. Not at first. He fed Her bodies, but bodies were not what She needed. Not dead ones, anyway. Good fertilizer, but insufficient for Her deeper needs.

It had taken time for him to figure out what She required, and then they had entered into their own symbiosis. Not that She needed him to entrap victims; rather, She needed him to clean up after Her, and he did so as the years piled on and the young murderer had aged and become something else, someone else. He kept Her hunting grounds clean, and if gratitude was beneath Her, there was at least the awareness that his efforts helped Her do what She did, and he could take the scraps She left behind for him.

[Besides being called out as such directly by Tyler Finn, this is the most overt reference to Cooper DeVille being the Black River Butcher. Whether there's any truth to this is in the domain of the dead. However, the Butcher's timeline of activity does parallel the timeline of many regional disappearances. —Ed.]

Others had come down the river, and She had taken them when they got too close, but it was the one who'd come and gone, the birther of Blossom, who had most pleased Madame Summerville. The whisper of her name bounced around in my skull, and the image of the young woman, like a ghost of a memory I'd never had:

Ashley Talulah Graham

"What made her special?" I asked.

And there was nothing special about her, at least to Madame Summerville, except for the confluence of circumstance that had given Graham the chance to escape with Blossom inside her. It had been the first time one of Her children had been able to fly free from the nursery, as incredible as that might seem.

[This is one of the more unusual claims in the Rivers blog entries, in that in the decades where Madame Summerville lurked in the ruins of the town, one would have imagined others could have been infectively colonized, carrying the plant pathogenic parasite elsewhere. The significance of "Blossom" is something only the entity can attest to. My purely speculative theory is that Madame Summerville's instincts evolved at this point, moving beyond simple reproduction to something greater in scope. —Ed.]

With Blossom, everything had changed. Madame had changed Her approach when the others appeared, and She had birthed the Flower Children, with Lia Larkin as the first of them, these new disciples.

Be fruitful and multiply.

It was the only commandment that mattered to Madame Summerville. There could be no other imperative for Her.

The Flower Children had been good to Her, good for Her. She had enfolded them and given them so much. How much greater than the wasps were they? How eager they were to spread Her far and wide. Their rituals were their own, fueled by alkaloids and intoxicants that flowed through Her, what they eagerly imbibed and brewed like the derelicts of the past, the Three Unwise Men squatting in Her crèche.

The mechanics of marketing and commerce were alien to Her, but She was content to allow them to pursue them if they meant that She might spread Her progeny. And they did.

She did not know Her progeny's fates, only that they would thrive wherever they grew. That was the blessing of Her caretaker who had let Her grow. Each time the Flower Children grew another crop and traveled away with it, She took some sort of satisfaction in it, without entirely knowing it for what it was.

Those moments of communion when She impregnated them were the only times She knew the others, for each carried Her seeds within them, forming a relationship with their seedlings, one that was for them and them alone.

This latest crop had been so successful, She didn't know what would occur when the last of them evanesced, as they called it. There was always the need for more, and when these others appeared—*The Seen,* as they called themselves—they would document the passing of the Flower Children and bring more to Her. This would be their calling.

"My calling?" I asked, chafing at this alien presence in my head.

Others would learn about Her, and they would seek Her out. Some might seek to destroy Her, which was why She was having the Flower Children spread Her far and wide. They would not find all of Her, so even if HE returned, some of Her would remain. This was the legacy of propagation, the sacred circle.

"Who is HE?" I asked.

The One That Got Away was Her answer, in a vision. The Machete Man. Not unlike the Old Man, but younger. HE had been quick. HE had nearly evaded Her clutching vines, had thrown himself into the river, out of Her lustful grasp. HE had been the first to get away, if not entirely.

In my mind's eye, I could see the exchange, the Lean Man who'd hacked at Her flowers and vines with HIS machete before diving into the river.

Although it wasn't a comprehensible emotional state, I felt this strange fear and loathing of the Lean Man, who lurked like a shadow, HIS machete dripping sap, clutched in HIS fist, evading Her at every turn. How unlike the others HE had been, how prepared for Her HE was, the torn and tattered flower scattered at his booted feet.

"Was HE the Swinging Man?" I asked.

HE was not the Swinging Man, the Burner of Her little servants. The Swinging Man was HIS partner. The two of them had come. They came now and then, those others. They took samples of Her and absconded with them. But not the way the Flower Children did; rather, it was more invasive. They clipped and cut. There would be more, because there were always more of them, these others.

"Hey, Ms. Rivers," Tanner said, and I could see that it was nearing sunset. My communion with Madame Summerville had eaten time and attention. "Do you want to stay here with Her, or do you want to come back up to the campsite?"

"No, I'll go with you," I said. I needed to get all of this down. I pointed to Sharon and Justin. "That's a wrap for now. We'll set up shots tomorrow."

Sharon and Justin nodded, as pie-eyed as ever. I didn't know why I was more together than the two of them. Maybe I was stronger. Maybe I was stranger.

> [There's a lot to unpack in this entry—the Lean Man is clearly Glen Fields, the missing Fawcett man, who appears to have escaped Madame Summerville, if the fever dreams of Holly Rivers are to be believed. I'd avoided talking about the Flower Children, but my own explorations of the area showed them to have been a very active group of propagators, selling summerviolets and summerviolet-related products in a variety of towns, using the ghost town as their base of operations. I don't have access to business records for the Flower Children, but the range of their VW van would have allowed for considerable access to the area, and they represented at a number of local art and folk festivals in their short time in operation. My own efforts to find out who may have purchased summerviolets from the Flower Children didn't yield much. —Ed.]

Circle, K?

I didn't quite have my bearings, but just based on the country road access to the ghost town, I was able to backtrack my way to the Circle K in just under an hour by way of a deerpath (?), sweating in the South Carolina humidity.

Tramping through the trees and underbrush, I felt better when I got farther away from Summerville. It's hard to put into words (but you know I'll at least try; writer's gonna write, right?). The air felt lighter, and the absence of the ever-present smell of those strange flowers helped clear my head.

It certainly looked weird, me walking with a crossbow over my shoulder with my laptop backpack containing the drone footage, wearing my *The Seen* logo-branded ballcap to try to keep the sun out of my eyes.

I felt like a survivor in need of rescue, but part of that feeling included an overabundance of caution. So, when the sun-bleached Circle K sign came into view, I got careful about approaching.

After all, DeVille was there wrapping up with that kid and his tow truck. They'd pulled it around back and dropped off the Fawcett Biotech van there, before DeVille gave the kid some money and he drove off. I saw them putting some old, drab tarp over the van, securing it with some spikes in the ground, like it was a tent. The overall effect was to make it look as nondescript as possible. The kind of thing somebody might not even notice while driving the winding country road.

The casual, even lackadaisical way this vehicle theft occurred gave me a very bad vibe. This was business as usual for them, clearly. DeVille went to his rocking chair and just rocked back and forth. It could hear the creak of the chair even from where I was:

Creak. Creak. Creak.

It would have been peaceful if I wasn't pretty damned sure I was spying on the Black River Butcher. I mean, does it make a difference if a serial killer is old or not? All of those ghostly cars on that side lot, just sitting there. Each one of those had been tied to victims of some sort, I was convinced.

Just because DeVille had gotten away with it didn't exonerate him. I'll admit that my evidence on that score was pretty slim. However, whatever was going on with him wasn't right. I knew that much.

From my downhill vantage point, I was figuring out how I might sneak up there, and what I might even do or say. While I was mulling over that, I saw the Flower Children—or some of them, anyway—roll up in their VW van.

What a contrast that was, the brightly-colored van and the washed-out Circle K, with four of the Flower Children—Tonya, Tressa, Tanner, and Sabrina, I think—they got out and chatted up the old man. I could hear hints of their voices and could see them pointing, could see DeVille shrugging and shaking his head.

Tanner walked in the shadow of the covered gas pumps and squinted this way and that, up the road and back, while Tressa talked to DeVille and Sabrina looked over the summerviolet display stand, seeming to talk to them.

I stayed low in the brush, keeping an eye on everything, while trying to stay unnoticed, ogled by jumbo mustard-colored grasshoppers that just watched me with their big bug eyes while they gnawed on grasses.

Tanner said something to Tressa and Tonya, and they went inside the Circle K, while Sabrina was singing to the flowers, before going to the trunk of the van and emerging with a tray of summerviolets and a watering can. They were the ones I'd seen when I'd poked around their van earlier.

She carefully filled the stall's empty rows with fresh saplings, and then went to the side of the Circle K and turned a spigot, filling the watering can. She then carefully gave each of the summerviolets a bit of a drink, ignoring something DeVille was saying to her.

Then Tressa and Tonya emerged from the store, shaking their heads. Tanner then directed the other Flower Children to get back into the van, which they did. Sabrina was last to do so, finishing up her watering of the summerviolets before she shook out the empty watering can and put it back in the van.

Tanner said something else to DeVille, before getting back into the van. Then they started it up and drove off, heading away from Summerville, driving slowly along.

They're looking for me, I thought. It was as clear as death. The way the road wound, the VW van quickly slipped from view, and it was just DeVille and me again. I glanced at my phone and could see that I still didn't have proper signal. DeVille had gone back to his rocking.

Creak. Creak. Creak.

I didn't know how far the Flower Children would travel before they turned back around and was still not clear on what I might even do. I had to get to a working phone. That was first on my list.

Then I saw something astounding: I saw a guy in a dirty Fawcett Biotech golf shirt emerge from the Circle K, toting a sawed-off shotgun. The Fawcett blue-and-yellow colors were clear to me despite the grass stains and grime, and the guy was wearing a blue Fawcett boonie hat that also had the logo on it. The guy was dirty and sweaty, his eyes wide as he confronted DeVille, who stopped rocking and stood up, hands raised.

I took this moment to get out of my hiding space and run across the street, could see the Fawcett man's eyes flick up at me before focusing back on DeVille, who had been edging closer to him.

"Don't do it, Old Man," the Fawcett Man said, then pointed the shotgun at me. "You, neither."

DeVille turned his head to look me over. I raised my hands.

"I'm not with him," I said. "Or them."

"No?" the man said.

"I'm part of the documentary team," I said, feeling idiotic, since this guy wouldn't know us from anything. "*The Seen.* It's a show, a web series. I saw DeVille take your van around the back of this place."

The Fawcett Man trained his shotgun back on DeVille, who gazed dourly at us both. The Fawcett Man looked like he'd been roughing it for the past several days.

"You been to the Temple?" the Fawcett Man asked.

"I haven't," I said. "My team went, but I didn't."

"Prove it," he said.

I didn't know how to prove that I hadn't done something, honestly. How does one even do that?

"I'm Tyler Finn," I said. "I'm a writer/producer. The rest of our crew went with the Flower Children. I, uh, reviewed the drone footage. What exactly happened to you?"

The mention of the drone footage didn't seem to put him at ease. If anything, it made him warier.

"You, what, hacked Jeph's drone?" he asked.

"Boys, you *both* need to settle down," DeVille said. "This is bigger than all of us. We might be on some old back country road, but people still do come through here. The Sheriff sees you holding me up, and he's not going to ask questions; he's just going to start shooting."

"Shut up," the Fawcett Man said. "Give me the keys to my van, Old Man. And you, you tell me what you saw on the drone cam."

"The Flower Children must have attacked 'Jeph' because the signal cut off," I said. "I played it back. I have it with me. I'm just trying to get to a phone."

"What good's a phone going to do you, Boy?" DeVille said. "Madame Summerville's got no use for phones."

At the mention of Madame Summerville, I felt myself get kind of twitchy. There was something in the way he said it.

"Those Flower Children are looking for you," DeVille said. "And you, Fawcett Man."

That seemed to anger the Fawcett Man, who looked at the cap DeVille was wearing.

"You've got some brass balls on you for wearing that cap, Old Man," he said. "Meant to bring it up last time. A souvenir you took from another employee that came out here?"

DeVille seemed offended by that.

"I support local businesses," DeVille said. "Traded some summerviolets for it, if you must know."

"Right," the Fawcett Man said.

DeVille pulled the van keys from a pocket on his overalls and held them out to the Fawcett Man, who shook his head.

"Hey, Mr. Tyler Finn, you take those keys from him," he said, keeping the shotgun pointed at DeVille's chest.

I walked up to DeVille, holding my hand out. He dropped the keys into my palm.

"I already saw you roll up and bring my van around back," the Fawcett Man said. "How's about we go get it?"

"Nossir," DeVille said. "Y'all better get out of here, is what I'm thinking. Madame don't like people messing with Her people."

"Go get the van, Finn," the Fawcett Man said. "Bring it around and fill it up. Mr. DeVille and I are going to have words."

"What's your name?" I asked.

"Glen," he replied. "Glen Fields."

BLOG ENTRY 15

(Holly Rivers)

Mid-Afternoon Delight

Ty had disappeared.

This was apparent when we'd come back to the campsite, and it had tarnished what had otherwise been a fairly blissful morning (I know what you're thinking; I was under the influence). There was no trace of him. In fact, the Flower Children had gotten rather squirrelly when they'd come back to find him gone.

What's more, Tanner had gone to the trunk of his VW van and been upset about something, as I'd seen him talking furtively with Tress, Tonya, and Evan. Then he called over the rest of the Flower Children and spoke to all of us.

After taking a few minutes to tend to their gear, Sharon and Justin were back at it, documenting it. The two of them had been almost robotlike after the Temple, going through the motions of normalcy without offering much in the way of commentary to me.

"What's going on?" I asked Tanner.

"Where's your buddy, Tyler?" Tanner asked, his ever-present smile a bit tight on his face.

"No idea," I said. "He said he was coming back here. What happened to the Fawcett van?"

"Oh, I'm sure Mr. DeVille took it. He was supposed to do it the other day, but I guess the storm screwed that up. Tonya, Tressa, Sabrina—you pack up the van and we'll go to the Circle K, see if Cooper's seen Tyler. Evan, you and the others look around here, see if you can find Tyler."

"Will do, Tanner," Evan said. The Flower Children, for all of their hippie vibe, buzzed around like bees—or, well, wasps—and got things in motion in short order.

"Do you want us to help?" I asked. "We can go with you."

Tanner looked me over a moment, then shook his head.

"No, you three can just help out Evan and the others," he said. "We'll be back soon. Your pal couldn't have gotten too far. He didn't seem like the outdoorsy type to me."

"Oh, he's not," I said. I could feel something squirming inside me, a sensation unlike anything I'd felt before. How many seeds were in me, anyway? This was one of those bizarre sorts of questions somebody asked themselves that they'd have never asked before becoming pollinated? Infected? Impregnated?

Some part of my brain was screaming about what had happened, but the rest of me was strangely matter-of-fact about it, even at peace with it. I imagined some biochemical subversion was taking place, bringing me peace and a feeling of wellbeing. Something else was inside me, and that was great, because it was part of Madame Summerville. That was the other part of me, the alien part.

"We'll find him," Tanner said. "If he's out there, we'll find him. Otherwise, Evan and the rest will. We know this area well. Joanna, you and Ruth take the footpath to the Circle K."

"What about the crossbows?" Tonya asked.

"Yeah," Tanner said. "Your friend Tyler seems have stolen our crossbows."

I didn't know what to think about that, no matter which way I went at it. I mean, crossbows? Who drove around with crossbows?

"Crossbows?" I asked.

"Yep," Tonya said. "Stole them right out of the back of our van."

Even Justin had something to say about that, piping up from behind his camera.

"Why do you have crossbows?" he asked.

"For hunting and self-defence, duh," Tonya said. "Guns are noisy. Crossbows are quiet. We like our peace and quiet around here. Nobody cares about crossbows."

My apparently alkaloid-addled brain didn't fire on as many cylinders as it had before meeting Madame Summerville, but journalistic questions still formed in my mind, even if blurrily.

"Have you shot people before?" I asked.

Tanner sighed, wanting to smooth things over. He opted for a non-answer answer:

"We'll talk about this when we get back," Tanner said. "Come on, let's go."

They got into the van and did a quick three-point turn to get out of there, Tonya's eyes hard one me was she went by.

"Crossbows," I said, but Sharon and Justin were back into their cataleptic state. I didn't know how I was somewhat more myself than they were, except that I hadn't been huffing on the flower garlands like those two had been, so maybe I wasn't as far up the Summerville on-ramp as they were. I felt a strange sort of hope that maybe Tyler had gotten away, without necessarily feeling that he'd been in any danger. Were any of us in danger? What was danger, anyway? Everything depended on your viewpoint and attitude, even your mood. And my mood was *good.*

Is this what being an unreliable narrator feels like? We hear references to them in stories, but you never really expect to find yourself in the position of *being* one. From a flora and fauna perspective, I was clearly compromised. Nothing I say past my time in the Temple should be trusted.

That said, I directed Sharon and Justin to go with Evan and the others to try to find Tyler, while I went to work on my blog entries. That's right—*everything* you've seen from me before now was written by me *after* being pollinated by Her. I wanted to document it all while I still had some wits about me.

Was I supposed to tell you that at the outset? I'm sorry/not-sorry. Would you have read it if you'd known that I was writing under the influence of Madame Summerville? Don't think so.

> [Holly Rivers brings up a good point here that many Seensters have raised since the Summerville Incident, which is that we cannot take anything Holly says here without a hefty handful of salt, whether or not what she observed actually happened. —Ed.]

The thing is, I don't know what I'm honestly communicating, if anything, or whether I'm writing what *She* wants me to get out there. That's the part I can't entirely wrap my brain around—does She want people to know about Her? Or would She rather it be a secret? Does She even understand what this is?

I don't know. All I know is that my fingers are flying, and I'm trying to capture all of it for the inevitable posterity that'll occur with my own evanescence.

Even catching myself capitalizing "Her" in this context is freaking me out. Since when did "she" become Her? The seeds inside me, nestled somewhere in my body, pumping me with chemicals and maybe even hormones, keeping me sedate, keeping me focused on this task.

It's like *Chordyceps* species, that fungus that takes over arthropods and turns them into zombies that climb at the top of leaves to wait to be eaten, so they can be transmitted to the next stage in their reproductive cycle. The horrific circle of parasitic life. I don't know how smart ants are, and we know they're not so self-aware, but at some point, self becomes non-self, and non-self takes over.

Where am I on that journey? Why would She want that getting out there? Why would She want people to know? Our audience is niche, but *The Seen* still has plenty of fans. She really wants us getting that out there?

How many people has She infected over the decades? My research put hundreds among the disappeared. Was each one a carrier? Did they travel to parts unknown to spread Her seed? Was that part of the plan, or some un-fathomably alien instinct?

I can't pretend to know how She thinks, or what, beyond propagation, Her agenda is. Maybe it's no higher than that. I'm getting philosophical, and I need Ty here. He'd cut right through it in his writerly way.

For now, it's my fingers that flick across the keyboard, capturing everything we've encountered so far. People will want to know. They will seek us out, once we, too, disappear. The way that I went after the Ladygirl Five.

I feel stupid about that, now. She told me about Ashley Graham, and that chewed at me, too.

Ashley Graham carried Blossom to Duke University. She did that. Only nobody found Graham or Blossom, which means that *somebody* did and kept it a secret. Somebody at Duke knows all about Blossom. Another mystery within a mystery.

And there was the matter of the Swinging Man. I paused to look up at him, dangling forlornly on that length of rope, the crossbow (!) bolts sticking out of him. That was a Fawcett Biotech man up there, I was sure.

Fawcett kept coming up, which meant that *they* knew about Madame Summerville, too. Damn, but I needed Internet access badly. I needed to search for things, hated having to rely on memory. But Fawcett had a big operation somewhere north of here. Someplace out by themselves, where they could conduct agricultural revolutions in peace.

Summerviolets could be a dandy cash crop. I'd since tasted the fruit, the jam, the tea. The scent of the soap. Madame Summerville was a gregarious and generous goddess—the products She offered were useful to those who were inclined to use Her. Most invasive species were pests; She wasn't a pest—She was a conqueror.

Had Her caretaker understood what she had nurtured? Was that road to Hell well-intended? I'd never know. Or, perhaps more on the nose, I wouldn't live long enough to find out. A biography of Her caretaker would have been meaningless to any of you reading this. All that mattered was understanding that Madame Summerville had exceeded the wildest dreams of Her caretaker, whatever her original intentions had been. Had she known she'd taken a monster under her wing? In those moments when she'd been swept away by the Black River, had she known? Were her last thoughts of Madame Summerville?

However, Fawcett was a place of ideas. They had to have dipped their beaks into this place and bred cultivars. I apologize for mixing my metaphors; I'm not quite myself. My only question—the journalistic question—was why Fawcett hadn't laid claim to the ghost town. Their people *had* been here. Their corporate research facility wasn't too far away—maybe a day's ride?

Watching the Swinging Man, it was all I could think about. Was some team of botanists, plant biologists, bioengineers, and biochemists turning seedlings of Madame Summerville into hothouse harlots that would make Fawcett piles of money? It was maybe beyond the scope of *The Seen*, but I did wonder about it.

And how would She feel about that? Would She welcome it, if it guaranteed Her a better life beyond the ramshackle ruins of Summerville? Given Her parasitic approach to pollination, would this be a symbiosis She would welcome?

Again, I was getting philosophical in the middle of my own burgeoning evanescence. That word again, like a playful finger running up my arm, toying with me, flirting with me: Oblivion's Embrace. The concrete understanding that something within would end me. Maybe these blog entries were to be my epitaph, something to remain after I had gone.

Whatever the case, I wrote and wrote, brought myself up to speed, so that everything would be there when we went into post-production. I didn't know if Sharon and Justin would make it, frankly. Or whether they'd even stay with *The Seen*. Maybe they'd become new Flower Children, once some of the others passed.

How did that work, exactly? Having witnessed Lia's evanescence, I presumed it would go much the same way with the others, would see other plants potted and, what? Taken elsewhere. From the Temple to the wider world. Not a factory farm, but a breeding ground, all the same.

This was how I was, how I would always be: I had to know. I had to know everything. From seed to seedling, I had to know how it ended.

Tagging & Bagging

Glen Fields was brusque with Cooper DeVille. Even under the bizarre circumstances of the moment, I felt uneasy with how he manhandled him, that shotgun never far from the center of his back.

"Where's your phone, Old Man?" Glen asked.

"On the wall over there," DeVille said. "Who you planning to call, Son?"

"Fawcett," Glen said. "My boss."

DeVille shook his head, scoffing.

"Fawcett can't help you none, Son," DeVille said. "You know how far they are from here. They're already in on it."

Fields just squinted at DeVille and scoffed back at him.

"We're already a couple of days overdue," Glen said. "Somebody will be wondering where we went."

"That a fact?" DeVille asked.

"That's a fact," Glen said. "Hey, Tyler, how's about you point that crossbow at this son of a bitch while I make a call?"

The look on his face made me think there wasn't much wiggle room in the request, so I took the crossbow and leveled it at DeVille, who sneered at me.

"Son, you're no killer," DeVille said. "This is *not* your kind of game."

"Shut up," Glen said, cradling the shotgun while he dialed. His face went all-business when it was clear he'd reached someone. "Wyndham? Yeah, it's Fields. I know. Sorry. We ran into some local trouble here. Nope. I don't trust them. I think maybe you need to send some more people here. For real? No, like sooner than later."

I could only imagine what the Wyndham fellow on the line might have said to Fields, but reading his face, it wasn't what he wanted to hear.

"You said to keep this quiet," Glen said. "I'm keeping it quiet as I can. Yeah. The storm. We thought we'd beat that, but we didn't. Something happened. Told you that this was biologist work, Johnny. Yeah. Yeah, I did. What did I say? Three days? Are you kidding me?"

Cooper chuckled at that, shaking his head again. I just scowled at him over the crossbow, not feeling very threatening, but hoping the broadhead of the bolt might carry at least a hint of menace I couldn't provide.

"What's the holdup? Yeah? Johnny, seriously," Glen said. "We were supposed to just—yeah, I know. Exactly. What do I care about budgets? Let Payroll worry about it. Yeah, you bet your ass. Jeph's missing. No. No idea where he is. He flaked out on me. These crazy flower kids turned up. The cult. Yes. I am *not* shitting you. No. Would I shit you? Exactly. The Flower Children. *Not* fooling. They have a VW van with it printed on the sides. I saw it. Can't miss it. Yeah. I want hazard pay. Hell, yeah. Yeah, you do. Big time."

I saw the Flower Children were rolling back into the Circle K. Glen and Cooper saw them, too.

"Gotta go," Glen said. "Three days, Johnny, or I swear I'm coming for you."

He hung up, jabbed the shotgun at DeVille.

"Looks like your pals are back, Old Man," Glen said. "How's about you send them on their way, and nobody gets shot?"

DeVille looked from me to him, heaving a sigh.

"You don't want to be reckless, now," DeVille said.

However, the Flower Children would have to be idiots not to notice that the Fawcett van had been pulled up to one of the pumps. Fields and DeVille came out, and I went with the two of them, putting the van between me and the Flower Children's VW, which pulled up on the other side of the island.

The same four Flower Children came out—Tanner, Tressa, Tonya, and Sabrina, and when they saw Fields and me there with DeVille, and our weapons, their smiles withered into winces and grimaces.

"Tyler Finn," Tanner said. "Looks like we found you after all. And you, Mr. Fawcett Man—Glen Fields. The Lean Man."

"That you did," Glen said. "Where's Jeph? My partner?"

Tanner and the others slow-stepped, hands raised.

"Your drone jockey? He's our new Swinging Man," Tressa said. "After he burned down Madame's favorite tree, it was the *least* we could do."

"Wasps," Glen said, spitting on the ground. "They got what was coming to them."

"And so will you, Lean Man," Tanner said. "You know, *nobody* gets away from Madame."

"First time for everything, I guess," Glen said. I could see the iron-hard looks on the faces of Tressa, Tonya, and Sabrina. What's more, I could see a couple other Flower

Children across the road, in the distance, having come the footpath way I had earlier. With the afternoon sun in their eyes, they didn't yet see us.

Tanner and the others kept slow-moving toward us, until Glen cleared his throat.

"This is a ten-gauge slide action," Glen said. "Math's not my strong suit, but I've got five shots here. That's one for each of you."

"No need to get violent," Tanner said. "We're peaceful."

"Like hell you are," Glen said. "Y'all serve that thing out there in town."

Tanner wasn't about to be intimidated. In fact, he was almost serene.

"You saw Her," Tanner said. "You desecrated our Temple. We thought you were dead. Or claimed by Madame."

"Oh, you haven't seen desecration, yet," Glen said, and shot Tanner in the chest. The shotgun blew Tanner back, knocking him clean out of his sandals in a splash of blood. While Tressa, Tonya, and Sabrina cried out, Glen cocked the shotgun again and fired shots into each of them, blowing fist-sized bloody holes in their chests. I could see the other Flower Children across the road, two women, straightening up and squinting in dismay at the spectacle.

Cooper DeVille made as if to run, drawing a pocket-knife, only to catch the last shotgun shell in the back, which sent him flying with a dusty grunt.

"Ohmigod," I said, almost dropping the crossbow, my ears ringing from the sounds of the shotgun.

Glen reached into one of his pockets and reloaded the shotgun, while I watched the Flower Children die from their wounds. The ones who'd taken the shots to the chest had saplings emerging from their broken bodies—these green and red bloodied blossoms that were flailing at the untimely breaching of their nesting places. I almost threw up at the sight of them, felt myself heaving, while Glen nodded to them.

"You see that?" he said.

"Christ," I said.

"Like Hell it is," he replied. "Help me get them into their van before somebody turns up."

We threw open the side of the VW van and grabbed the fallen Flower Children by the arms and legs, mindful of the grasping, bloodied vines that thrashed around through their copious bodily breaches. That image would haunt me for the rest of my days, the way the vines boiled bloodily within the grievous wounds Fields had inflicted on their hosts.

"Fine batch of saplings, here," Glen said. "Bumper crop."

"No way you could have known that," I said.

"Seeing is believing," Glen said. "I hid and watched them do their thing. We gotta burn'em. We gotta burn all of it."

It was in that moment that I saw Tanner sit back up, gazing at us with dead eyes, the saplings in his chest—three of them—quivering, open-blossomed, while the vines twisted and took control of his ruined body. He reached for us with bloody hands, and Glen fired another shot at him, again in the chest, the shotgun tearing into the fragile blossoms.

I could see Tressa, Tonya, and Sabrina struggling to rise, too, looking on with sightless eyes and bloodied faces, guided by parasitic puppet strings in the form of bloody green roots, vines, and rhizomes.

"Mother of Hell," I said. Glancing at the summerviolet stand, I could see the saplings there thrashing about, their blossoms flexing at they seemed to watch us. The ones remaining in the van were moving, too. The whole place was seeming to move, and pollen filled the air, whether by manmade accident or ungodly design.

"We gotta burn'em," Glen said, firing shots at the legs of the Flower Children, counting on the power of the shotgun to help cripple them. Still they crawled for us, their mouths working, the vines pulsing beneath their skin like green veins, leaving smears of blood on the ground like giant snail trails as they made their way toward us, trailing thorny vines in their wake, seeking futile entry in the hardened, unforgiving ground.

Things were getting well out of hand at the Circle K, as Glen and I dealt with these bloody, crawling Flower Children-things. We grabbed them by their legs toward the summerviolet stand, while they fought us soundlessly, blood gurgling from their mouths, with ever-more puffs of psychoactive pollen filling the air around us, the dizzying scent of it making the ground shift beneath our feet as we went.

If I hadn't been so busy doing that, I'd have taken some pictures, but there was a profound sense of urgency, here. Glen ran into the Circle K and came out with a gas can he quickly filled up from the pump, pouring it all over the bodies of the Flower Children and the saplings. Wherever the gasoline touched them, they recoiled. I was never more thankful for the pungent power of petroleum products.

"Get the ones out of the van," Glen said, and I did so, glancing at DeVille, who had not moved since he'd been shot.

Glen then tossed a lit match at the summerviolet stand and the whole thing whooshed into a towering column of fire. Only then did I take out my phone and take some shots, as we watched the Flower Children twitch in the blaze, the shoots and vines that had animated them bursting in the fire, sending up white smoke as they burned, followed by brown and black smoke as the wood and gasoline burned fiercely. While their mouths worked, there was no sound beyond the bursting of stems and blossoms in the firestorm as the skin of their hosts blackened in the blaze.

"Holy Hell," I said. Glen lit a cigarette and watched them burn without saying a word. Then he glanced at DeVille's body.

"What about him?" he asked.

"I don't think he was infected," I said.

Glen shook his head.

"Volunteer, I guess," he said. "It takes all kinds. Let's throw that old son of a bitch on the fire, too. Just in case he needs to get something off his chest."

I told him about my suspicion that Cooper may have been the Black River Butcher, and Glen just smiled to himself.

"Guess that makes us heroes, doesn't it?" Glen said, managing a long drag on his cigarette, flicking ash at the bonfire we'd made.

"Or something," I said. Would anybody approaching these bodies even see the traces of plant life that we had seen? Or would it only be burned bodies that they saw? Five people murdered by shotgun blasts at point-blank range?

We heaved DeVille onto the fire, adding him to the conflagration. I worried about having a fire so close to the gas station, but it was preferable to the monstrosities we'd just witnessed. My mind raced at the mechanics of this, even as my hands shook from the post-adrenal nerves that struck. They'd been infected by the flowers, by the plant.

"What about the others?" I asked, glancing at the now-empty field across the road. The smoke line from this fire would draw attention from somewhere, I was sure. I was grateful that the storm had rolled through the other day, or we'd have had a wildfire burning here for sure.

"We've got their van," Glen said. "They're not going anywhere."

I immediately thought of Holly and the others, of Lady-girl, while Glen popped the security camera videotape from behind the counter, looked for any others. I saw a number of tapes on the shelf and I instinctively grabbed them, put them in some tote bags, while Glen tossed the current tape onto the bonfire, watched it burn a bit, before flicking his cigarette butt onto the fire as well.

"Our car is there," I said.

"Well, then," Glen said. "Let's fill everything we can with gasoline and supplies and go pay Summerville a proper visit. You can take the VW; I'll take the company van."

Back & Forth

Joanna and Ruth had come running back, crying out as they'd come, which had gotten the other Flower Children riled up. Their words were strange jumbles, took me out of my nonstop blogging.

"They killed them!" Joanna yelled. "Tanner, Tressa, Tonya, and Sabrina! They're dead!"

Evan and Layna took the initiative, while I had Sharon and Justin record it.

"Who killed them?" Evan asked.

"The Lean Man," Ruth said. "And *their* missing man! He helped!"

Ruth pointed an accusatory finger at us.

"Who, Ty?" I asked.

"Yes," Joanna said. "Him. He was with the Lean Man. They gunned down Tanner and the others, just gunned them right down."

I knew Tyler better than anybody, and even in my brain-fried state of infection, I couldn't imagine him doing that. The Fawcett guy, though? Who knows what he might have been capable of, after all?

"Sharon, Justin," I said. "Get over here."

The two of them walked over, filming me as they did so, their eyes blank, the garlands writhing at their necks, the flowers attentive.

"Take those off," I said, grabbing at them, while the Flower Children were trying not figure out what to do next. Sharon and Justin were somewhat pliant, let me remove their garlands, which I tossed aside.

I noticed when I pulled them off of them that the living garlands had been slipping tendrils *into* their necks, and each one came out reluctantly, like removing a splinter or worse. It had taken longer than I expected, leaving stigmata-like bleeding pinholes in the skin around their clavicles and back of their necks. The garland vines slithered in my arms, and I threw them away even as the slender bloody vines slapped against my hands. They had been growing on them. If I wasn't in a sedated state, I'd have lost my mind as I'd seen those ghastly garlands dripping with the blood of my friends on their twitching tendrils. Drops of their blood spattered the ground around our feet as they sought a safer place to grow.

"Get in this instant!" I said.

"Where are we going?" Sharon asked, her head seeming to clear a little. I wanted to vomit as I saw the bloody garland vines trying to find purchase along the ground, with a relentless intensity that called to mind parasitic worms.

"Away from here," I said, "Quickly, now."

Evan saw us and called out.

"Where are you going?" he asked. "We need your car."

"Back in a second," I said, turning on Ladygirl and wheeling us out of there, kicking up gravel in the faces of the Flower Children as they ran after us. Evan sprinting to try to catch us, but I just gave Ladygirl more gas and left him in the dust.

This was in the spirit of self-preservation, mind you. We had to get distance between us and Summerville.

"Why are we leaving?" Sharon asked, sitting beside me as I drove us quickly up the rough country road that got us back on the proper rural roadways. She was clutching her temples as she spoke.

"Because if that Fawcett Man catches us, he'll kill us like the others," I said. "Tyler doesn't know what happened to us. We can persuade him, maybe."

I don't know whether this was my own will to survive speaking here, or whether it was Her guiding my thoughts. All I knew for sure was that I didn't want the Lean Man catching me. The memory of my communion with Madame Summerville lingered in my mind.

The road chain was thankfully down since the others had gone before us, so I quickly took a right, heading away from the direction of the Circle K.

"That's not the right way," Justin said, his hand stealing to around his neck, where the bloody holes in him were still dripping, running down his chest, staining his shirt. I wondered if the flower crown that Lia Larkin had worn had burrowed into her own skull when she'd evanesced. The thought of it made me shudder, while the alien part of me loved that imagery.

"Shhh," I said, spinning the wheel and completing the turn. Ladygirl drove like the dream that she was, drifting over any bumps as smoothly as if she'd been a parade float.

"What are you doing, Holly?" Sharon asked. I was relieved that without the flower garlands, some semblance of cognizance was coming back to them. The remaining part of me felt enormous relief that Ty and I had taken ours off. One of those simple decisions that had made a difference.

"We're not ripe, yet," I said. "Our seedlings aren't ready. Understand?"

Justin wasn't recording this, for which I was happy. Of course, my documenting of this reveals it to you, but by the time you see it, it'll be too late. The fact was that I just wasn't ready to die just yet.

And, to their credit, they understood what I was talking about. They felt it as strongly as I did. When my cell service came back, I'd talk to Ty. I'd explain. Or maybe I'd persuade him that we weren't infected. He didn't know. He hadn't been there. The need to convince him began to consume me, and while I knew it wasn't the real me thinking this, I couldn't stop it. The seedlings could drive some obsessions at this stage, harnessing instinct to their own ends.

"This way takes us to Fawcett," Sharon said. "Right? Somewhere out there?"

"Somewhere," I said, looking back at the river-hugging cluster of trees that camouflaged Summerville. Somewhere in there She reigned. And while the Flower Children might have remained to defend Her, I knew that She *wanted* us to escape. I felt that in the coiling in my guts.

"What about Ty?" Sharon asked, looking around us at the highway-hugging green trees interspersed with yellowed fields, along the rolling road.

"We'll catch up with him," I said.

"What were those Flower Children talking about? About the Circle K?" Justin asked.

"I don't rightly know," I said. "We've filmed a ton of this. We need to make sense of it all."

Sharon just looked at me from the passenger seat, her eyes no longer so blank, but more characteristically New Jersey-reproachful. She'd mopped up her neck wounds with a wet nap, grimacing in pain as she did so, letting out quiet curses with each application.

"Those things were growing on us," Sharon said.

"Yeah," I said. The full emotional impact of it was muted by the seedlings, I was certain, as Sharon moved on to other matters.

"We still don't know what happened to the Ladygirl Five," Sharon said. "All of this was for *nothing,* Holly."

"Are you kidding?" I said. "We know exactly what happened, Sharon."

She didn't seem convinced, so I just drove, keeping an eye on the rearview mirror, to see if anyone was pursuing us, but the winding roads were empty. How empty this place was. Full of woods, swamps, rivers, bugs, frogs, plants, and nothing, too.

"I don't know what happened," Justin said. "Not exactly."

"That's because you were busy filming, Stupid," Sharon said. "I heard everything. I heard Her speaking to me. The rustling of the leaves."

I let them bicker, because it freed up my mind to plan what was next. We needed to get the raw footage and recordings back to Charleston, where we could work on it, create a decent package, something that made sense. That was key to it. Failing that, I needed to get somewhere with decent Internet so I could upload the footage and information we had to our *Seen* servers in DC.

Before that happened, we needed some footage of Fawcett Biotech. That was basically a pit stop before we went east and hit Charleston. Fawcett was the blue and yellow bow that tied it all together neatly.

The thing was, I didn't know how much time we had. From what I'd gleaned from Tanner and the others, they'd been at it for weeks, or, at most, a couple of months. I couldn't be sure, and they weren't the best at making it any clearer.

For us, the only thing we knew was that we were freshly infected. Whatever Madame Summerville intended (and I wished I'd had the time to stay with Her longer, that I might have better known Her will in all of this), we had a set amount of time to get things done before we evanesced.

Worse, we had less time before our own wills were superseded by the parasite. The truth was, I wasn't sure how many of my thoughts were Hers and how many were mine. You don't know what it feels like, having a goddess blossoming inside you. You don't have *any* idea how it feels.

Lia had cried and talked about pain, but I felt no pain. Maybe it was the pain of the birthing or her coming apart. The way I felt could only be described as euphoric. I felt *good*. Like warm and full of powerful purpose. You can't know how that feels—that sense of purpose—of being entirely aligned. Maybe zealots or fanatics felt it. Maybe the delirious or the insane. Not certain, but I felt like I was going exactly where I needed to go.

And that felt good.

BLOG ENTRY 18
(Tyler Finn)

Burning Questions

When Glen Fields and I got to the Summerville road, there was nobody around. No Ladygirl, no Flower Children. Not a soul was there but him and me, and we parked the vans on either side of the road, turning around so we faced away from the Jut, just in case we needed to make a quick escape.

Glen got out of his Fawcett van, brandishing the shotgun.

"Hey, there, Flower People," he said, barking it out. "Got something for you. Me and my pal. We're here to talk to you."

I got out with the psychedelic crossbow and the quiver of bolts.

"Who's got something to say to me?" Glen asked. We listened a bit, but all we heard was the babbling of the Black River and the rustling of late afternoon trees. The silence was otherwise pervasive, as strong as the scent of the flowers. I could see the garlands on the ground where they had been tossed and felt some relief which swiftly became dread as I saw them squirming bloodily, vines and roots seeking our direction in reaching twitches. Holly and the others had made their escape. I don't know what I was bracing for, but not finding their corpses on the road was a blessing.

Fields grabbed one of the cans of gasoline and splashed it on the garlands, taking some satisfaction in the way they moved when exposed to the fuel. He tossed his cigarette down on it and we watched the garlands burn. I could see them sizzling in the flames until they burst and succumbed to the fire.

"Y'all want to play hide-n-seek, is that it?" Glen asked. "You seen what I did to your peeps? Now, this can go easy or hard, you know? The harder you make it, the worse it's gonna go for you when I find you."

There was no answer, and we made our way to the Jut and looked across the river, and could see the Flower Children there, looking up at us. They looked like strange forest spirits, standing there on the sea of green leaves, red flowers moving around them, their faces devoid of expression, their eyes like marbles.

"Come get us, Lean Man," Evan said, cupping his hands at his mouth so we could hear him. "That sawed-off shotgun isn't good for anything but up close. Let's see you dance with the Madame again. We think you got lucky last time."

Glen pushed his boonie hat back on his head and gave his forehead a half-handed scratch.

"Well, now," Glen said. "He's got a point, there, Ty. But first things first."

He drew the machete that hung from his hip and strolled over to the tree that held the line that kept the Swinging Man hoisted overhead. He cut the line and had me lower it to the ground. It was heavier than I imagined, and the buzz of flies about it was as nasty as the stink of it as it came closer.

When it reached the road, collapsing in a heap, Glen walked over and took off the mask, grimacing as he looked it over.

"Sorry, Jeph," he said. "I can't bury you properly, Brother."

He gave the body a shove and it went over the side of the Jut, landing with a dismal splash. We watched his body float downriver, propelled by the flood-fed water. Glen pulled a little bottle of whiskey he'd lifted from the Circle K and took a drink, then poured a dram over the side. He handed it to me, and I took a swig as well. I hadn't met Jeph, but having watched his drone footage, I'd at least gotten a sense of him.

"You sons of bitches took your shot," Glen said. "It's our turn."

"Try it," Ruth yelled back up at us, her blank eyes wide. "Just try it."

Glen took another swig of whiskey before pocketing the flat-faced bottle. "Night's coming sooner than later. We'd best get this place lit up before these loons come after us, Ty."

"We could just get out of here," I said. Having already helped Fields burn DeVille and the others at the Circle K, I felt a certain queasiness at the prospect of torching Summerville and the remaining Flower Children. He clearly sensed my reticence, looked me in the eye while we went to the vans to get the cans of gasoline.

"This is a war, Tyler," he said. "That thing over there in town, it attacked me. It infects people and turns them into its slaves. We have to end this. What's more, the company I work for is neck-deep in the stuff. They already have it; they just want to get rid of wild strains of it so they can corner the market and keep it all quiet. They'll be here in a few days. We have to leave them only ash and bones."

Putting it that way, yeah, it made sense. However, it didn't make it any easier. I wasn't a killer.

"I'm not right for this kind of work," I said.

"You're all I've got," he replied, taking a pair of full gas cans, urging me to take some, too. "I've got a shotgun, you've got a crossbow, we've got some cans of gas. We need to step to it."

My pragmatic mind was working through it, the way it always did. This was a production like any other, at least in the mechanics. It was like the work Holly and I did for *The Seen.* It made me wish the others were here to film it. As it was, there'd only be my word that something had happened at all. Which was very on-point for *The Seen,* when I really thought about it.

"We don't have a way to ford the river," I said. Glen shook his head.

"I used an inflatable raft to cross the river," he said. "Those hippies took it. It's probably in their van, there."

We went through the VW van and, sure enough, there was a deflated Fawcett Biotech-branded raft and paddle.

"See? They couldn't resist keeping it," Glen said. "I'm just glad they didn't shoot it up with their damned cross-bows."

He took an electric pump from the Fawcett van and used it to inflate the raft.

"What are we going to do?" I asked, feeling stupid for asking it, but wanting to see where Glen's head was at. He was patient with me, looked me in the eye as he laid it out.

"We cross the river with these cans of gasoline, and we start setting fires," he said. "This is pure slash-and-burn we're talking about, mind you. I've been through that route before, and the plant's got defenses. We need to burn our way to Her, let me just say that. Once there, we start choppin' and burnin' Her to the ground."

He'd lifted a couple of hatchets and another machete from the Circle K, among other gear, which included a Colt Python he'd found behind the counter, the blued steel revolver looking particularly formidable. I put on one of the mesh belts, securing my own machete and hatchet on opposite sides, with the crossbow on my back. Glen handed me the Colt Python in a leather holster.

"You ever shoot anything?" he asked.

"Targets, yeah," I said. "My dad and me, when I was young."

"Well, alright," Glen said. "That's a beauty right there. I'd keep it for myself, but the shotgun takes two hands, and I'd rather have both of us carrying, just in case. It's got .357 magnum loads, which have a kick to them. Old man had a box of shells with it."

He handed me that box as I nodded, moving the stuff on my belt to allow for the holster at my hip. The weight of the weapons was reassuring, and I felt strange standing there like this. However, the memory of the Circle K loomed large, and I wouldn't let something like that get away from this place.

"When Jeph and I turned up, that big wasp nest was in that tree, but we burned it down," Glen said. "If we hadn't done that, those lil' buggers would have stung us half to death and then some. However, that didn't happen because we took them out. Same applies with the Flower Children. They're Her servants and protectors. It's all about layers of defense with that thing over yonder."

"I can't just kill those people," I said.

"Let me worry about them," Glen said. "And they're not people, anymore; they're plant-things. I don't know what they are now. Slaves? Thralls? Drones? Whatever they *were*, they're Hers, now. And they'll not hesitate to lay their lives down for Her. Push comes to shove, I gotta know you won't flinch, Tyler."

The earnestness in his tone made me want to agree to it, despite my reservations. I wanted to interview Fields and really gain insight into the work he did as Fawcett. He knew more about what was going on there than he let on, but I had no doubt about his determination to end Madame Summerville in her namesake town.

"I won't flinch," I said, flinching. "I was the one who took away their crossbows, put'em in the trunk of Ladygirl, the car we drove in on."

Glen chuckled, taking a sip of whiskey, holding out the bottle for me. I shook my head, and he took another sip.

"What did you run into in town?" I asked.

"Worst nightmare of my life," Glen replied. "Biggest plant I've ever seen, this side of a tree. Flailing vines, thorns, pollen turning everything blurry. But She's still just a plant, whatever the hell else She is. She needs helpers. We take care of them, and it'll be just Her and us."

He glanced at the fading daylight and sighed. We knew that sunset was coming, and that it would come sooner to the ghost town, so we got to it.

We trekked down the slope with our raft and cans of gas, acutely aware that we'd passed into the shadow of the Jut, where the Black River flowed. We could see the big red trumpet blooms watching us, bobbing on their tangled vines, which seemed to slither in the darkness. There was no sign of the Flower Children.

Glen and I loaded up the raft, and he took point with the shotgun, while I rowed us across the river. It was weirdly lit, with the sun still in the sky, casting a golden-orange glow at the tops of the trees and painting the clouds in the sky, but where we were was a sea of blackened branches. The river reflected both the light and the darkness in ripples, and we could hear the tree frogs serenading each other, competing with the crickets. Somewhere far away, I could hear a crow cawing. It felt like it was a world away.

We crossed the river, reaching the other side in a few minutes, with Glen jumping out and tying down the raft. The sea of heart-shaped leaves shivered at our presence, making Glen snicker.

"She knows we're coming," he said, grabbing one of the metal cans and splashing the leaves with fuel. It could have been the shadows playing with me, but I swear they recoiled from the touch of the gasoline. "Cut down the flowers wherever you see'em."

He drew his machete and slashed at them. To my relief, the red flowers easily gave way when cut. Our machete steel sang out as we cut, and there was a pleasant sort of rhythm to it, the music that we made in attacking the plants.

"They can puff pollen in your face if you let them," Glen said. "Put you right under if you get a full whiff of it, if the flower's big enough."

I instinctively hacked at some of the blossoms that were hovering nearby. I'll admit that the vibe rekindled my wariness earlier, what had made me bail on the excursion Holly and the others had taken.

"You've seen this?" I asked.

"Yep," Glen said, alternately hacking with his machete and splashing gasoline as he went. I copied his own actions, just from the opposite side of our walk. In that manner, we wended our way into town and kept the jabby-stabby plants somewhat at bay. Glen got a bit philosophical about it as we did so. "Our ancestors came to this New World and had to hack and slash their way through it to make a home for themselves. That's all we're doing."

I could only imagine the conflagration that would ensue once we lit this place up. Glen laughed as he watched the leaves react to the gasoline.

"Madame's no fan of the gasoline, that's for sure," he said, while I watched the last of the sunlight banish itself to the clouds overhead. We were in darkness.

"When do we light this stuff up?" I asked.

Glen pulled out a metal lighter and bent down and lit some leaves, pleased when they ignited, sending a line of fire down the path we'd traveled, while I lit my own side with a disposable white lighter I'd picked up from the Circle K. My own pyrotechnic efforts weren't as smooth as Glen's had been, with clusters of leaves bursting into flames fitfully, which made Glen chuckle as he watched.

"You gotta leave a little stream between them, so they'll catch," he said. Then he whipped a splash of gasoline with a pivot of his own gas can, amused when it burst into flame as it landed on the withering leaves. "The storm we had will probably slow us down a bit in terms of burning stuff, so we need to be sure to save some for Her. She's going to need to be drowned in the stuff."

The fire had messed up what night vision I had, and I could only imagine the Flower Children somewhere in the brush, waiting for a moment to strike.

Glen got us to Main Street, where we really went to town with the gasoline, pouring it on the old, ruined buildings and plants alike, igniting them. Despite the thunderstorm of the other day, things did burn. This included mats and sheets of skinny dangling vines, which shriveled in the flame.

"Too bad Jeph's not around to see this," Glen said, taking out a blackberry fruit pie he noshed on while watching the flames spread. "He had a gizmo on his drone that was a bona fide flamethrower."

"I saw on the replay," I said.

"Then you know," Glen said, savoring the fruit pie a moment or two before tossing the waxy wrapper onto the fire, watching it sizzle and contort as it burned.

"Murderer!" cried Ruth, somewhere from the shadows. "Heathens!"

At the sound of her voice, Glen raised the shotgun, wiping the crumbs from his lips with the back of his hand.

"Come on out, Little Sister of Summerville," Glen said. "Let's have a look at you."

"You'd like that, Infidel," Ruth said.

"We'll do no such thing," Joanna said from somewhere else in the shadows.

The arrow flew between us, thunking into a tree, startling us both. The Flower Children had been prepared after all, it would seem.

Two more arrows hissed by us, one nearly creasing my nose as it went into the ground. And two more arrows flew from other directions still, and it became apparent to Glen and me that we were surrounded by Flower Children.

"Too little, too late, Apostate," Layna said to our right, behind a tree, firing an arrow that found its mark, landing in Glen's upper thigh. He cried out, cursing.

I drew the Python and fired a shot in Layna's direction, the kick of the revolver catching me off-guard, while the sound of it echoed around us, making my ears ring. I'll confess to some reluctance to shooting these women down, not entirely because I feared what they might become even if I managed to hit them. I had no idea how far along they were.

Glen yanked the arrow out of his thigh with a grunt, and I could see that the arrow was a target arrow, not a hunting broadhead, which didn't make it any less dangerous, but at least meant that pulling one out might not be as bad as it might have been. Three more arrows came in, missing us.

An arrow struck me in the back, sticking out of my backpack, and I could see Dara half-lit by the fires we were making. Without thinking, I pivoted and fired two shots from the Python. One of them cut her cheek, while the other went through her throat, knocking her off her feet as she choked on blood.

"Damn, Tyler. Nice grouping," Glen said, cutting down Ruth with a shotgun blast as she rushed us in the wake of Dara's being dropped. He worked the slide and ejected the empty shell, even as two more arrows came at us.

I tried to charge Layna but tripped on some thin vines that caught my ankle, sending me face-first into cutting leaves that hacked at me, while Layna nocked another arrow. In the light of the gasoline fires, I could see her flat eyes upon me. I raised the revolver to take a shot at her, only to have more of the carpet of vines lash themselves across my outstretched arm, yanking it down. The shot I fired nailed her in the thigh, spinning her and sending her arrow whistling off skyward.

I fished out my machete with my other hand and swung at the vines, cutting them with ringing sounds of the sharpened steel as I parted the vines, heedless of the cuts on my arms as I did so.

Glen limped toward Joanna, who was readying another arrow as he shot her with the shotgun, making her do a backflip from the force of the impact at such range.

My own fight with the vines was turning in my favor as I rolled and sliced, while Layna staggered toward me with an upraised knife, having tossed aside her bow. It was a hunting knife, but she bore it in an overhand stab that I managed to parry with the machete, severing her hand with a swipe of it. To my shock, she didn't even cry out as her hand fell into the underbrush, but just glowered down at me with her mouth snarling, her other hand clawing at me.

She blasted away from me in a splash of blood as Glen fired his shotgun again. My hands shaking, I cut myself free of the vines, getting to my feet, while another arrow hit me in my backpack, this time closer to my neck.

Turning, I could see Joanna drawing another arrow. I fired two shots into her with the pistol, dropping her. Then, to my horror, I saw Dara, Ruth, and Layna sit back up, dead-eyed, the hint of vines trembling and boiling beneath their skin, animating them.

Absurdly, in that moment, I thought of them as the "Far-Alongs" as a way of classifying them. It was perhaps something I could tell myself to have a sense of order to what I was observing.

The Far-Alongs came at us again, hands outstretched, while the saplings inside them fought to come out. I did not know how this played out with the servant-slaves of Summerville, but it was a ghastly vision mercifully drowned in gasoline as Glen lit up the two near him.

And still they came, making not a sound even as they burned, with only Glen's own ringing machete swings severing their legs and dropping them.

Layna groped for me, and I cut off her other arm at the shoulder with three blows of the machete, then took a leg at the knee, dropping her. Still she fought to reach me, the saplings inside her seeking to grasp me with their bloodied green vines uncoiling from the wounds I'd made.

I scrambled back from the horror of Layna, not caring that I was being cut by the leaves, only wanting to get away from this thing. Glen tossed more gasoline on her, and the nearby fires were all too ready to ignite her. I watched her burn as I made my way back to Main Street.

Glen was pouring some whiskey on his leg wound, chuckling again as he saw me yanking the arrows out of my backpack.

"Accidental body armor," Glen said. "Smart guy."

"You okay?" I asked, looking at his leg. Glen took a swig, shrugging.

"Fit as a fiddle," he said. "You tell me: how many Flower People we still have?"

I walked over to Joanna's lifeless body, and poured some gasoline on it, igniting it, just to be on the safe side. To say that felt ghoulish was an understatement.

"I think maybe only Evan," I said. I wasn't great at math and hadn't exactly taken a census of the Flower Children. But, as I looked over the burning bodies of Layna, Joanna, Ruth, and Dara, I thought maybe that was it.

"Cool," Glen said. "Let's hit the Temple, then. Sacrifices must be made."

[This encounter forms the heart of what came to be referred to as "The Summerville Slaughter" and this is the only account of it outside of the conjecture of local law enforcement. Are we to believe that the parasite had turned the Flower Children into plant zombies? Can we trust Tyler Finn at his word, here, or is this some after-the-fact justification for a mass murder? Seensters overwhelmingly support Finn's motivations here, although some think it was all made up, possibly a pollen-influenced hallucination. The idea of the "Far-Along" is an interesting classification on the part of Finn that can only be verified in the wake of violence, which is a potentially useful justification for the violence. Much like the pod people of *Body Snatchers* fame (infamy), only more insidious because a Far-Along won't reveal themselves in ways that a pod person otherwise might. —Ed.]

The Burial Plot Thickens

What am I going to say? What's the right thing to do in my situation, I ask you? We reached the Fawcett Biotech facility after driving until sunset, and the three of us parked on the outskirts of it, far from the otherworldly blue-white brutalist flying saucer stacks they represented, with dark wings of windows between layers, and a forest of broadcast antennae on the top floor. When I say we reached the facility, what I really mean is that we drove along one of the roads that led to it, where all the plants were growing.

Two things jumped out at me while driving on that stretch—there were a lot of white crosses on the shoulders of the road, where people had died. The little memorials were dotted along it in a profusion that was uncanny. There were speed limit signs and DRIVE WITH CAUTION signs intermittently along it, many of them studded with bullet holes.

And, perhaps related to that was the pollen that wafted across the road created a euphoric hallucinatory experience for those of us upon it. I felt it, we all felt it. If we hadn't already been infected by Madame Summerville, who knows what might have happened to us. Maybe I'd have wrecked Ladygirl and we'd be memorialized like those phantom people and their little white crosses.

There were fences and screening apple trees growing to block the view of the casual observer who might be driving through. It was designed to seem unexceptional and boring—an industrial horticulture center, growing crops well away from prying eyes.

But once we got close enough, we saw Madame Summerville growing on endless trellises, tended by blue-and-yellow Fawcett drones that flew around like hummingbirds or bees (or wasps). These vineyards (?) were massive, and were protected by parallel lengths of razor fencing, with cameras aplenty, with Fawcett lozenge signs declaring that it was private property and that anybody trespassing would be arrested and fined.

However, they weren't even the most impressive thing. Rather, imagine a sea of blood red trumpetlike flowers in row after row going as far as the eye could see, the heavenly scent of them bringing back that intoxication Sharon, Justin, and I all felt. To say it was bliss didn't do it justice; it was something grander than that. All of those flowers, those children of Madame Summerville, holding court. Being pampered by their handlers.

The handlers wore Fawcett-branded hazmat suits and gas masks, incredibly enough (had to be hot in those, yes?) They looked like biological warfare revenants moving between the rows with claw-tipped poles, with drones flying around them, monitoring them, tracking the growth of the vines.

Had it begun here for Her? Had She escaped from this place? Or had She grown in Summerville and some of Her had been transported here by employees of Fawcett? I couldn't know, despite the dream-vision-hallucinations I'd experienced before. Something I felt inside me, however, was that She wanted me to see all of this. Perhaps to understand what I was dealing with.

To say I was "up against" it was absurd; this was quite beyond me.

She *wanted* me to know. As sure as the day was waning, I knew. I stepped out of Ladygirl and set up to have Justin and Sharon record me.

And while I'd been impregnated by Madame Summerville, I wasn't yet Her puppet. I didn't like bosses; it's why *The Seen* existed, a chance for me to be myself. Finding my voice was important to me, and letting myself be heard, whether or not anyone listened. This was for our Seenster fans.

We owed it to our audience to let *The Seen* be seen one last time. I understood that this would be our last episode, at least for Sharon, Justin, and me. I had to find Ty, to talk to him and let him know what we knew. He'd been smart to not fall for what we had. I felt that as strongly as I felt the euphoric effects of so much summerviolet pollen.

"This is Holly Rivers at the Fawcett Biotech Agricultural Science Facility Number Seven, located in a remote part of South Carolina," I said. "Behind me are what some call 'summerviolets' but they don't really have their own name, at least for those of us outside of Fawcett. Heaven knows what *they're* calling them. What we at *The Seen* have uncovered is something far worse. We came out here trying to track down the Ladygirl Five, but what we found was what, exactly? Nature run amok? Bioengineering led astray? You can see these crops growing. Whatever their precise origin, Fawcett has big plans for them."

Justin understood the assignment, doing a soft pan that looked magical on playback, catching the sea of red blossoms and the sunset, the golden hour glow of it all. I loved Justin in that moment, wished Ty was there to witness it with me.

"What those plans exactly are, we don't know," I said. "But what you've seen on the documentary should give you pause. If you see these plants in the wild, cull them. If you see products made from them, boycott them. Boycott Fawcett."

Inside me, the seedlings quivered, pumping me full of bio-chemical blockers that made me tranquil and compliant, but I fought through them as best as I currently could.

"Don't let *them* have the final say, whatever that say ultimately is," I said. "The Ladygirl Five stumbled onto something, and we might never know their fate. Some of you out there do, however. Some of you know just what I'm talking about."

I could see that Sharon and Justin were uncomfortable, too, or blearily succumbing to the pharmacological trickery Madame Summerville's children instinctively knew how to inflict upon their hosts, or the windborne waves of pollen that blew over us.

Not sure how much longer I might be able to keep going, and fearful that Fawcett's drones, which watched from the confines of their well-tended vineyards, were already reporting our presence on the periphery of their property.

"This is Holly Rivers, signing off for now," I said, motioning for Justin to cut. I could see the flowers closing as the sun set, just as I saw the drones flitting back to the Fawcett headquarters and could see some of the masked workers turning their black-masked eyes on us from afar. We had been seen. "We have to get out of here."

We stowed our gear efficiently, and that's when I saw the crossbows Ty had stashed in Ladygirl's trunk. He'd put them there, had stolen them from the Flower Children van. And speaking of a van, I could see a blue and yellow one far down the road, having come from the Fawcett facility, heading our way from a great distance, like a mirage that happened to be all too real.

I got us back into Ladygirl and did a U-turn, drove like hell back to Summerville, gripping the wheel tightly with fingers that weren't entirely my own.

BLOG ENTRY 20
(Tyler Finn)

Sacrificial Bonfire

Summerville was burning. Glen had a knack for arson. We even worked out a system between us, once we emptied our first four cans.

"Go back to the raft, get as many cans as you can pile in there," Glen said. "And there are two cannisters in the Fawcett van. Jeph's special mixture—Jeph Juice. Be sure to get those."

He smoked a cigarette while leaning on a signpost for First Street. We'd chopped so much vine in the center of town as we'd made the fires that my arms were aching.

"What about Evan?" I asked, looking around.

"You see him, you shoot him," Glen said. "Don't hesitate. You know I'll do the same. Just get back here with that stuff. We've got to burn this place to the ground, Tyler. Ash and bone, remember?"

"Ash and bone," I said.

"And bring me another bottle of whiskey," Glen said, tossing the empty into the fire, smirking as the remaining alcohol whistled into flame. "I'll be waiting for you."

I went quickly, my nerves raw as I made my way through the smoky fire, the scent of pollen mixing with the burning of underbrush and vines. Beyond the brightness of the blaze was the woodsy darkness and inky black of the river. The raft was where we'd left it, and I untied it and rowed back across the river. It was easier without Glen aboard. He was lean, but weight was weight.

Hearing his shotgun fire once, then again, made me whip my head around. Had Evan made his move? What would await me when I'd returned? I had to resist the urge to turn back and try to help Glen out. Getting the incendiaries was what mattered most at the moment.

Stumbling up the slope, I couldn't imagine how I would possibly get everything back down without wiping out. Another shotgun blast broke the deathly peace of the early evening.

This'll sound crazy, but I could relate to how vampire hunters or soldiers felt. You know how they're always so serious in movies? This was like that. Nobody else would know what Glen and I had done, why it mattered, and what the consequences of our actions were. This was war, and we were waging it the only way we could.

> [Admittedly, part of my rationale for getting these accounts out there, so people can understand what actually took place at Summerville, versus depending on media narratives that don't have the on-the-ground facts. Assuming that Tyler is communicating in good faith here, this is the real story at the heart of what's a mystery to those coming to it from outside. —Ed.]

I grabbed four more cans of gasoline, and the special plastic containers which held Jeph's Juice (it's what he had scrawled on the handmade labels for it). I got enterprising and found a pole in the Fawcett van and slung the cans and cannisters on it, using it like a yoke to make it somewhat less difficult to descend. I remembered the whiskey, stuffing it in a back pocket.

While I was descending, I heard another shot, then nothing. Thankfully, where we were was away from most anything else but woods, river, and swampland, so we weren't drawing attention that might have come in other places. I reloaded the Colt Python and holstered it.

I got tripped up over halfway to the bottom and cursed as I slid-tumbled to the riverbank, careful to recover the damned cans before any plunged into the river. Another shotgun blast sounded, which brought me some reassurance. If Evan had overcome Glen, I wouldn't have heard that. More likely, Evan (or Madame Summerville— yeesh) was having a go at Glen, and he was using the shotgun to keep them at bay.

Without another thought, I bathed in the Black River, if only to get the blood and mud off of me. Not exactly a baptism, but necessary. If I was to wade back into the hellscape we'd been creating, a little water couldn't hurt. I've never hopped into a river at night, but with what had gone down at Summerville, I didn't have time to be un-nerved. I emerged dripping, slipped back onto the inflat-able raft, and rowed my way across, heading toward the raging fires that were burning everything they touched, save for the path we'd cut to Main Street.

The fires we'd set were burning brightly, and gave Sum-merville a hellish glow, turning all the trees into silhou-etted specters. I tied off the raft and got out my pole and hoisted it up as steadily as I could, the cans and can-nisters clattering with bell-like tones as I did so, pulling out my machete as I went, just in case Evan popped up somewhere.

"Hey, Glen," I yelled. "It's Ty. Don't fucking shoot me, Bro."

"No worries, Ty," Glen said. "It's been…festive…since you left."

Not sure what that meant exactly, I just headed back up the trail, up Main Street, to our rendezvous point at First Street, where Glen was leaning, smoking, the shotgun held casually in his other hand. Around him were some shattered vines, as well as the ventilated and dismembered body of Evan, who gazed sightlessly up at the night sky. His hands, trailing bloody vines, tried to crawl away, looking almost like spiders in the firelight.

"Christ," I said. "What happened?"

"He attacked me, of course," Glen said. "And kept coming, just like the others. If not for my limp, I'd have made quicker work of him, but the son of a bitch kept after me. Do me a favor and douse him, would you?"

I set down the cans and poured some gasoline on him. The saplings in him had been blasted with the shotgun, and I could see from the machete cuts on his arms and legs where vines had held him together, like he was some macabre marionette. I was more than relieved that I'd missed out on this particular bit of carnage.

Once I'd finished pouring gasoline on him, Glen flicked his cigarette butt at him and Evan's corpse burst into flame, the heat wave coming off him like a slap in the face.

"Got my whiskey?" Glen asked, and I tossed him a bottle, which he drank with relish. "Everything alright up topside?"

"Looked okay to me," I said. "Nobody else around but us."

"And Her," Glen said, turning his gaze to Temple Street. "Let's finish this."

He held out his hand and took the pole I'd used to haul the fuel and used it as a kind of walking staff, grunting with each step.

"Save the Jeph Juice for last," Glen said. "This part is going to get gnarly. Remember, I've been through this before."

The oblique awareness of this didn't bring me comfort, because I wondered how the heck Glen could have survived the whatever-it-was that waited in the Temple. He seemed to know my thoughts, as he held up his machete.

"Man's best friend out here," he said, lighting another cigarette. "Madame Summerville sure doesn't like machetes."

We made our way slowly, lighting more gasoline fires as we reached the Temple. I imagined what Holly and the others might have seen in this twisted place. A cracked cathedral, a mound of ash at the far end of it, and ropy vines intertwined overhead, bearing orange fruit the size of cherries. It was like being in a garden of the gods, with bundled berries hanging heavily from tangled vines in a ruined building surrounded by fire, while fat blossoms swayed to a rhythm only they knew.

Although the flowers we'd seen and cut had been big, they were nothing compared to the monstrosities that awaited us in the Temple at the far end. They were the biggest flowers I'd ever seen, and their faces were locked on us.

"There you are, Sweetheart," Glen said. "Remember me? The Lean Man has returned."

The thick vines coiled and flexed, while the flowers bounced back and forth, almost hypnotically amid the psychedelic scent the plant threw off. I wished Justin was here to capture it, and then remembered that maybe he had earlier.

It led to another disquieting thought—if Holly and the others had been here, this thing would have attacked them, wouldn't it? Where had they gone? Had they ditched me?

The vines whipped at us, with Glen raising his machete to slash at them, spraying amber-colored sap on the floor of the Temple, even as I was lighting up the gasoline I was spilling.

"Yeah," Glen said. "Burn it down, Ty."

Roots charged at us from the ground, displacing bricks as they went, and snagged our ankles, much like the smaller ones had caught me before, only these were far stronger. I struck out with my own machete, severing them, falling to the cracked and broken ground, while Glen cursed, emptying his shotgun at the massive plant at the heart of it all.

I poured gasoline left and right, igniting it, grateful for the cascading conflagration as it found further fuel with which to burn.

Glen had traded the shotgun for the hatchet he carried, swinging hard for it. Each blow the hatchet struck resounded heartily, splashing amber sap like blood on the floor of the ruined church. Backlit by the blaze, I felt like we were fighting some giant squid, with the vines acting like tentacles. One set of them coiled around my gasoline can-holding arm, yanking me back, while I swung with the machete at the thick vine.

As we fought this thing, I had a strange, pollen-carried vision that while Madame Summerville bore the *appearance* of a plant, that it was in many ways far more than that. Or else it embodied an alien existence beyond anything we could imagine, being merely men.

"Mind the flowers, Brother," Glen said, and I could see he was right. The big blooms were angling at me, trying to lock onto my face. I swung wildly with my machete, severing them, stomping them even as I struggled to free my caught arm from the vine. The bulbs broke and bled glossy sap that was thankfully flammable, igniting readily when kissed by fire. Whatever this thing precisely was, fire *could* hurt it. I took great solace in that.

Glen was being enfolded and squeezed by the trunklike vines, cursing as he chopped with one hand and dumped gasoline with the other hand. The plant had him around his midsection in a pythonlike grasp, its daggerlike thorns sinking into his skin as it gripped him.

"Get the Juice," Glen said, wheezing as he dropped his cigarette, which caught the gasoline vapor and exploded into flame. I had freed my hand from the vine—or, more precisely, I'd freed the vine from myself, for it was still wrapped around my wrist, squeezing tightly, thorns jabbing into my flesh like syringes. I poured more gasoline and lit it up, happy that it kept some of the other vines away.

I half-ran, half-stumbled my way out of the Temple, grabbing both plastic cannisters of Jeph's Juice and went back in. Glen was on the ground while Madame Summerville burned, vines slamming every which way, including striking the mound of ash, which filled the already-saturated air with clouds of it, making it hard to see clearly. The firelight shone in beams through the fractures in the cathedral walls, while ash and pollen wildly waltzed with sparks.

Dodging the vines, I poured some of Jeph's Juice onto the blazing plant, pleased when the sticky stuff landed and exploded into flame. Glen pushed his way free of the vines, even though one of them still squeezed his midsection, and blood ran from the thorn wounds he'd suffered.

He couldn't speak, so I poured more of the Juice on that offending vine that held Glen, and some of the sparks from the existing fire caught it and went up. Once it was on fire, that vine tossed Glen away, while the plant-thing sought to save itself.

I'd never seen anything like this in my life, and if I hadn't been in such danger, I'd have paused to photograph it. As it is, the memory of that moment in the Temple would join the others that I had, the things I'd never forget.

"Toss'em!" Glen yelled, and working together, we lobbed the cans of Jeph's Juice at the heart of that big bonfire, gratified when they exploded into a syrupy fireball that enveloped Madame Summerville. The heat of it alone was incredible, and we tumbled away from it, watching this botanical beast burn. Glen clutched his stomach while we watched it burn from the back of the Temple. He lit another cigarette, puffed on it a bit before speaking. "Now *that* is a beautiful sight."

"Sure is," I said. In that moment, I finally did pull out my phone and take some photographs. The digital camera didn't entirely comprehend what it was looking at, but I tried to frame it as best as I could, as we watched Madame Summerville die. And she did not die easily, willingly, or readily, for she clawed for us with her thorny vines, even as the fire consumed her ripe flesh. But as animated as she had been, the fire was somehow more alive in those moments, until she was lost in the flailing blaze.

There was joy in this victory, that overwhelming sense that we had prevailed against this alien thing, and Glen and I took alternating swigs from the whiskey bottle I'd brought him.

"A good start," he said. "A damned good start. This was the easy part, you know."

"How so?" I asked, handing him back the bottle.

He pointed to the rest of Summerville.

"The Queen is dead, but She's got a ton of subjects," Glen said. "You gotta burn the rest of this place down, Brother. And then there's Fawcett. She's made that place what it is."

"Let's get to it, then," I said. He shook his head.

"It's on you," he said, patting his lean stomach, the rivulets of blood lining his body where the thorns had pierced him as well. "She's in me, too."

"Wait, what?"

"Told you I had run into Her earlier," Glen said. "She had a go at me the first time."

He grimaced, drinking the rest of the whiskey.

"You got away, though," I said.

"Not entirely," Glen said. "Madame stole a kiss before I went into the river. I woke up downstream, on a riverbank. Felt Her inside me. *You* gotta end this. I did what I could, but sooner or later, She wins. She always wins, if you let Her in."

I couldn't believe it, but then remembered when they'd called him "Apostate"—the Flower Children had somehow known that he'd been infected by the summerviolet, only he'd been able to resist it, at least to a point.

"Flower Power," Glen said. "Mind the blossoms. Like I said. Burn it all and get out of here. And it's only the start. Fawcett's breeding them. Whole vineyards growing as a cash crop. Plot after plot of them. Hectares. I don't even know how many."

He smoked and drank and bled, looking exhausted and sad.

"I didn't connect it," Glen said. "Not entirely. A job's a job, you know? They had us wear protective suits in the fields, where there were so many growing. I thought it was stupid. Funny, even. The stupid Fawcett superplant. The reverent way they worked with it, like it was something sacred. Seeing this growing wild, I don't know, I really could see it for what it is. There were stories, but stories are just stories. Rumors and so on. This isn't a rumor. Fetch me that shotgun, wouldja?"

Shaking, I staggered my way to it, brought it back. I couldn't fully process what Fawcett might be doing with such a thing as the summerviolet.

The gleeful words and antics of the Flower Children, the products and byproducts they made with it. It seemed goofy, even ridiculous. Patented plant parasites? Or maybe nobody outside of Fawcett knew about that. The big secret at the heart of their proprietary product.

Fawcett was just another pawn of Madame Summerville, whether it knew it or not. The scope and scale of it terrified me. I imagined massive fields of summerviolets, carefully tended by Fawcett Biotech workers just like Glen, paid well to keep quiet and do their jobs.

Seeing Glen's wounded contrition, I could see his anger and regret at being so ill-used. He didn't confide in me what his mission had been, and even if I'd inquired, I don't know if he'd be able to tell me the truth. But in those moments we shared in Summerville, there had been a kind of baptism by fire.

Glen had gotten to his feet, and held out his hand to take it, putting a lone shell into it. He nodded over my shoulder.

"Go ahead and burn the rest of this cursed place," Glen said. "Burn me last."

"What about going to a doctor?" I asked. "A hospital?"

Glen laughed.

"Fawcett'll have their experts scoop me up and put me in a research lab," Glen said. "No thank you. At least this way, it's on *my* terms."

"We can fight it together," I said. "Fuck Fawcett."

Glen managed another, drier laugh, shaking his head.

"I'm not going to make it, Brother," he said. Even thinking about it upset me, but he gripped my forearm with his free hand, looked me in the eye, his eyes bright in the firelight beneath the brim of his hat.

"You burn me like the others," Glen said. "You hear me? Don't get all squeamish on me, now. I don't want some hellplant sprouting in my innards when I'm gone. I don't want some Fawcett flunkies recovering my remains and taking them back to their corporate horticulture labs to make soap, breath mints, or hand lotion from the things that killed me. That happens, and what we did here is all for nothing."

He let me go with a push, and I walked away from him, seeing Glen in silhouette, the Temple ablaze behind him. Then I turned my back on him and spent the rest of the night lighting Summerville on fire, until I'd run out of cannisters and places to burn, except for the one I'd reserved for him.

When the shotgun blast finally came, I didn't flinch.

Curtain Call

Ladygirl was thirsty by the time we got back, and I'd seen the fire burning long before we'd gotten there. In the darkness of night, that big fire burned so brightly, and I'd awakened Justin to film it, but he protested that it was too far away and the road too bumpy to get a decent shot.

"What do you suppose it is?" Sharon asked.

"It's Summerville," I said. "Somebody burned it down. Burned Her down."

That stirred them both, not necessarily to action, but to a bleary kind of awareness that didn't usually come this time of night on a road trip.

"Who?" Justin asked.

"Who knows?" I said. "We'll find out."

Thankfully, the Fawcett van hadn't followed us after we'd taken off. Rather, they must have stopped where we'd stopped to see what we'd been looking at. I doubted the employees there fully knew what we knew, and even if they did, it wasn't entirely clear how much they'd care. Part of their jobs meant not making things needlessly complicated for their bosses.

Despite the seedlings curling up in my stomach, it was nice driving Ladygirl at night with the top down. The night sky overhead was gorgeous, and I felt a strange peace, which could have been whatever narcotics the seedlings were pumping me full of without my knowledge or consent. And who knew what exposure to all that pollen meant for us. Were our lungs and bloodstreams brimming with summerviolet pollen, now? It only made sense. None of us sneezed or coughed, so our bodies must have welcomed it. That subtle bodily betrayal stung.

Who's to complain when I felt good in the first time in so long?

The Summerville bonfire got bigger and bigger as we got closer, and I felt like something major had occurred while we were gone. My original plan had been to drive to Charleston, but that strange sight at Fawcett had put me off—those workers in the hazmat suits tending their vineyards and the drones whizzing about, while the red blossoms watched. Doubling back had been the only thing that made sense.

Overshooting Summerville confused Sharon and Justin, but when I told them we were going to fuel up at the Circle K and hopefully take shots of what might have transpired there, they understood.

The Circle K at night was haunting, with just a few lights on, the kind that concealed more than they revealed. Nothing looked out of place until we were pulled up and could see the badly burned bodies in a pile by the side.

"Justin, you know what to do," I said, while I tried to pump some gas. It didn't work, and Sharon, exasperated, went inside and activated the pumps. I fueled up Ladygirl while Justin filmed the burned bodies and Sharon came out, having taken a box of tissues to wipe down everything she touched. She chucked the box to me, and I carefully wiped down everything I'd touched.

Don't judge me harshly here, because I wasn't in my right mind; I was living under the influence of Madame

Summerville. It colored my perceptions of everything, a kind of amber haze that softened the impact of awareness.

"Can't believe the police haven't showed up here, yet," Sharon said, resting a hand on her hip.

"They're probably saving gas money," Justin said. "It's a drive out here."

"We should pop in on Summerville, take some shots," I said. "How'd you know how to work those pumps, Sharon?"

"Summer job," Sharon said. "Somebody cleaned out the videocassette closed circuit camera archives, too. Nobody'll know we were even here, provided you didn't leave prints. This is a crime scene."

All three of us knew better, based on what we'd overheard before we'd taken off. We were careful to leave as little trace as we could. Before implantation (?) I would never have done something like that. Afterward, it only made sense. I honestly could not tell you whether that was something my old self thought of in the confines of my new reality, or whether the alien seedlings drove the impulse.

"Let's just take a peek at Summerville," I said. "We need footage."

"You *always* need footage," Sharon said.

"Fire footage is the lifeblood of good filmmaking," I said, getting into Ladygirl, waving for them to follow. We got out of there as inconspicuously as we could. If a deputy or highway patrolman came along and confronted us, what would I do? I didn't know.

"Oh, is that what we are, now? Filmmakers? I thought we were independent journalists," Sharon said. There was no point in arguing aesthetics or journalistic ethics with Sharon in our current conditions. The reason we kept her with audio work was because she had no vision. Not that she ever wanted to hear that.

The fact that we hadn't even discussed what had happened to us worried me. It really made me wonder what was going on in their minds. They had to be experiencing the unusual sensations I was. Maybe the seedlings were already affecting our minds in even more insidious ways.

As I saw it, all of the accumulated footage and recordings we'd gotten added up to something major, something that would make *The Seen* stand out. The key was editing it all together and wrapping it up in a tidily marketable package. And for that, I needed Ty. In retrospect, I can't even say how I knew that he'd be there, but it was just a feeling that he would be, if he wasn't already dead.

I pulled in carefully, and the light was so otherworldly, with this fire consuming Summerville, with nothing but darkness around it. The Flower Children and Fawcett vans were parked facing outward, but I didn't see anybody.

We parked Ladygirl, and I had Sharon and Justin get their gear so we might record it. In the dark of night, this blaze was incredible footage. We might be able to sell it to local new outlets.

As our eyes got used to it, I could see that a figure was sitting at the Jut, watching it burn. What a sight he was— the lone STOP sign nearby, in silhouette, too.

"Ty?" I asked, and he turned, looking at us, seeing through us somehow.

"Holly," he said. It wasn't a question. *The Seen* team was back together. Sharon and Justin walked up, and everybody expressed their interest in seeing Ty back with us again. Of course, he wasn't quite *with* us anymore. Madame Summerville had seen to that.

"Did you set those fires?" I asked. He was drinking some gin from a skinny bottle.

"Pretty much," Ty said.

Justin zoomed in on the firestorm.

"Where are the Flower Children?" I asked.

"Dead," Ty said, meeting my gaze in the firelight, which meant that only half his face was illuminated, while the rest was in shadow. I didn't want to spoil the moment by asking Justin to film it, but thankfully, he did, anyway. He was just that good.

"The fire department will probably be here soon," I said, feeling nervous. I didn't want the authorities getting involved in this. Ty took another swig from his gin.

"I was wondering whether you'd be back," he said. "Where were you?"

"We drove out of here when things went crazy," I said. "We filmed stuff over at Fawcett. That place is bizarre, and we didn't even get too close."

Somewhere, a siren sounded, and I got more nervous.

"Let's get out of here, okay?" I said.

"Did SHE infect you?" Ty asked. "Don't pretend that you don't know what I mean."

The look in his fiery eye, what could I do but tell him the truth?

"No," I said, glancing at Sharon and Justin, who didn't correct me. "The Flower Children let us film their ritual.

We have it on film. They sacrificed Lia to Madame Summerville. It was insane."

Ty smiled to himself, shaking his head.

"And just like that, they let you go?" he said.

This required adroit negotiation on my part. Tyler was no fool. Meanwhile, the siren was getting louder.

"Can we talk about this elsewhere?" I said. "If you set these fires, we need to *not* be here."

"Fine," Ty said. "Let's get the hell out of here."

The coldness in his tone disarmed me. There was a story here, and I'd have to get it out of him, obviously. In the fiery darkness, I didn't see what a mess Ty was. We went to Ladygirl and I got us out of there. Before we left, however, Ty asked me to pop the trunk, and he stashed a few things in back. Then we left without a backward glance, Charleston-bound in the dead of night.

I tried to get Ty to talk, to say something about what had happened, but he was hardly helpful, giving curt answers, terribly noncommittal, lost in his own thoughts. He and I had a strong rapport, both personally and professionally, and not being able to read him made me uneasy.

"What happened?" I asked.

"What?" Ty replied.

"The fire," I said.

"Controlled burn," Ty said.

Sharon scoffed, while Justin dozed.

"Didn't look controlled," Sharon said.

"It was," Ty said. "Burned the ghost town right to the waterline. Dozens of cans of gasoline. All it took. Despite the storm the other day, the place was ready to go."

Ty was a world away, and this was coming from me, who was on the express train to evanescence. Did he know about us? Did he suspect?

"The Far-Alongs tried to fight it," Ty said. "The Flower Children were mostly Far-Alongs."

I asked him what those were, and he explained it to me, his own taxonomy for Madame Summerville's victims, disciples, and protégés. Hearing him talk about the "Far-Alongs" was creepy. He unloaded it on us, and I think that was his intention. Sharon and I were grossed out by it, but he kept going.

"The seedlings grow inside their victims," Ty said. "And they gradually take control. But it's not just that. Their bodies become vessels for the seedlings. Eventually, the Far-Alongs ripen and split apart. Like Lia. What you filmed, I'm thinking."

The memory of Lia was an unpleasant one. I didn't want to end up like her. Maybe I could get myself checked into a hospital, and they could perform surgery to remove the parasitic plants inside me. I had to hold out hope for that.

"However, if you face down a Far-Along before they burst, that's when something even worse happens," Ty said, turning to look Sharon and me over. "They become like bio-zombies. Worse than pod people. Animated by the plant-things infecting them."

"Gross," Sharon said. "That's really gross, Ty."

"Worse in person, let me tell you," Ty said. "The Far-Alongs aren't happy to go that way. They'd rather burst when they're fully ripe, not before. Madame Summerville has it all worked out. Not sure the timetable for it, but when you're freshly infected, your behavior's altered, but there's still enough of a sense of who you are to limit what it can make you do. Over time, though, that fades as the seedlings become saplings inside you, and then you're like a human cherry bomb, ready to explode from within when the time is right. However, I'm thinking that if a noob gets infected and killed too early, the seedlings can still sprout from the corpses, which act as fertilizer."

"Eww, Ty," Sharon said. "Just stop. It's awful."

"Just a theory," Ty said. "Those Flower Children were all Far-Alongs; it was just a question of how far along they were in their infective cycle."

I didn't know when my tipping point might arrive, when I'd stop being me and would become an extension of Her. I'd been impregnated recently. A trip to the right hospital might mean I had a chance of surviving. They'd have to be able to spot it if they scanned us. The seedlings within us could be seen. How would their removal go, though? What if a surgeon didn't remove it all? I thought of the garlands Sharon and Justin had worn, the way they'd sunk into their skin. And all of the pollen we'd breathed, as I said above. How many routes of infection were available to Her?

Ty was watching me, studying me. He knew I'd lied about us being impregnated. You ever get that feeling when somebody just knows you're trying to put one over on them? That's the way Ty was looking at me.

Now, I'd be remiss if I didn't bring this up, but I thought there was an opportunity for another scoop for us—we could get someone to film the removal of the plant para-sites inside us. That would be a medical first, yeah? Med-ical history made by *The Seen*. On top of everything else we'd filmed, it would be a major scoop. The challenge would be having Justin film it, so we could retain the rights. I wouldn't settle for any old academic medical center hack video marketing team to do the work. It had to be *The Seen* doing it, because we'd do it right.

Everything was an opportunity, see? *That's* how I got through life. Even as I was white-knuckling my way to Charleston at night, infected with a horrid plant parasite and keeping my best friend and business partner in the dark about it, I was trying to figure out a path that could make it all work out.

"You three were all infected," Ty said. "Fess up, Holly."

"Okay," I said, after being quiet far too long, feeling the shame bubble up inside me. "Yes, we were. Madame Summerville grabbed us and it happened."

"I knew it," Ty said. "But so was Glen. He was the Fawcett guy, the missing one. He helped me kill the Flower Children and your Madame Summerville. Even as it was growing inside him, he resisted it. So, maybe it's possible, at least until you become a Far-Along."

That sliver of hope hit me hard, the possibility that this wasn't a death sentence. Hell, I'd be content with having a scar down my chest if it meant I could be free of this thing.

"Okay," I said. "So, that's our plan. Sharon, Justin, and I undergo surgery to remove the things. We film it—maybe you film it, Ty. Or Justin films Sharon and me, and you film Justin. Something like that. We fold that into the larger story. The story of the century."

"Except what about Fawcett," Sharon asked. The roads were so dark out here. It was easy to feel both free and terribly isolated.

"Yeah," I replied. "Ty, we saw that Fawcett's growing summerviolets. Like a ton of them. We're talking fields of them, like some toxic vineyard."

Ty sighed, and I felt his concern.

"No way is Fawcett going to let us out them on this," Ty said. "Not going to happen. Did they see you filming?"

"There were drones," Sharon said. "And cameras. There were workers in hazmat suits. They'd have to have been blind not to see us. It was Holly's fault. She just *had* to stop and have us film it."

I glanced back at Sharon, and the two of us glared at each other a moment. We both carried our respective secrets. Although we'd all been infected, I didn't know how far along Sharon and Justin were. They'd worn those freaky garlands far longer than I had. Maybe they were more infected than I was. I couldn't trust anyone but Ty in the car. I couldn't even trust myself.

"Okay," Ty said. "We need to ditch Ladygirl, once we clean her out."

"No way," I said. "Ladygirl slaps. I'm not parting with her."

Ty was exasperated, I could tell from his tone.

"They saw you, Holly," he said. "There aren't too many dots to connect between what happened at Summerville and us. And those dots become a straight line if we're pushing some crazy story on the Web about what really happened there."

There was no way I'd consider spiking this story. Yes, I wanted to be cured, but I also wanted to lay claim to this amazing story. As I saw it, it was reparations for what we'd undergone.

Maybe Fawcett would work a deal with us to pay for our silence. Then again, maybe they'd just kill us and reclaim their property. The one thing even Ty and I could agree on would be that if Fawcett was banking on summerviolets being a big cash crop, they wouldn't let anything get in their way, and we were nothing but collateral nuisances to be swept out of the way.

"How about giving Ladygirl to Isabella Allen?" Ty asked. "Just give her the car after we've cleaned her up? Just walk away? The whole reason you bought her car was for *this* story."

"Yeah, but I'm attached, too," I said. "What's Isabella Allen going to do with her? Probably just stick her in a garage under a tarp. At least with me, Ladygirl has a fighting chance."

Ty was patient with me, took a breath, while Sharon scoffed.

"You've got bigger problems than Isabella Allen," Ty said, drawing the pistol he'd been carrying.

Duking It Out

I told Holly to stop the car, but she refused. Even with the pistol pointed at her, she didn't stop.

"You're *seriously* pointing a gun at me, Ty?" Holly said. She affected being wounded, but how much of that was just a mask? There was no way of knowing.

Sharon glared at me from the back seat, some hint of her true self in her angry eyes, while she elbowed Justin awake.

"What are you planning to do, Tyler?" Sharon asked. "Shoot us dead? I thought you wanted to get us to a hospital."

The thing was, I didn't know what to do. Holly had lied to me about being infected. Maybe that was just a bad call on her part, or maybe it was something worse. It could have been Madame Summerville commanding her to say that. We'd killed her in Summerville, but maybe she was a gestalt organism of some sort, and her malevolent spirit lived on wherever she grew.

"Don't be an asshole, Ty," Sharon said, while Justin was waking up.

"You're all three walking, talking biohazards," I said. "Maybe they can help you at the hospital, or maybe not. More likely, the CDC, Homeland Security, and/or Fawcett will send people to take you away. And, quite possibly, me, too."

"What the hell are you doing, Ty?" Justin asked. I shifted in my seat so I could keep tabs on all three of them.

"It's all about *you,* eh?" Sharon said.

"Look at yourselves," I said. "Holly, you're wanting somebody to film the extraction of the parasite? Like anybody's going to let any of us walk after whatever they do takes place? Our lives are finished from this point onward."

Holly shook her head. I could see her trying to work through a way to reach me.

"We could make our lives mean something," Holly said. "This matters, Ty."

When I'd burned away the remaining wild summerviolets in the ghost town, after Glen had killed himself, I did a lot of thinking. Arson apparently helps you clear your head, and as I fought my way through that burning town, the summerviolets attacking me at every turn, I had time to get my head on straight.

Knowing what to look for made all the difference. Evil hides in the shadows, behind facades, misinformation, and lies. That's how it thrives. Deception is the armor of evil.

I'd used up every container of gasoline that Glen and I had taken from the Circle K to get Summerville ablaze. And every time one of those summerviolets burned, it thrashed and popped, tried to snag me with its cutting vines. The blossoms filled the air with the intoxicating pollen in a bid to enslave or knock me unconscious.

While I'd waged my war on them, I'd hoped that Holly and the others had escaped. I didn't know if they'd been infected. As long as it was an unknown, I could have some hope for them, a happy ending. Sitting on the Jut, getting drunk on gin, I'd felt like I'd won the Battle of Summerville simply by surviving. I'd felt a sense of triumph, even if it was just me sitting there, watching it all burn.

And then they showed up. And then Holly had lied about being infected, as if I wouldn't figure it out. Where did that leave me? Was I expected to trust anything they said from that point on? Until they became Far-Alongs and murdered (or infected) me?

As the only uninfected person in the car, I had the moral burden. The others couldn't be expected to act in good faith. Sure, they *seemed* in control of themselves, but they weren't. Sooner or later, whatever was left of them would be hollowed out and they'd be puppets for the plant parasite, the way the Flower Children had been.

To abandon them would be a betrayal of my moral responsibility. The only acceptable step I could see was getting them medical care, where the seedlings might be removed. Glen probably would have simply executed them by the roadside before driving Ladygirl into a wall.

But what would I do? Further, what if they didn't agree to go to the hospital? There was that, as well. Holly seemed motivated for now to take that course of action. However, what if Sharon and Justin balked at it and tried to run off? Was I prepared to gun them down?

Additionally, anybody seeing me do that would think I was the bad guy, just another shooter taking it out on innocent victims. How would that look? Who knew how that might play out in the autopsy? Maybe the medical examiner would open them up and the saplings might burst out and attack them, and then we'd have a breakout infection in a hospital. Or perhaps Fawcett and/or the government would send agents to recover the bodies and make them disappear.

Maybe I shouldn't have downed the gin before finding myself in this situation, but I hadn't planned on them showing up.

"Earth to Tyler," Sharon said, her caustic tone shaking me out of my reverie.

"Yeah, this matters," I said. "Holly, we have to get you three to a hospital. That's the only way forward. We're just going to have to take our chances on someone being able to get those things out of you."

Holly nodded warily, while Sharon and Justin just looked at me, at my pistol, uncertainty the only sure thing about them. Then something came to me.

"We need to head to Duke," I said, just blurting it out.

"Duke?" Justin said. "Dude, that's like over a dozen hours away from here."

Holly understood.

"Ashley Graham," Holly said. "That's where *she* went. You're saying somebody there knows what's going on."

"They might," I said. "They should. If nothing else, there's more expertise there than what we'll be finding at a community hospital around here. No offense, but most of the doctors around these parts likely haven't seen anything like what you have. And anybody hereabouts who knows what's going on has to be in Fawcett's pocket. So, we head up to Duke. While we're on the way, I'll do some research once we've got decent Internet access and I'll try to zero in on some plant biologists and surgeons. Maybe somebody multidisciplinary. Also, we need to upload everything we have to our servers. All of the footage. Everything."

"Sure, Ty," Sharon said. "You must feel like that person who was running late and missed out on a plane crash."

As ever, Sharon didn't get me. There was no survivor's guilt with me. I didn't feel guilt; I was more scared than I'd ever been, and I was the one holding the gun.

"Somebody over there knows about Madame Summerville," I said. "You three will just have to hold it together."

"All well and good," Sharon said. "But are you going to just hold us at gunpoint the whole way, Ty? That might play out here in the dark, but during the day? We'll be pulled over. Probably arrested. Especially you. Somebody's going to have to swing for all that arson and murder. Somebody'll hit that Circle K and see your handiwork."

"That was Glen," I said. "I only helped."

"An accessory after the fact," Sharon said, locking eyes with me. I pointed the pistol at her.

"I'm trying to help you, Sharon," I replied. "Whether you want it or not."

She just stared at me, scorn etched deep into her face. On her best days, she was a pain in the ass. Nowadays, who could know?

"I can see that, Ty," she replied. I didn't have to justify myself to her. She was the half-person at this point, not me.

"I'm trying to get you three a way out of this," I said. "I could just blow you three away, take Ladygirl, and drive off with all of the footage. At least this way, you have a chance. And I'm in the minority here."

"How about you put the gun away, Ty?" Justin said. His eyes weren't as hard as Sharon's, were more conciliatory.

However, it didn't mean anything. Maybe the seedlings were making him seem that way.

"I'm going to put it to you as clearly as I can," I said. "If I put this pistol away and any of you try to mess with me, I'll shoot you dead. None of you are Far-Alongs, yet, which means that a bullet or two will drop you. We just need to manage a thirteen-hour drive to Duke and a data dump to our DC server along the way as insurance. Let's see how that goes. What's more, if Fawcett has been minding us, they might not expect that we're headed to Duke; they might think we're going back to our rental at Charleston. They could be waiting for us there."

Holly smiled at that, her face underlit by Ladygirl's dashboard lights.

"You're so marvelously paranoid, Ty," she said.

I made a show of holstering the revolver.

"Putting the pistol away, now," I said, stealthily slipping the machete from its scabbard and keeping it by my right leg in the shadows. Just in case.

I waited for them to jump me, but nobody did. I pulled some amphetamine from my backpack, more of the loot stolen from the Circle K and downed it, while Sharon and Justin looked on. Even Holly gave me a sidelong glance.

"You don't trust us, Ty," Holly said.

"I've seen what your kind can do," I replied.

"Our kind," Sharon said. "That hurts, Ty."

Thirteen hours. I could make it that long, right?

BLOG ENTRY 23
(Holly Rivers)

Road Trip Rashness

Poor Ty. He had to try. I don't blame him for that. There was a sweetness to him that I envied, to be honest. We drove through the night, refueled when we'd crossed the border into North Carolina. He'd stayed awake all night. We all had, except for Justin, who conked again. Sharon just lurked in the back, lost in thoughts she chose not to share with anyone.

You might think we infected folk shared some kind of common bond, like a telepathic thing, but while still in our old bodies, that root-and-vine rapport didn't exist, yet. We were seedpod people, waiting for the right moment to burst. Fruit had to ripen before harvest. Even thinking that way grossed me out, and I wondered if the seedlings put that in my head.

I didn't know how it went for Ashley Graham, carrying Blossom inside her. Me, I felt like myself, except for the barely perceptible nagging of Madame Summervile's seedlings inside me.

What kind of plant grew inside a living body? I thought way too much about orchids, the way they parasitized trees. And mistletoe. I thought an awful lot about mistletoe, which was another parasite. People loved mistletoe around the holidays. How many knew that it was a parasite? That in the ancient times, it stood out as still green when the snow fell because it drew strength from the trees it was feeding on.

Thinking about orchids and mistletoe brought me a peace in what was trying circumstances. When Ty had drawn that pistol, the look in his eyes frightened what was left of me. He'd never have done something like that before. I had no doubt that he'd have made good on his threat to blow us away now, though. Whatever had happened at Summerville had ruined him as surely as it had ruined us. For as harshly as Sharon judged him, I knew Tyler was going through some things.

We took a break at a rest stop where there was Internet access, and Tyler and I furiously updated our blog entries while Sharon watched us and Justin slept in the back of Ladygirl. Ty also went through the raw footage files Justin had taken and uploaded them to our server. He watched us the whole time we were doing this, making sure nobody got behind him.

We saw on the Net that the local news had covered what had gone down in Summerville, with area reporters talking about a scene of arson and murder between an apparent Mansonian cult called "The Flower Children" and some Fawcett Biotech employees. Authorities were actively investigating two crime scenes, with numerous bodies burned beyond recognition.

I was anxious to get going, but Ty insisted on getting as much uploaded as we could, which took a few hours we weren't sure we had. He fretted about Fawcett coming for us, and Sharon and I used that fear to persuade him to get us rolling again. The seedlings in me were content to wait, which made me want to move all the faster.

We listened to the radio broadcasts while driving north to Duke, and I was almost happy to see purple-blue thunderclouds on the horizon, heralding rain. It let us close up the convertible, which made it cozier. Does that make me seem shallow or something, thinking about coziness at a time like this? Never argue with the cozy, man.

I told Ty that I was tired from driving, that we needed to take another break, and he and I filled up our laptops with blog entries during our break, which Ty uploaded to our server. I was lying about needing a break. I could have driven for days. Whatever Madame Summerville did to the human body, fatigue didn't come into it. Hell, I was energized.

Sharon and Justin noodled around a Waffle House we'd stopped at while Ty and I blazed away on our keyboards. As crazy as it sounds, I was proud of Ty and me, being *The Seen* machines we both were, trying to get everything to our servers. Nobody appreciates how much effort goes into production. People probably think it's just point-and-shoot, but so much planning and data transfer is involved in the process.

"I think those two are played out," Ty said. "I'm watching."

"You think?" I asked.

"It's like anything else," Ty said. "Some people can smoke their whole lives and not get cancer. Others get sick and die from it at a young age. Alcohol, all of it. Things affect people differently. It's gotta be the same with the summerviolet. And they wore those garlands longer than we did. Those wounds on their bodies. They're probably even more infested than you are. The summerviolet's probably growing all through them."

It was as good a theory as any other. I only knew how I felt. I still felt like myself. The Flower Children had been at it for a few months. They'd built an entire cult religion around their experience in a matter of months.

I didn't see myself doing that, although visions of myself as the High Priestess of Madame Summerville held an appeal, a braided vine and flower-flecked crown on my head was a lovely image I found hard to shake. Were the seedlings sending those signals to my brain, along my neuronal pathways?

"If they get screwy, I'll help you do them in," I said. "I promise."

Ty looked sad.

"I wish I could believe you, Holly," he replied after a moment that went far longer than I wanted it to.

"So do I," I said. I moved to put a hand on his shoulder, but he flinched, and I didn't press the issue.

"I appreciate what you're trying to do for us," I said. "It's sweet. It's…human."

Ty smiled more bitterly than I'd hoped he would, shaking his head. He snapped shut his laptop, slipping it into his bag. I could see the holes in it from the arrowheads the Flower Children had shot at him. I would have been terrified. I wanted to praise him for his bravery but didn't think he'd believe that any more than he believed anything else I said. The loss of trust between us was painful, like a spiritual wound we both carried.

"Once we get to Duke, I want you to review our footage, I'll share access to my blog, and you can see what you can make of it," I said. "If nothing else, you'll have that to occupy you while we're undergoing whatever the hell we're undergoing at Duke."

I wasn't going to fess up that I feared what might happen to me at Duke, that maybe we'd arrive too late and they'd have to cart us off somewhere else, and that I'd never see Ty again.

The rain had started to fall, all sweeping squall line and juicy raindrops that splashed everything they touched.

Sharon and Justin came running out, slipping in the back. They smelled of hasty breakfasts and secrets.

"Let's get out of here," I said, and off we'd rolled, just as the storm came down hard on us. Part of me—which part, right?—was glad for the storm, because it would have helped the firefighters deal with the blaze that Ty had set.

What a weird group we were—the writer-arsonist and the seedpod production people on our road trip together. Not at all how I thought it was going to end up when we'd first set off.

Sheets of rain fell, but Ladygirl was smooth as glass on the ride as I slowed down a bit to deal with the storm. Even with the wipers on fast, it was hard to see.

The news we heard on the radio implicated one Glen Fields (31 years old) and Jeph Wales (27 years old) in a shootout with the Flower Children, in two crime scenes that included the Circle K, where owner-operator, Cooper DeVille (84 years old) had been shot in the back by the same shotgun that was later recovered at Summerville.

At the Circle K crime scene, four as-yet unidentified people had been gunned down and hacked with machetes before being set on fire, in a scene that was called by local sheriff, Jasper Johnson, as "the most brutal crime scene I'd ever seen in twenty years as sheriff."

Authorities found a total of six badly burned and dismembered bodies at the burned-out ghost town of Summerville, along with the body of Glen Fields, who had apparently expired from a self-inflicted shotgun wound before being consumed in the blaze. Preliminary reports indicated that he'd been shot with an arrow before succumbing to the flames he'd allegedly set.

Further, the body of Jeph Wales had been found downriver by some fishermen, wearing a Fawcett environmen-
tal suit and being in an advanced state of decomposition.
He had been shot by a pair of crossbow bolts and his
time of death was earlier than the other victims of the
Summerville Slaughter.

The Flower Children were known in the area, being active at art fairs and seasonal festivals. A number of locals
were interviewed talking about them and had nothing
but good things to say about them.

Identities of some of the victims were being withheld
pending the notification of next of kin, but Sheriff Johnson was pretty confident that there had been some kind
of escalating confrontation between the Fawcett employees and the Flower Children.

Fawcett Manager of Field Operations, Johnny Wyndham
(54 years old), confirmed that Fields and Wales had been
contracted to do some fieldwork at Summerville as part
of a larger project, and that he'd spoken to Fields, who
had alluded to "some local trouble" on their call, asking
for assistance. He had said that they had been putting a
team together in response, but logistics required a three-
day delay in Fawcett personnel being able to get there.

A curious aside to the investigation that authorities
mentioned as that the shotgun used on the victims was
traced to one Ethan Allen (33 years old), who had gone
missing two years earlier, along with several others.

"The Ladygirl Five," I said. It always came back to them.

"Glen snagged the gun from DeVille," Ty said. "The old
man had it at his Circle K. Along with the Colt Python."

"Juicy," I said. "DeVille must have cleaned up the crime
scene of the Ladygirl Five, taken that shotgun as a souvenir."

"They didn't mention the pistol, which either means that they're keeping that under their hats, or maybe they think Jeph used it, or that the fires burned away that evidence or something," Ty said. "Somebody's bound to notice that the camera and SD card was missing on the drone. Anybody finds that and we're toast. Persons of interest at the very least."

Despite the precarious nature of our situation, I took real satisfaction at gaining some of the puzzle pieces tied to the disappearance of the Ladygirl Five.

"Was DeVille infected?" I asked. Ty shook his head.

"Didn't seem to be," Ty said. "Nothing came out of him when we burned him."

He looked sick at recalling that, and it made me wonder why DeVille was allied with Madame Summerville, despite apparently not being infected. Why would he ally with Her? The visions washed back into my memory, of Madame Summerville working with him, the bizarre symbiosis they had.

Sheriff Johnson had also spoken with Noah Arkes (24 years old), who had been contracted by DeVille to tow out the Fawcett Biotech van from the Summerville location. Authorities were looking to talk to the owners of a 1975 sky blue Cadillac Eldorado nicknamed "Ladygirl"—including an unidentified young black man who'd spoken to both Arkes and DeVille. Arkes was working with police sketch artists to try to come up with a composite of the mystery man who'd been at the scene, reiterating that this person was not a suspect in the murders, but might shed some light on what had happened.

"Oh, shit," Ty said. "We've got to ditch the Circle K videotapes. Gotta burn them or something."

He grabbed his *The Seen* cap and jammed it low on his head. He explained about the towing of the Fawcett van, which authorities thought might have been the precipitating event in a conflict between the Flower Children and the Fawcett employees.

We drove through the storm and got a can of gasoline at one of the stations when we refilled. We were about five hours from Durham. Ty was very nervous until we'd driven out of the way and stopped at an empty park, where Ty tossed the videotapes into a trashcan and lit them on fire with the gasoline, before toting four colorful crossbows and tossing them into the trashcan to melt and burn. We watched them burn.

He held onto the Python, looking at us all in turn.

"I *should* get rid of this," Ty said. "But I'm thinking maybe I shouldn't."

"You couldn't shoot us, Ty," Justin said, folding his arms. Ty just met his gaze without expression and pointed to the machete and hatchet at his hips, resting his hand on the revolver. Sharon nodded grimly.

"Okay, there, Grisly Adams," Sharon said. "Point taken."

We watched the stuff burn and melt a moment longer before Ty directed us to leave before anybody saw us out there. It looked clear to me, but you never knew.

We got back into Ladygirl and drove off, leaving a burning trashcan in our wake. As we drove away, Justin grumbled in the back seat.

"Those Pythons are worth a bundle," he said. "Especially vintage ones. You could clean up if you sold that sucker."

"Not a chance," Ty said. "Literally the last thing I should do."

"Just saying," Justin said, scrolling on his phone. "Depending on the year and condition, you could sell that for maybe a couple thousand dollars. Good walking-around money, Bro."

"Just stop," Ty said. "At least this way, if somebody pulls us over because we're driving Ladygirl, we won't have a bunch of evidence tying us to the Circle K and Summerville. Not sure how cleanly ballistics turns up with badly-burned plant-zombie corpses."

"Hiding evidence," Sharon said. "Criminality somehow suits you, Ty."

After the storm passed, we put the top down and drove as casually as we were able to, Ty keeping the radio on in case anything else came through. The fact that we'd crossed state lines hours ago didn't make any difference to Ty, who was increasingly restive.

Ty got it into his head to have Justin film us talking, just leveling about our experience at Summerville. After all, nobody knew that we'd even been there, except for Noah Arkes, who had seen and talked to Ty.

"You're reading too much into it, Ty," Holly said. "Sounds like they think it was a scrap between the Fawcett guys and the Flower Children. We're not mixed up in it."

Having the top down made a difference. I liked feeling the sunlight on me and didn't know whether that was a result of the seedlings inside me. Best not to think too much about that. Still, part of me *did* think about it:

Seeds

Seedlings

Saplings

Sprouts (?)

Shoots (??)

Was that how it went? We were implanted with seeds, which then embedded themselves in us. After an unspecified period of time those seeds became seedlings, taking root inside our bodies in some surreal and grotesque manner, influencing our minds and behavior through the application of hormonal and biochemical agents that made us receptive vessels for the parasite.

The fact that neither the pollen nor the seeds generated an immune response from us meant that the summer-violet was very adroit at insinuating itself into its hosts, which brought me a bushel of brooding.

At some point, the seedlings became saplings, which were probably at the front-end of the Far-Along taxonomy Ty had envisioned.

After an again unspecified time period those saplings were ready to sprout. We'd seen that with Lia, where she'd literally come apart. If one weren't tended to by the likes of the Flower Children, one would simply find a sapling growing. Eventually, if all went well, it would get bigger, sending out shoots, so it could spread. It would grow its own clusters of flowers and eventually be ready to infect others.

I was thinking about that far too much. Everything hinged on the timeframe of our impregnation. We were in the seed/seedling cycle. We didn't yet have saplings in us. We couldn't. Until we had medical experts examining us, there was no way of knowing how deep the infestation went.

From Ty's account of the Far-Alongs, there came a point where victims were truly like pod people being puppeteered by the parasite.

The organism was sentient, either directly or indirectly, in that it could affect our thoughts at some point. How that drove our behavior afterward was anyone's guess. I privately resolved that I'd keep a record in the form of these blog entries, so that there'd at least be documentation of it. I'd tell Ty when we had a moment. Since he'd already been feverishly uploading files when he got the chance, it was a logical thing for me to do.

"Are we there, yet?" Justin asked, and nobody laughed.

"Maybe four more hours," I said. "If traffic's not a problem."

"Or if we don't get pulled over," Sharon said, sounding pretty desolate. I wanted to know how they were feeling, so I chimed in.

"How are you two feeling?" I asked.

"Meh," Sharon said. "This whole trip has sucked, Holly. I'm blaming you."

"I'm alright," Justin said. "Stomach's in knots, but I got some great footage. Should be a killer episode, assuming Ty doesn't botch the postproduction."

Ty glowered over his shoulder, but Justin was nonplussed.

"Overproduction is your baseline, Ty," Justin said. "All I'm saying."

"He's right," Sharon said, and, weirdly, everybody laughed. Not hearty laughs, but laughs, all the same. Like a glimpse of sunlight in a storm, there was the barest hint of hope in that moment, the friends and comrades that we'd been. Doing production work brought that out in everybody, I thought.

Ty sighed and held his hands up.

"I'll be gentle with the rushes, I promise," Ty said, taking out his tablet, which he'd been charging since the Waffle House. "Let me film you. Like last words or something."

"Jesus, that's grim," Sharon said.

"A chance for you to say what you want to say," Ty said. "Your own words."

His sincerity was undeniable, and we all agreed to do it, provided that Ty did it, too. Sharon insisted on going first, and we let her.

BLOG ENTRY 24
(Tyler Finn)

Three Strikes

[These digital testimonials were a curious sidebar for *The Seen* team, seemingly thought of as a way of them sharing thoughts and feelings for posterity, but also being something else that I don't think Tyler Finn necessarily intended. Seensters have repeatedly played these and analyzed them, attempting to find something of value in them. —Ed.]

The clips I shot weren't fancy; they were more low-fi out of necessity and design. It took some persuading to even get them to let me film them. I was adequate with a camera, but still shots and video were different things. I told the others that each person got to say their piece without interruption, which wasn't easy, given this crew. They humored me…

SHARON'S LAST WORDS

Ty wants me to do this, and I'm going to tell you that I hate being filmed. Hate. It. I think he wants to give me a chance to have my own say about what happened at Summerville. What can I even say? Lots of plants growing like crazy there. I saw a young woman explode in this temple. Lia Larkin. She was one of the Flower Children, and they carted her to their Temple and she blew apart atop an ash pile. It was gross. I was just capturing the sound for it and had headphones on. I heard all of it. The crunching, splashing, screaming, chanting. All of that. Even the sounds of the plants. I could hear the plants.

This was before it went after Holly, before it went after me. I blacked out. I don't remember. The pollen's like a drug. It takes hold of you. It makes you see things. Not hallucinations, exactly. More like something else, something more intimate. Like a narcotic haze. You walk through a waking dream and you're not sure of your place in it.

I'm sorry Mom and Dad. Sissy. Trish. They're saying I'm infected, impregnated, whatever you want to call it. I feel fine. Okay, not fine. I should never have been on this fool's errand of Holly's. But you know how Holly is. She's persuasive. I love and hate her for it. The things we've gotten into over the years, just because she gets something in her head and goes for it.

Lia screamed and wept when they carried her to the Temple. I don't know whether it was out of pain or ecstasy. Maybe both. When they took those bloody plants from the ruin of her body, potted them and everything, it was all too much.

Will I scream when my time comes? If it comes? Ty thinks the doctors at Duke will be able to remove this thing inside me. I hope he's right. I pray he is, which says something, because I'm not a thoughts-and-prayers kinda gal.

She stopped and waved me away, cursing me out. Sharon didn't like feeling vulnerable, and I guess this exercise brought that forward for her. Justin offered to comfort her, but she wouldn't take it. Unable to make her feel better, Justin wanted to go next, while Holly pretended to concentrate on the road while listening to everyone else. I knew her too well to think otherwise.

JUSTIN'S LAST WORDS

Look, man, hold it steady. I should just shoot this myself, no? There's nothing I can say that Sharon didn't already touch on. I filmed it all, saw it all go down. Like she said, I don't feel any different. I hope we go to Duke and they're like "You're okay, Justin." I'll be a happy guy.

What went down at Summerville was weird. I'm used to letting my footage speak for me, you know what I mean? If Ty edits it alright, you'll see what I'm talking about. You won't need my input if he doesn't botch it.

My stomach's been in knots since we left. It's not painful. If anything, I feel great. Everything's more colorful, you know? The colors pop. I'm not seeing things, but I am seeing colors. It's like being high all the time. We went to a Waffle House and everything was just vibrant. That's the word for it. VIBRANT. Even my breakfast was vibrant—chocolate chip pancakes with bacon. I was HUNGRY, man.

I don't think anything's wrong with me. Sure, I saw weird stuff go down at Summerville, but that pollen was everything. You could smell it—like cinnamon and citrus, other spices. It smelled wonderful and it messed with my head. Best high I ever had, tell you the truth. Grams of that stuff would sell. I'll bet those Flower Children did a brisk trade on the side with that summerviolet pollen.

I'm saying that I'm not quite sure what I saw. I haven't seen the footage since I shot it. I just hope I caught everything that needed to be caught, because it was a trip.

He stopped, mostly because Sharon was staring at him from her side of the car. Justin took things as they came, which probably made him good at indie filming. He just caught things without getting shaky or shaken.

"My turn," Holly said. I was amazed she'd been as patient as she had been. Unlike Sharon and Justin, Holly's last words were in profile, with her driving, glancing every now and then at me. Otherwise, her eyes were on the road.

HOLLY'S LAST WORDS

I don't believe in last words. Except, you know, when you die. I always wondered how that even happened back in the day. Like if you were on your deathbed, what would you even say? Who had the presence of mind to say something poignant or clever with their last breath, versus saying something stupid or senseless?

What's more, did others simply embellish those last words, make them better than they actually were? That's entirely possible. Probable, even. We all can't be wits.

My motivations for traveling to Summerville were to uncover a mystery. I wanted to know what happened to the Ladygirl Five. It obsessed me. When I saw Lia Larkin die—sorry, evanesce—I'd never seen anything like that. I had tried to get away, but Madame Summerville had caught me. Her vines had taken hold and I couldn't escape. The blackness Sharon spoke of? Felt that.

The violation of the parasite. I felt that, too. Dead like death.

And then I wasn't dead. I was reborn on the forest floor. Not a forest, I know. But when I looked up at the trees and vines, it's how it felt. Rebirth.

Depending on how much you know about Madame Summerville, you're thinking maybe I'd be outraged and terrified. I get that. I should be feeling that. Maybe She won't let me feel that, though. That's why I have to let somebody open me up and take Her out of me.

All I know is that the me that I was before the seeds were implanted in me isn't the me that's here now. I'm still in the driver's seat, literally and figuratively. Or maybe that's just what She wants me to believe. Don't know.

Ironic that we're taking Ladygirl back to Duke. Maybe we're driving the same route Ashley Graham took with her stolen car a couple of years ago. Poor Ashley didn't have anyone but herself with her. At least we have someone to talk to.

Ty, you have to promise me that you'll do the best you can with all of the footage. People need to know what's really going on.

"I promise," I said. And I meant it.

MY LAST WORDS

I'm not letting Justin take the camera; I'm just shooting myself out of a sense of fairness. Look, we've uploaded the footage to our servers, and while my friends are being operated on—assuming we can get anyone at Duke to help us—I'm going to try to get caught up on the blog entries and get the rest of it uploaded.

I may even get some of the blogs to our website portal, for you Seensters out there, so you know what we've been up to. Not sure if that's something I want to do before we get the episode together. We're trying to educate and alert, not entertain, here.

My friends are all in a bad situation, and we're trying to fix that. My hope is someone can help us and we'll maybe not laugh about this one day, but hopefully be able to talk about it. No way am I ever forgetting what I saw in Summerville. I saw heroism and evil. It's given me a lot to think about.

Whatever happens, I want to make sure people understand that Fawcett Biotech is involved in this. No idea what kind of response they'll mount once they find us. Probably armies of lawyers will march after us, but the truth has to get out there. People have to know.

Mom, Dad, everyone—no matter what they might say in the legacy media, just know that we tried to do the right thing, even before we knew what that was.

[This video clip abruptly ends, so I'm not sure what else Tyler may have wanted to say. You can see his emotion in the footage we were able to recover. —Ed.]

BLOG ENTRY 25

(Holly Rivers)

Full Disclosure

We got to Duke in a total of eighteen hours, allowing for our blog and file footage uploads along the way. Ty had managed to find some plant biologists and surgeons there on the Internet while I drove us. They were people who might be able to help:

Gennifer Sherman, PhD, Plant Biology

Laurel Lee, PhD, Plant Biology

Reed Roswell, MD, Thoracic Surgery

James Briarton, MD, Cardiothoracic Surgery

Ty had emailed Drs. Sherman and Lee and had mentioned that we had become infected by some kind of plant parasite. He'd said as much after he'd done it, and Sharon in particular had been irked by that.

"You told them?" Sharon asked.

"I did," Ty said.

She leaned forward in the back seat, glaring at Ty.

"If they're in league with Fawcett, you will have signed our death warrants, Ty," Sharon said. I saw Ty's hand steal toward the pistol at his hip. He tried to be circumspect about it, but I saw. I didn't say anything—whether that was me or Madame, I couldn't say.

"Either way, you three need to be treated," Ty said.

"Still, I don't like it, Ty," Sharon said.

His phone rang about an hour after he'd sent that email, and he answered, didn't put it on speaker, just kept an eye on us while he talked. I wasn't angry about it. Why should I be? He was only trying to help. Whatever the seedlings were putting in me, there was still enough me left to feel gratitude that he was there for us, whether or not Sharon or Justin did.

"This is Tyler," he said, answering. "Yes, Dr. Lee. My friends were exposed to something. Some kind of plant parasite. A vine-thing with red flowers. Trumpet-shaped. Yes. Fragrant pollen. I think they were infected. We thought Duke might be a good place to go. Yes. I looked up some of your faculty. Drs. Sherman, Roswell, and Briarton. I only contacted you and Sherman, because it's a plant thing. Yes. No, we haven't. We're about two hours away. We didn't know what else to do. Yes, I've seen what happens. We all have."

"Put it on speaker, dammit," Sharon said. Ty held up a finger.

"I'm going to put you on speaker, Dr. Lee," Ty said, and he did, and we introduced ourselves quickly.

"Mr. Finn, you were right to reach out to us," Dr. Lee said. "How long ago were your friends infected?"

"Three days ago," I said. "Approximately."

"Okay," Lee said. "That's early enough that we ought to be able to do something about it. I'll talk to my peers."

"Have you seen this before?" I asked, not wanting to just keep quiet and drive.

"We have," Lee said. "Or, more indirectly, we've found one of these plants growing on campus. It's in our Botany Plot, now."

[Duke University hosts the Botany Plot, which is a protected, limited-access field where faculty can conduct large-scale, in-ground plant experiments. I'd love to be able to access it but haven't been able to. Seensters suspect that "Blossom"—the summerviolet that had infected the missing Ashley Talulah Graham, is growing there. This cannot be confirmed or denied. —Ed.]

"Blossom," I said. The word came to me from somewhere deep inside. It came from Her. The memory of the vision I had with Madame Summerville in the Temple.

"Blossom?" Lee asked. "Not certain what that means. We'd found corrupted traces of human DNA in it."

"Ashley Talulah Graham," I said. "She'd been infected with the parasite around two years ago. That sample came from her."

Lee was quiet on the line a moment.

"That's correct," Lee said. "At least in terms of when the sample turned up on our campus. We didn't correlate it with any specific person. How'd you determine this?"

"Lucky guess," I said. I wasn't about to go through the whole process of discovery or anything about me communing with Madame Summerville. "Do you think you can cure us?"

"We have tested infection on lab animals," Dr. Lee said. "But you'll be the first infected humans we've directly encountered."

The skies were cloudy again, and it looked like more rain would be coming. I just tried to keep us driving steadily toward Durham without unnecessary complications.

"You have the facilities to treat my friends?" Ty asked.

"We do," Lee said. "Just get here and we'll do what we can for you."

"And please tell me you're not tied to Fawcett Biotech," Ty said. Again, a brief pause from Dr. Lee, which made me edgy.

"Some of my peers have research grants with Fawcett, but I don't," Lee said. "I'll coordinate with some of the surgeons in the School of Medicine and see who might be able to help. Why are you worried about Fawcett?"

How much tea was I prepared to spill in that moment? How trustworthy was Dr. Lee? Did that even matter at this point?

"We filmed a major horticultural effort at Fawcett that seemed to involve the Summerville species," I said. "If this is some bioengineered specimen of theirs, they may not take kindly to people getting wind of it."

"I'll be sure to be discreet," Lee said. "Just get here and we'll see what we can do."

"Two hours," I said.

"Thanks, Dr. Lee," Ty said, hanging up. Sharon was miffed, while Justin had slept through it all. Sharon gave him a swat or two to wake up.

"Are we there, yet?" Justin asked.

"No, we're not there, yet," Sharon said. "But Ty went ahead and contacted the people at Duke. Hope you're ready for surgery, Justin."

Justin cracked his neck and shoulders, was paranormally blasé about it all. Of the three of us, he seemed the most reconciled to his condition. This could have been his generally genial nature, or it could have been a bell-wether for his own issues with the summerviolet seedlings inside him.

Sharon's own behavior could have gone either way. If the seedlings were compelling her to feel upset about their possible removal, there might have been resistance on her part. Or maybe that was old Sharon being irritated by circumstances beyond her control.

Speaking only for myself, I did hope this gambit paid off. I wasn't ready for my own evanescence, yet. Who among healthy—sorry, functional—humans really wants to disappear? We don't. Even introverts want to be seen by *someone,* don't they? Being seen was an acknowledgment of our existence.

Though She may have carried an iota of Ashley Graham's DNA, Blossom wasn't her. It was like when a virus infiltrated a cell and took it over; while that cell might wear the trappings of its own former existence, it had ceased to be what it was, with only a ghost reflection of it remaining.

I didn't yet want that for myself.

I wanted to live.

Operational Theater

Drs. Lee and Sherman were there when we arrived, wearing Duke Blue hazmat suits, which included gas masks. Campus security were there as we'd rolled up early Friday morning, before the campus was active.

At the sight of Ladygirl, some of the campus police elbowed each other and pointed. They remembered the last time that Cadillac had showed up on their campus. I was positive of that. I slipped the Python and its holster into the glovebox, moving as discreetly as I could.

A university media relations administrator named Amelia Jackson was there in her own hazmat suit, holding out clipboards for us to sign. Jackson's voice was authoritative despite the mask, rendered through a speaker.

"These are nondisclosure agreements from our Office of General Counsel," Jackson said. "As well as waiving of liability in the event of unforeseen outcomes experienced during the procedure."

We all signed, while Holly cleared her throat.

"A condition for undergoing surgery is that my partner, Tyler, can film it for our own use," Holly said. I could see everyone looking at me, which was creepy with the ones wearing the gas masks, who gazed silently at me with those horrid, lifeless mask eyeholes like shark eyes.

"Provided the liability waivers are signed, we don't object to this, so long as all of you sign consent forms for this," Jackson said. "And use it for educational purposes only, versus promotional purposes, without directly tying the procedure to the University through identifying marks, logos, staff, facilities, or branding."

"Fine," Holly said. "Justin, get the consent forms from the trunk. We always have them handy."

Justin did as she directed him, and we filled them out, handing them to Jackson.

"Okay," Jackson said. "The University accepts no responsibility for any ill effects occurring from this procedure, including disfigurement, maiming, disability, or death incurred from the attempted removal of the infective agent."

Justin handed me his good camera, his prized possession, and muttered how I might work the thing. I let him talk a moment before cutting him off.

"I've got it, Justin," I said. "Don't worry about it."

Jackson looked around us, as morning ground on.

"Security, form a perimeter on these subjects," Jackson said. "Let's get inside without drawing any more attention to ourselves than necessary."

Drs. Lee and Sherman were walking with us, examining Holly and the others with penlights, taking notes on tablets, while we went inside.

Holly looked at me a moment before they were whisked away, reaching out and clasping my hand a moment. Her hand was cool to the touch, and held the keys to Ladygirl, which I pocketed the moment she handed them to me.

"If we don't make it, make sure our story gets out somehow, Ty," Holly said. "Thanks for being there for us. And for, you know, *not* shooting us."

"Sure," I said. And then they were gone. Once out of sight, Jackson took off her mask, looked me over a bit. She was a white woman with long, brutally blonde hair and cornflower blue eyes. She was about my height and wore a suggestion of a smirk more often than not as she talked to me.

"Were you part of what we saw on the news?" Jackson asked. "The incident in South Carolina?"

Not wanting to give away anything, I played dumb.

"Incident?" I asked, while she walked me through corridors toward the observation area for surgery, past unmarked doors that seemed clinical in comportment.

"Since you were traveling, maybe you missed it," Jackson said. "Some kind of mass shooting and arson event took place over there. A lot of people were killed."

"Wow," I said. "That sounds crazy. My friends and I are part of a show called *The Seen*. We do documentaries as part of an ongoing Internet series. We were looking into disappearances in South Carolina."

"Right," Jackson said. "How'd your friends get infected by this alleged parasite?"

"They got exposed," I said, feeling awkward, like Amelia Jackson could look right through me with those blue eyes of hers. The observation area was nice, and I could see them prepping the room for surgery, with people moving about intently, wearing scrubs, masks, and hairnets.

"How'd they get exposed? How'd you even know what had infected them?" Jackson asked as we took our seats overlooking the operating room. Everything smelled antiseptic, almost cloyingly astringent. "You have to admit, the cognitive leap to 'plant parasite' is steep, Mr. Finn. Is there a story you want to share with me? In confidence?"

Some part of me wondered how they'd managed to get a surgical team together so quickly. It was one of those tiny warning voices one sometimes got in one's head and so often failed to listen to.

She was pumping me for information, and I knew how crazy it sounded. Her tone was measured, even preternaturally calm, which was to put me at ease, but did the opposite; it put me on alert. I expected FBI or DHS agents to come bursting into the observation room, looking to take me down. Maybe CDC researchers, if any of them had been made aware. Atlanta wasn't that far away.

"And arriving here in that ill-omened Eldorado, too," Jackson said. "I had been here a couple of years before that whole thing blew through. It's the same car. That whole missing persons bit we had to endure. The media sure loves it when a white girl goes missing, doesn't it? If I never hear the name 'Ashley Talulah Graham' again, it'll be too soon. People disappear all the time. And yet here you and your friends come rolling on up in that same damned car."

I knew that had to look strange and did my best to represent Holly.

"Holly bought the car at a police auction," I said. "She got a little obsessed about the 'Ladygirl Five' as she called the people who disappeared."

"Oh, I know the story, Mr. Finn," Jackson said. "It's an urban legend by now. And yet, here you are. And right after something went down at that overgrown ghost town. The police are looking for you as a person of interest or a witness. You know I already told them you were coming."

"I didn't do anything," I said, feeling less convincing that I might otherwise be. "Why'd you do that?"

"I don't want us getting dragged into another media circus, Mr. Finn," Jackson said. "Drs. Lee and Sherman seem to think there's something to this that ties to their department indirectly, and the Administration is willing to humor them up to a point. However, Fawcett Biotech has been very generous with grant money. I don't want to jeopardize that relationship. If Drs. Roswell and Briarton are able to cure your friends, I'm okay with that. If Sherman and Lee can publish some papers about whatever-this-is and elevate our profile in academia, I'm okay with that, too. Everything else, *not* okay with it."

She maintained her cool composure, and I did my best to mirror it.

"The plant parasite works through its flowers," I said. "Some kind of anesthetic or narcotic pollen that incapacitates its victims. Then it implants seeds in its hosts."

"You *saw* that?" Jackson asked.

"They experienced it and told me," I said. "Ms. Jackson, the moment they do CT scans or whatever on their bodies, they're going to see the growths inside them."

Jackson's smooth face wrinkled in disgust.

"That's disgusting," she said.

"Just wait until they open up my friends," I replied, setting up Justin's camera on a tripod. Justin loved doing handheld, but that was his style, not mine. "You'll never eat a garden salad again."

Two surgeons appeared to be in the room, with another one looking on. Holly was the first one they rolled in, and I could see her glancing up at me, her eyes wide but bright, not with that doll-liked aspect I'd seen on some of the Flower Children. She looked calm, and I wondered how they managed to set up diagnostic imaging so quickly. I would have imagined that it would take days to get them on the table. It was almost as if they were ready for us.

Or possibly they had an on-call team ready for events like these. That possibility filled me with angst, because that made me think that despite the assurances of Dr. Lee, Fawcett Biotech must be involved.

I began filming, while Jackson watched me, seemed to anticipate my question.

"We're lucky you reached out to us before you arrived," Jackson said. "It helped us prepare for your arrival, to get the necessary experts lined up. They're going to use an endoscopic approach, which is minimally invasive. Given the relatively recent impregnation of the subjects, that should work best."

Glancing at Jackson, I could see her eyes were locked on me. It made me uneasy. Something wasn't right. I feigned disquiet about the camera, stopped filming.

"What's the matter, Mr. Finn?" Jackson asked.

"Something's off with the camera," I said. "I need to talk to Justin. He's our regular film guy."

"He's in surgical prep," Jackson said.

"Okay," I said. "Then I'll be right back."

Jackson watched me get up, looked concerned. I trotted up the steps to the exit, glancing back, seeing her on her phone.

Moving as quickly as I could while still appearing casual, I made my way through the corridors to exit the building and reach the parking lot. I could see that there were three Fawcett Biotech vans parked nearby, including some men near Ladygirl.

"Excuse me," I said to them. They wore blue suits with yellow neckties and wore Fawcett Biotech lozenge-shaped lapel pins. One of the men was a middle-aged Latino man with slicked-back dark brown hair, while the other was a younger Asian man with a black-haired brush cut. The Latino spoke up. Both of them smiled confidently at me.

"Is this your car?" he asked.

"Who wants to know?" I asked. The Latino man, who was tanned and tall, had a trim beard, held out a hand for me to shake.

"I'm Ernesto Salazar," the man said. I shook his hand. "This is my partner, Michael Chen. This car was spotted outside of our agricultural facility in South Carolina yesterday. You are?"

"Tyler Finn," I said. "Nobody trespassed onto your property."

Salazar smiled at me.

"We have it on good authority that some of your friends may have had an incident with one of our plant products," he said. "We're here to make sure there weren't any adverse reactions."

I resisted the urge to film these men right there and then, to put them on the spot, but didn't want to be overly provocative, which would only make me look bad.

"Adverse reactions?" I said. "Is that what you're calling them?"

"Calling what?" Chen asked. The two looked completely bewildered. It was the kind of rehearsed, practiced bewilderment that a couple of corporate shills had mastered early in their careers.

"My friends are undergoing surgery," I said.

"We know," Salazar said. "Fawcett's got some experts tending to your friends. They're lucky we got here. Honestly, we thought you'd film the procedures before you attempted to flee. For your little show."

"You're, what? Company cops?" I asked.

"Something like that," Chen said. "We'd like to offer you compensation for the footage you've so far acquired. Including what we suspect might be stolen property of Fawcett Biotech."

The drone camera footage.

"Like what?" I asked.

"Drone footage, as well as the drone camera," Salazar said. "With all that went down near Summerville, you can understand why we might want to better understand what happened. We lost two employees."

Tactically, I was hamstrung by these two. What might happen to me if I resisted? The three vans looked as threateningly innocuous as they could be.

Salazar pulled an envelope from his inside pocket. I could see the Fawcett logo on it.

"We're willing to put all of this behind us for a nondisclosure agreement from *The Seen* and a generous out-of-court settlement, Mr. Finn."

"Oh, we're already talking legal action?" I asked.

"Not yet," Salazar said. "But soon. Hear us out, first."

I took the envelope, which was thick, and I set down the camera to inspect it. It was an agreement that *The Seen* would refrain from revealing what we'd uncovered in the course of our efforts over the past few weeks, both leading up to and culminating in the events at Summerville and afterward. If we honored this agreement, Fawcett Biotech would pay us $2.5 million.

"Are you kidding me?" I asked.

Salazar shook his head, holding out a blue Fawcett pen.

"I assure you, we are *not* joking, Mr. Finn," Salazar said. "The work we're doing at Fawcett is very important to us, and we'd like to keep it as discreet as possible. Incidents like what happened to your friends get us off on the wrong foot as we're rolling out new product lines."

Salazar and Chen looked like they could just as easily pack me in Ladygirl's trunk as get me to sign another NDA.

"I can't sign something like this without Holly and the others signing, too," I said.

"Oh, they'll sign, once they're healed," Chen said.

The morning sun was up, and yet, despite the heat and humidity, I was the only one sweating. These two Fawcett men were as coolly collected as I'd seen anyone ever be.

"I should have a lawyer look at this document," I said.

"We have lawyers," Chen said. "Meaning Fawcett. They are very, very interested in what you *think* you saw. If they felt that your interests ran counter to Fawcett's, you could find yourself locked down in litigation for at least a decade, Mr. Finn. From what we discovered when investigating you, we don't think *The Seen* could afford this, especially looking at your more recent numbers. Just sign the NDA, give over the stolen property, your film and photography, and we'll all walk away from this better off than we are right now."

"Our physicians are treating your friends," Salazar said. "Think of that, too. They're saving your friends' lives. If we didn't think you were our friend, Mr. Finn, we'd not take those extraordinary steps on their behalf."

The heroic thing would have been to somehow take these two guys down, jump into Ladygirl and take off, exposing whatever the hell went on here for the world to see. Or was that the careless, reckless, foolish thing?

"Fine," I said, signing the NDA. Salazar and Chen never wavered in their benevolently threatening smiles.

"Fantastic," Salazar said, pulling a blue and yellow Fawcett envelope from his coat pocket. "Once we have the stolen property and the recordings, we'll be on our way and this'll be yours."

Chen whistled and one of the Fawcett vans rolled up, and some burly Fawcett Biotech employees came out. They were beefy men with glowering, no-nonsense visages. One of them scooped up Justin's camera from the ground, put that in the back of the van.

"How about you pop that trunk, Mr. Finn?" Salazar asked. I took the keys to Ladygirl and opened the trunk. "Hell of a nice car. They truly don't make them like this anymore."

"Ah, here it is," Chen said, holding up the camera we'd taken from Charlene. "Where's the SD card, Mr. Finn?"

I went to my backpack and resisted the urge to give him a blank one. That was the right move to make, because Chen checked.

"What's in that gym bag?" Salazar asked, pointing.

"Additional SD cards and lighting gear," I said.

"Yeah, take those, too," Salazar said.

The employees took them and threw them in the back of the van.

Chen looked at me closely, taking a leisurely breath.

"What about your tablet and laptop?" he asked.

"Fine," I said, turning it on and making a point to delete the photos I'd taken with the tablet, while Salazar and Chen looked on.

"We could just confiscate them, if that'd be easier for you," Chen said.

They were the most accommodating corporate thugs I'd ever encountered. They the only corporate thugs I'd ever encountered, for that matter. I finished deleting my photos and showed it to them. When they were thoroughly satisfied, I put it away.

"Why don't you just kill us and bury our bodies in a swamp somewhere?" I asked. "Make us disappear. Isn't that how that usually goes with this kind of thing?"

Salazar smiled and laughed.

"If we wanted you all to disappear, we'd not go to the trouble of removing the implanted seeds from your friends," he said. "You'd all disappear, one by one. That's how it 'usually goes' with these situations. Accidents happen, no matter the precautions a person might take to avoid them."

I really wanted to be recording this conversation, but the way they were monitoring me, there was no way I could do it without being noticed.

"Really?" I asked, keeping everything as conversational as I could.

"Yeah," Salazar said. "There's about a three-month gestational cycle from implantation to sprouting."

"Three months?" I replied. Chen looked at Salazar with a covert nervousness, making me think he worried that his peer was revealing too much.

"Some variability between subjects," Salazar said. "That's just the average, which is longer than earlier interactions. Seems like the organism has moderated its approach compared with years past."

Why was he even telling me this? Was he that confident that he saw no danger in it? Or perhaps since I'd signed the NDA that I had nullified myself as any sort of threat?

Chen walked to the van and came out with a Fawcett Biotech gym bag.

"We've got an *alternative* narrative for you, Mr. Finn," Chen said. "About the disappearances. Ever heard of the Black River Butcher?"

"Of course," I said.

"Perfect," Chen said. "That makes this easier. We've got a bunch of anecdotal evidence about the Black River Butcher. Take this and make your episode about it. Everything can be the same, except for the part that implicates Fawcett Biotech's products."

He held out the bag and they waited for me to take it. Not wanting to leave him holding the bag, I took it, opened it to see what was inside. There were videotapes, cassette tapes, digital cameras, paper files, and more. It was a trove of conspiratorial collateral.

"What is all of this?" I asked.

"Black River Butcher stuff," Chen said. "Grist for the rumor mill. People love serial killers, Mr. Finn. You know that. Killer plants? That's so much harder to swallow. But unsolved murders, cold cases, and disappearances? Squarely in people's conceptual wheelhouses. Better than killer plants from outer space, don't you think?"

Salazar put a hand on my shoulder and leaned in, his brown eyes earnest.

"It's a far easier story to sell," he said. "With your $2.5 million in your pockets, just think of how *The Seen* could get a higher profile from it. Maybe a comeback for your web series. Wouldn't that be something?"

"But it's bullshit," I said.

"Is it? There *was* a Black River Butcher," Salazar said. "The late Cooper DeVille. It ties it all up nicely. Cleanly. No loose ends."

I wished Holly was here, but she might have gotten us all killed with her mouth. Even now, I couldn't imagine how I'd explain it all to the rest of the team.

"You're asking us to tell a bogus story," I said.

"It's simply *another* story, Mr. Finn," Chen said. "Just as true, and far more believable."

I threw the Fawcett bag in the trunk and closed it with an authoritative clunk. Salazar and Chen just watched me. Overhead, white puffy clouds lazed across a beautiful blue sky, without

"I'm supposed to believe that you lot had this whole Black River Butcher material on-hand for this contingency?" I asked.

"Contingency planning is central to what we do at Fawcett, Mr. Finn," Salazar said. "Biotechnology is rife with contingency planning. If it's a balm to your indie journalistic ego, let's just say that nobody in traditional media got as enmeshed in the story as you four did. The Ladygirl Five was a curiosity that captured attention for a few news cycles, but nobody threw themselves into it quite like your little team did. Not that it matters. Nobody would believe it's even possible. You'd ruin your own reputations if you went public with a story like this. It would look stupid. Insane, even."

"Your signing the NDA showed that you're a sane and sensible man, Mr. Finn," Chen said. "Someone we can deal with. And who knows? If your Black River Butcher story does well, maybe Fawcett can hire your team to do some PR work for us down the road. Fawcett remembers friends and allies."

My friends were the ones being operated on, and I was the one who was feeling nauseous. I don't know what I expected, but it hadn't been this. Salazar handed the envelope to me. It was made of thicker stock, and I opened it, seeing the check for $2.5 million, made out to *The Seen*. I closed it and just held the thing daintily, like it was toxic.

"What is Fawcett actually up to with the summerviolets?" I asked.

"Quaint name for them," Chen said. "They're a supercrop, with a wide range of uses and industrial applications. Food. Textiles. Soap. Perfumes. Tea. Other beverages. Pharmacology. Medicine. And so on. Fawcett has invested a ton in it. It's not our fault that it's a dangerous plant to grow. Under careful, best horticultural practices, it can be safely grown and tended. And exclusively by Fawcett."

"How long has your company known about the Summerville..." I didn't know what to call it. Outgrowth? Strain? Subculture?

"Oh, we've known about it for a long time," Salazar said. "We kept our eye on it, studied its effects from a safe distance."

The epiphany hit me like a chill wind. The summerviolets had originated there. Fawcett had learned of it and patented it in the wake of the passing of the town and had allowed it to serve as a breeding or proving ground for it. It would have allowed them to engage in human experimentation without getting their hands dirty.

"When Ashley Graham drove to Duke with it, that was unanticipated, but we took appropriate countermeasures," Chen said. "These days, academia is always eager to have well-heeled benefactors. We worked with our academic partners hand in glove with that offshoot. Again, everybody wins."

"Except Ashley Graham," I said.

"People die every day, Mr. Finn," Salazar said. "Ms. Graham died for science."

My mind was spinning. Everybody knew about the banality of evil, I felt. But the blitheness of it? And my own complicity in their casually psychopathic business schemes?

"Mr. Fields and Mr. Wales had been tasked with exterminating the Summerville outgrowth," Chen said. "The Flower Children represented an outcropping that we hadn't factored in. When what you call 'summerviolets' began showing up at regional flower festivals, we sent agents to recover them and realized we needed to do something about those flower fanatics. While Fields and Wales didn't exactly carry out their mission by the book, the end result was acceptable. We've got employees on-site right now, working with local authorities to make sure nothing survived there. After all, we don't want the media reporting on some biological incident occurring in a small rural area. People panic so easily."

Salazar glanced at his watch.

"If you run into anything else that is pursuant to our work, please don't hesitate to call us any time, 24/7," he said. He and Chen handed me their business cards, crisp and bone-white:

> Ernesto Salazar, Property Protection Services
>
> Michael Chen, Property Protection Services

"What if I went public with this anyway?" I asked. Salazar and Chen chuckled, exchanging glances.

"Just another crank," Salazar said. "Our lawyers would have a defamation field day with you, Mr. Finn. You couldn't afford to fight us. Do yourself a favor and run your Black River Butcher story. It'll be worth your time and money."

"A great return on your investment," Chen said.

The workers went back into their vans, while Salazar and Chen walked to a blue and yellow Fawcett Biotech company car, all smiles as they waved to me, driving off.

I pocketed the check and drove off as well, heading quickly in the opposite direction.

BLOG ENTRY 27
(Holly Rivers)

Seeding Doubt

I awoke in a recovery room, tended to by Fawcett Biotech personnel who wore royal blue scrubs and yellow masks. The entire thing had felt like a dream, but when I awoke, I didn't feel Madame Summerville inside me anymore. Gone were the pushes in my psyche, the compulsions and errant thoughts and alien feelings.

Sharon and Justin were in beds nearby, and the three of us were in good post-operative spirits. The attending physicians—Drs. Roswell and Briarton—were upbeat and agreeable. Both of them looked like the models of stereotypical surgical excellence that they were: middle-aged men, tanned and in their prime, with admirable bedside manners for surgeons.

"You three are lucky you got to us when you did," Roswell said. "The seedlings had implanted in your tissues but had only just begun sending out tendrils. Another week or two and they'd have been inextricably intertwined with your organ systems. Removal would have been life-threatening. As it stands, you three should enjoy a complete recovery."

I was relieved by this, and the only thing that intruded on this feeling of relief was Tyler's absence. When I asked Roswell and Briarton as well as the nurses about it, nobody knew where Tyler had gone.

"For now, just rest and recover," Briarton said. "We tried to be as minimally invasive as possible, but all surgery is bodily trauma, and you three need to rest to get better."

My mind was focused on whether Ty had gotten the footage, and I'd been disappointed to find that our cell-phones had been accidentally wiped in storage, where they'd been placed too close to some diagnostic imaging equipment, and I didn't actually remember Ty's phone number. We'd always just pinged each other; there hadn't been a need for knowing each other's numbers.

"Sharon, do you remember Ty's phone number? Justin?" I asked.

"No," Sharon said. "Why?"

"I want to touch base with him," I said. They knew I'd wanted to have him film the procedure, and I worried that maybe somebody had gotten to him. The recovery room we were in was a double, which could have housed four people, so Sharon, Justin, and I had plenty of room. The walls were antiseptic white with blue and yellow stripes on them in dynamic forms that instilled a sense of corporate confidence.

"About the, you know, thing?" Sharon asked. I nodded. The three of us looked pretty good, all things considered. We were in hospital gowns and in our respective beds. Both Sharon and Justin had bandages around their necks, where their wounds had been carefully treated.

"Do you remember what happened?" I asked.

Sharon met my question with a prolonged eyeroll. "Of course I do."

"We should have Ty film our reactions to it," I said. "Before and after. Our recollections and reflections."

Justin scoffed at the idea.

"Nobody will believe us," he said. "They'll think we're insane. Or frauds."

That was a risk, naturally. Any kind of subject matter that strayed from the well-worn path of acceptably strange was likely to be treated that way. However, we'd uncovered something very bizarre and people needed to know. Our audience would trust us. They would take that journey with us.

However, I needed to talk to Ty, so we could strategize. We'd uploaded the material to our servers. That was critical.

"Who's paying for our hospital stay? For our surgery?" Sharon asked. Then Amelia Jackson came in, smiled at us in turn.

"Fawcett Biotech is paying your medical bills," Jackson said. "You three are very, very lucky."

Her smile had a lot of wattage, but it didn't reach her blue eyes.

"I'm assuming Fawcett hasn't done this before?" I asked.

"Not during Phase I or Phase II, no," Jackson said. "But we're in Phase III, now."

I was making mental notes, wishing to hell I had a voice recorder with me to capture this. Frankly, I wondered why Jackson was being so open about it, but then again, maybe our NDAs emboldened her.

"Phase testing?" Sharon asked. "Are you kidding me? Is this a clinical trial?"

Jackson patiently half-smiled, taking our bothersome inquiries in stride.

"Fawcett has been exploring the wide-ranging effects of the Summerville strain," Jackson said. "What you call 'summerviolets'—an adorable name, by the way."

I was trying to imagine what Phases I and II were, let alone Phase III. Were they covertly doing human testing? Was that what this was? Why had they even left us alive? Or was this still part of the test? Seeing how people might recover from exposure to Madame Summerville?

"What's it *really* called?" Sharon asked.

"That's a company secret, I'm afraid," Jackson said. "The three of you will need to rest and recover for the next seventy-two hours, as we keep you under observation."

"To see if you got all of it?" I asked.

"Yes," Jackson said. "If any of you feel odd or unusual, please contact a nurse. There are call buttons on your beds. If you feel anything like what you felt when you were infected, that's what we're talking about, here."

"And after seventy-two hours?" I asked.

"You'll be cleared to leave," Jackson said. "You've already filled out the required paperwork, and there won't be anything else to do on your end except leave with our blessing. We'll have meals brought to you at appropriate intervals. You're just encouraged to rest and recover."

Everyone here had been so accommodating and even pleasant, it was setting my teeth on edge. Maybe it was my years in DC, but this wasn't how I had been expecting it to go.

"Where's Tyler?" I asked.

"Haven't seen him since he fled the operating room amphitheater," Jackson said.

"Fled?" I asked, glancing at Sharon and Justin, who looked as displeased as I was. Had they done something to Ty?

"Was somebody chasing him?" I asked.

"No," Jackson said, laughing softly to herself. "Nothing like that. We were preparing to observe your procedure, Ms. Rivers, and I think Mr. Finn got squeamish and left in a hurry. I hadn't thought anything of it—people often get that way when observing surgical procedures. It's quite common. And then I got engrossed in your procedure. By the time I learned Mr. Finn had been gone, it was at least an hour later."

They got to Ty somehow, I thought. Or they did something to him.

"I need a phone to try to find him," I said.

Jackson feigned some concern and confusion.

"I believe some Fawcett representatives had met with him," Jackson said. "Offered a large sum of money to gain access to all of the footage you'd shot, on condition of a nondisclosure agreement where your film company would not broadcast *anything* tied to Summerville."

Sharon and Justin both exclaimed in frustration and outrage, while I was trying to decipher what had happened.

"Ty's not authorized to sign on behalf of the rest of us," I said. "We're partners. We're a collective."

Jackson simply shrugged. "The Fawcett representatives were satisfied with his cooperation, and they now have possession of all of the footage, as well as the Fawcett property your team had allegedly stolen from one of the company's trucks. It's all very above board."

I moved to get out of bed, but my body was worn out, and wasn't pleased with that decision, letting me know that I should just wait. The implicit legal threat about the stolen equipment was left dangling out there. I didn't take the bait.

"Fawcett paid Ty off and he let them take our footage," I said. Something was hinky about it; Ty wouldn't have done that without good reason. They'd forced his hand somehow. Or he'd pretended to play along, knowing we'd backed up our stuff on our servers. That's what had happened. I trusted Ty. In fact, the way Ms. Jackson was putting it, it was willfully done in a manner to make us think badly of Ty.

"How much money did they give Tyler?" Sharon asked.

"I'm not privy to the amount," Jackson said. "Only that it was a large sum. The intention was for it to be split four ways. That was my understanding."

I went into my head a bit and tried to process this information. Ty had reached out to the plant experts, some of whom clearly had ties to Fawcett. Fawcett had learned about it, likely because one of the people Ty had contacted alerted them. They'd set up some surgical triage—or, perhaps more likely (thinking of Phase I and II, whatever those were)—they had them on-site and ready for this scenario.

While Sharon, Justin, and I were being operated on, the Fawcett people leaned on Ty and got him to sign an agreement of some sort. They had also confiscated our phones, so there'd be no way for us to talk to Ty. And no way for him to talk to us. As the three of us were recovering, Ty seemed to have vanished.

"Are we prisoners here?" I asked.

"You're our special guests," Jackson said.

"We're going to sue you," I said. "You can't do this to us."

Jackson shook her head, the smile never fading.

"You already waived your right to legal redress," Jackson said. "That's not an avenue open to you. You'd illegally acquired access to proprietary crops belonging to Fawcett Biotech as well as some of our equipment. Fawcett is the injured party, here."

"We were infected," Sharon said. "Impregnated. Whatever you call it."

"Exposed," Jackson said. "And Drs. Roswell and Briarton saved your lives. That has to count for something. You have your lives to live. Would you have rather died out in a field, splitting apart like Lia Larkin?"

The mention of Lia quieted all three of us. The memories of it were just too fresh—all the blood on the flowers and leaves. The way the bloodied vines thrashed to find purchase as her broken body fell away. I didn't even think to ask her how she could possibly have known about that. Had they been monitoring the Temple even then?

"I didn't think so," Jackson said, her smile moving from something faux-benevolent to something far more forced and masklike. "We expect a full recovery from the three of you, and never anticipate our paths to cross again."

The sense of violation I was feeling was profound and as all-consuming as the seedlings of Madame Summerville had been.

"We need to find Ty," Sharon said. "He has to answer some questions. How long have we been here?"

"It's been two days since your procedures," Jackson said. "Your bodies underwent quite a shock, and even being young as you are, there was some system stress."

I refused to believe that a minimally invasive endoscopic procedure would have laid us out for a couple of days. Ms. Jackson (and Fawcett) was jerking us around. My mind worked. Whatever had taken place between Ty and Fawcett, it had left Ty shaken enough that he'd split. And he may have attempted to contact us. I believe he would, just as he wouldn't have risked coming back here.

"Now, if you'll excuse me, I have other matters to attend to," Jackson said. "If you need anything, your nurses are just a call button away, as I'd said earlier. And I think Drs. Sherman and Lee are likely to visit you in a day or two."

The plant biologists. I imagined there was some kind of surveillance in this room. The whole thing was another setup. We needed a phone we could trust. I had to find one and talk to Ty, assuming I could even find his phone number. If I even had Internet access, I might be able to contact Ty from *The Seen* website.

Jackson produced a trio of nice, silvery tablets and handed them to each of us.

"Obviously, we don't want you to die of boredom in here," Jackson said. "We have great WiFi in this suite. We just want you to relax as much as you can. We know you've all been through a lot."

I was confident that the complementary tablets were packed with malware that would indicate anything we said to whoever was watching. I mimed "no" to Sharon and Justin, trying to be as discreet as possible.

Amelia Jackson turned on her sensible heel and went to the door to the recovery room, rapping it with a knuckle. The door buzzed open, and out she went, before it locked.

"Locked," I said, glancing at Sharon, who was all frowns. For once, I was right there with her, in emotional lockstep.

Locked & Loaded

The drive back to Charleston had me thinking the entire way. What was I going to do? I didn't want to check back in on Holly and the others, who may have already been in the clutches of Fawcett. And speaking of being in Fawcett's clutches, there I was with a check and a bunch of their bogus (?) Black River Butcher B-roll in a bag.

I'd put the top up on Ladygirl, wanted to keep as low a profile as I could. The local news was still touching on the Summerville Slaughter, with authorities opining about leads in the case and how they were leaving nothing behind.

The responsible citizen part of me (did that count as a conscience?) thought I should go talk to Sheriff Johnson and unload what I may have known about the slaughter, but as a black man driving by himself in the Carolinas in a car he didn't own, I wasn't eager to talk with the police about the matter.

This'll sound weird, but I didn't put it past Fawcett to have planted that Butcher material on me in hopes that I might do just that. Then again, there was the matter of the check, and what Fawcett might have been up to with that.

Whatever was going on at their facility, they didn't want it getting out badly enough that they tried to pay us (me) off. Or else they were framing me. There was always that, too. That was the problem—I could see all sorts of angles, none of them clear…

Avenue A: Was I to believe that they just happened to have this Butcher-related footage waiting for someone to come along and use it?

Avenue B: Why would they pay us off when they could simply kill and disappear us?

Avenue C: Why did they offer to cure my friends? Did they even do it?

Avenue D: Were they *really* expecting us to make a Butcher-related episode instead of what we'd sought out to film in the first place?

Avenue E: Were they still watching us? Tailing me? Maybe they held off from killing us because they suspected we may have had copies of our footage, and they were waiting to see what we did with it.

I tried calling Holly and the others, and it just went to voicemail for each of them. I asked them to call me back, but nobody did. I glanced now and then through the rearview mirror but couldn't spot any tails. Then again, I wasn't a cop; would I even recognize a tail if I saw one?

Could they be waiting for me to deposit the check to somehow entrap me in a scheme of their own? But Salazar and Chen could have packed me in one of their vans without difficulty.

I needed to clear my head, so I went to a Waffle House along the way—the same one Sharon and Justin had been to on our drive to Duke. Then I went about completing the blog entries I had made, bringing things up to speed. I uploaded this to our *The Seen* server, and maybe if/when Holly and the others reappeared, they'd find all of this. While wolfing down some breakfast, I jotted down a note to Holly, which I'd include with the check:

HOLLY—

I HOPE YOU AND THE OTHERS ARE OKAY. ENCLOSED IS THE CHECK THE FAWCETT BIO-TECH PEOPLE (ERNESTO SALAZAR AND MI-CHAEL CHEN WERE THEIR NAMES) OFFERED WHEN THEY CONFISCATED ALL OF OUR SUMMERVILLE FOOTAGE.

SINCE YOU WERE ALL IN SURGERY, I WASN'T SURE WHAT TO DO. MY SENSE WAS THAT THESE GUYS WEREN'T GOING TO TAKE "NO" FOR AN ANSWER, SO I ROLLED WITH IT. IT'S A LOT OF MONEY. THEY GAVE ME A BUNCH OF COLLATERAL TIED TO THE BLACK RIVER BUTCHER STORY, SEEMED TO WANT US TO RUN WITH THAT INSTEAD OF OUR SUMMERVILLE STORY. I DON'T KNOW WHAT TO TELL YOU. I DON'T EVEN KNOW IF YOU'LL GET THIS. I DON'T KNOW WHO TO TRUST. LOOK FOR ALL OF THE FILES ON OUR SERVER.

THEY MADE ME SIGN AN NDA UNDER DURESS. I THINK WE'RE ALL HOGTIED LEGALLY BY THEIR VARIOUS NDAS. HOWEVER, IT'S POSSIBLE SOMETHING COULD BE SALVAGED. I REALLY WANTED TO CASH THAT CHECK AND HEAD FOR THE HILLS, BUT I HELD BACK BECAUSE I FEEL LIKE MAYBE THAT'S WHAT THEY WANT ME TO DO.

I'M LEAVING THE CHECK WITH YOU SO YOU'LL KNOW THAT I'M NOT LEAVING YOU HANGING. I'M ALSO GOING TO SEND YOU THE STUFF THAT THOSE FAWCETT GUYS GAVE ME. WHETH-ER OR NOT YOU TURN IT INTO SOME KIND OF EPISODE IS ON YOU AND THE OTHERS. I'M KEEPING LADYGIRL FOR NOW; HOPE YOU DON'T MIND, BUT SHE AND I HAVE SOME BUSINESS TO ATTEND TO.

I'M NOT GOING TO TELL YOU WHERE I'M GOING, BUT YOU'LL KNOW IT WHEN YOU SEE IT. LET'S JUST SAY THAT I'M GOING TO BE OUT IN THE WEEDS FOR A SPELL.

EVANESCENTLY YOURS,
TY

I may end up kicking myself for what I'm setting out to do, and I'm sure as hell not going to incriminate myself by documenting it here. All the loose ends I could tie up are tied up. Assuming Holly and the others haven't been disappeared (or worse), they should be able to make sense of it.

The thing is, when you're face-to-face with evil—not rhetorical evil, but the real stuff, you can't just look the other way and still be a good person. Those Fawcett fellas made their play, and maybe it'll prevent us from running our episode the way we wanted. But Holly's smart. She'll come up with something—nobody squares a circle with a steadier hand than Holly Rivers.

Me, I've got other things in mind. Best wrap this up. My To Do List is packed full. Just know that I'm setting off with no regrets and hope anybody reading this gets why I did this.

> [This is Tyler's last known *Seen* blog entry. If there are others, Seensters, let me know, because I haven't seen them. —Ed.]

BLOG ENTRY 29
(Holly Rivers)

Endgamesmanship

Okay, so what the hell am I to do with all of this? I'll backpedal so you'll not get as disoriented as we were and will try to not get mired in the details. Drs. Sherman and Lee looked us over. They seemed satisfied that we weren't still infected. Amelia Jackson was there as well, monitoring everything everybody said.

None of us used those tablets to do or say anything incriminating, which was part of our agreed-upon approach while we were under the care of the medical personnel. With our clean bills of health, Sharon, Justin, and I gathered up what belongings we had (not much—more on that later) and we worked out how to get back to Charleston.

We got some burner phones and after putting our heads together, we were able to remember Ty's phone number. We called him, but he wouldn't pick up. If I know Ty, it's because he didn't know the numbers and wouldn't answer. I left him messages:

> "Ty, it's Holly. Where the hell are you? We're okay. Weirded out, but okay. Call me back."

I tried sending text messages, but he blocked our numbers. We all tried, and he blocked us all. Sharon was peevish, Justin was annoyed, and I was concerned.

When we eventually reached our rental in Charleston and I saw the package waiting for us, everything changed. We were floored by the check Fawcett had cut for us. Hush money, yes. But holy hell, what a sum! The

Black River Butcher Bag™ as we called it was a bountiful pile of Butcher-related content.

It was a circumstantial breadcrumb trail that led to the late Cooper DeVille's doorstep at the Circle K. With him dead and no close or distant relatives to take offense at the character assassination rooted in the Fawcett Files, he was perfectly positioned to be a patsy.

And here's the thing: DeVille *was* up to something. His proximity to Madame Summerville could not be ignored. We'd still have to do the vetting, but it was a host of victims they were trying to pin on DeVille.

Having danced with Madame Summerville, I felt unencumbered and clear-headed while reviewing the material. I also read through Ty's blog entries, and seeing his headspace laid bare like that, I felt for him.

Ty was going through some stuff. If the authorities learned that he'd been at the Summerville Slaughter, he might even end up in jail. Is it murder if you kill a pod person? How is that adjudicated? Or did people even care?

We had a meeting, the three of us, happy to be alive, sitting on the side porch, feeling a sea-scented breeze blowing through from some unseen path to the ocean. I'd brewed some sweet tea and we drank it in relative silence until Sharon spoke up:

"What are we gonna do, Holly?" Sharon asked. Justin was quick to chime in, affecting a chill vibe that I was confident he didn't feel.

"It's a lot of money," Justin said. Sharon didn't seem convinced.

"It's not that much money," she said. Justin was visibly annoyed, which was measured in the furrowing of his fuckboy brows.

"For *us,* it's a lot," he said. "They could have simply killed us."

That part definitely stuck in my craw. What kind of world were we in where we simply expected a rogue corporation to off us instead of dealing fairly with us? Maybe they *weren't* dealing fairly with us; perhaps it was just another form of screwing with us.

Fawcett Biotech was doing bad stuff at their research facility. The payoff (being honest here) was just the minimum they had decided they could get away with to neutralize us. Then again, maybe we were overestimating our influence in all of this. Maybe that sum was all they thought we were worth.

Ty understood the implied menace in it, which was why he just disappeared without cashing the check, and why he kept quiet where we were concerned.

Me, I was trying to think through it all. When Amelia Jackson let slip about Phases I–III, I doubted that was some casual error on her part. What did those things mean? Did she say them *knowing* I'd be curious what they meant? Was it bait for another trap? And since we'd been in their clutches, why even bother to entrap us afterward? Paranoia was a mirror maze, and Fawcett was the Minotaur. Or maybe Madame Summerville secretly was.

"Legally, we're screwed," I said. "Fawcett will go after us if we broadcast anything we filmed."

Sharon's eyes flicked my way, one of those hard glances that were hers to give.

"What do we do, then? Run a bullshit Black River Butcher story?" Sharon asked. "Pocket the payoff?"

"It's not complete bullshit," I said. "DeVille was clearly up to bad things at that Circle K. I imagine the VINs on those vehicles there gel with some of the disappeared at the very least."

"Which would mean that the local police are maybe in on it," Sharon said. "Or else are really lazy and/or careless."

I was feeling what Ty had been feeling. That the Butcher story might have been a setup of another sort, a way of getting us caught up in some local law enforcement scandal that might eat up attention and divert it from the reality of Madame Summerville.

Had *we* become the patsies?

Another thing was nagging at me, based on what Drs. Sherman and Lee had said when looking us over. It had been Dr. Lee who'd said it, almost casually. In the moment, I hadn't fully understood it, but now, sipping sweet tea, it came together for me.

"In many ways, what you call the summerviolet behaves unusually for a purported plant exospecies," Lee said. "It *looks* and maybe acts like a plant, but it's a ruse, a grotesque parody of a plant. It doesn't depend on pollinators yet throws off prodigious amounts of fragrant, psychoactive pollen. The flowers are a means of infecting hosts, not attracting pollinators. Its vines can be smooth or thorny, depending on its situation. It manages to be active in its own defense but is not ambulatory. Dr. Sherman and I have our theories about it. There is a sentience to it. It is dependent on others to help itself spread, and so it has adapted itself to ensnare hosts."

"You're all in bed with it," Sharon said. "You and Fawcett."

Lee looked chagrined, but Dr. Sherman spoke up.

"We're studying it," Sherman said. "Our research has helped Fawcett mitigate the more dangerous aspects of the organism."

"Right," Sharon said. Both biologists looked at us with a degree of patient irritation.

"When the organism originally appeared, hosts were fatally compromised by it—infection was a rapid death sentence," Sherman said. "We wouldn't have been able to save your lives if not for our research. The people at Fawcett are domesticating it. We're evolving it. Or it's evolving with us, becoming acclimated to this environment."

"Making a profit from it," I said.

"It's still a process of domestication," Sherman said. "What you three experienced in Summerville was an unfortunate side effect of the processes of the organism. It's no different than being stung by a jellyfish on the beach. You got in the way, and the nature of the thing took over—it has a drive to reproduce itself in what it considers a hostile and alien biome."

It was one of those ridiculous, rationalized statements only someone who was fully compromised would even make. The plant parasite was an invasive species from gods knew where.

"What happened to the seedlings the surgeons removed from us?" I asked.

"We split them with the Fawcett people, as per our arrangement," Lee said. "You had twelve seedlings inside you from your exposure. These came from the mother organism, so they are particularly valuable, given that it's been destroyed at the site."

The thought of "our" seedlings growing in some lab here and at Fawcett offended me. That those things had been living inside us was grotesque. While I was relieved to have them removed, I would never emotionally or psychologically recover from the infestation. Trauma was trauma, even if the organism hijacked our bodies and minds to make us feel fine at the time.

I wanted to talk to Ty about it, just to better understand what he'd experienced. Instead, I'd see news stories about some unknown party—an arsonist—burning fields in the area. Fawcett vigorously spoke out against this individual, indicating that they were clearly mentally unbalanced. Fires were being set all over the region, and authorities were unable to pinpoint the perpetrator. Nobody needed to persuade me that this was Tyler. I *knew* it was him.

Further, someone had accessed our blog entries and selectively posted them on our *Seen* substack. The Seensters had been eating that up and discussing among themselves about what was *really* going on out there. The postings were carefully redacted—names were changed or eliminated, but details were there, nonetheless.

We decided we'd play ball with Fawcett and cobble together the Black River Butcher story. The check was ours and I'd deposited it, vowing to keep a quarter of it for Ty, should he ever show up again.

The Seen Episode 38: "Butcher's Bill" went out a few months after our misadventure in South Carolina, to fervid appreciation by our audience, although it was overshadowed by the rumors swirling around the blog posts and how Tyler was missing. The Seensters sensed that we were holding back, and we caught a lot of flak for that, having to account for his absence. More than a few Seensters inquired about the Ladygirl Five, wondered why we'd dropped that story.

At the height of the flurry around all of this, a fire broke out in our brick-and-mortar facilities in DC, which led to the destruction of our server. This occurred at the same time there had been a denial-of-service attack on our computer systems. This led to the annihilation of the files and footage we'd accumulated on our trip. The authorities weren't able to figure out who did it, and we went through a lot of hoops and hurdles trying to account for perpetrators. Some of the investigators even asked us if maybe Tyler had done it. I disabused them of this notion as much as I was able, even if I couldn't rule it out entirely. Once somebody went off the grid, anything was possible.

Sharon and Justin parted ways with me after that, deciding they'd rather take their share of the Fawcett money and get on with their lives, while I took to doing paranormal podcasts as a way of ensuring that some sliver of *The Seen* might remain. Rumors among Seensters flew about how I'd somehow driven everyone off, and how I was secretly working with Fawcett Biotech to undermine my own team's efforts to get to the truth. That rumor was particularly wounding for me, as I'd given years of my life to *The Seen,* trying to make it succeed. For those who knew me, the idea that I'd sacrifice all of that for Fawcett was offensive.

A group (?) calling itself "The Weedkillers" released unofficial and unredacted transcripts of *The Seen's* "Lost Episode" that revealed everything we'd discovered, which fed right into the conspiracy theory-focus of some of the subsets of Seensters, who'd argued with others about the veracity of the Lost Episode. The Seenster factions were broken down into those who believed what we had uncovered (54%) and those who thought it was a self-serving hoax (46%).

I don't know why Ty hasn't contacted me since everything had happened. It breaks my heart, and I hope to run into him someday. I have to know what's going on. With him, with us, with everything.

[This is Holly's last *Seen* blog entry. Not because she died; rather, because she has tried to move on with what's left of her life. —Ed.]

PART III:

DOWNSTREAM

BLOG ENTRY 1
(Lyle Hawthorne)

Easter Eggs & End Credits

> [This might seem presumptuous to further include myself in this story beyond my editorial commentary, but I have a few things to add that I feel like should be included in this documentation of what happened in that ghost town in South Carolina. I'm just going to put down what I know and leave it to you to decide what exactly happened. —Ed.]

You're caught up on everything that went on over the past year. I drove to Facility Number Seven, filmed it myself. The Fawcett Biotech facility looks like a cluster of discs arranged atop one another, with a circular tower in the center. Around it grows the meticulously tended vineyards where the summerviolets grow.

The impression of the place is that it looks like an alien outpost. Especially from a distance. The unique nature of the crop that they're growing, and the waves of golden pollen that blow across the sky around it, looks, well, otherworldly. That's the only fair way to put it.

Since my book, *The Unseen: The Lost Episode,* came out, Seensters have badgered me with questions about the Summerville Incident whenever I show up at Seenstercons. I've seen the "Where's Ty?" buttons and pins relating to it, tee shirts, chapbooks, maps, eyewitness accounts, and more. Fawcett Biotech has been as close-mouthed as ever about it.

The official story as told by Amelia Jackson, who is now the Media Relations Director at Fawcett, is that the entire story was cooked up by some eco-extremists out to tar the reputation of a leading biotechnology company. The standard tagline is: "At Fawcett Biotech, We Do It for YOU. Our superfoods and all-natural crops are produced with consumer wellness in mind."

Neither Sharon nor Justin (now married) will speak of it. They're living in a spacious home on acreage somewhere near Asbury Park. They categorically refuse to talk about anything Summerville-related, no matter how many times I tried to get them to discuss it.

Holly Rivers has continued her podcast work and has shown up at Seenstercons to do Q&A sessions about what happened. She is always careful to caveat her answers in a manner that doesn't specifically impugn Fawcett Biotech. I've been to some of those panels and I swear I could see some Fawcett people in their royal blue suits and yellow neckties standing in the back. Strange men, big men, wearing aviator sunglasses. Always watching.

I know she sees them, because I saw them. Holly just entertains questions about alien invaders and past episodes of *The Seen,* and the inevitable inquiries about either the Lost Episode or whether new episodes are coming. When questions about Tyler Finn come up, she's painfully gracious:

"We all want Tyler back," Holly said. "Me, most of all. Tyler, if you're out there, please talk to me."

Holly's always ready with a Sharpie to agreeably autograph *Seen*-related merch from that niche crowd of avid Seensters, and her podcast keeps going, always in the shadow of her work on *The Seen.*

She knows me. I'd like to think we're friends after a fashion. At the very least, she knows I'm an ally. We never talk, because I think she's afraid to. I think she's never not aware of how far down the dragon's gullet she'd traveled before coming back up. There's survivor's guilt, and, I think, less reflected upon—survivor's relief.

I'm afraid to add this here, just because I don't know who might be reading it, but Tyler Finn reached out to me. We knew each other because people in paranormal indie media always seem to know one another. I guess I could call it an occupational hazard.

He'd showed up at my place in Pittsburgh in the form of a sealed letter slid under the door with a message:

> Blue Stew's: Tonight. 6:00 p.m. —TF

Blue Stew's is a nice-n-noisy bar on the South Side of Pittsburgh, the kind of place where you can just unwind without feeling like you're on display, and where you can manage a bit of privacy, despite the locals pounding brews and patty melts with gusto. The brassy bar had big mirrors and a great big Thirst banner over it proclaiming that The Thirst is First! Thirsty, the lightning bolt-shaped mascot gave me a winking thumb's up, flanked by blue and orange cans of Thirst. The Fawcett lozenge is at the bottom right corner of it, as it's one of their flagship products.

I went there as nondescriptly as I could, getting there about fifteen minutes early, but Tyler was already there. He saw me, waved me over. I sat across from him, looked him up and down.

Tyler wore his *Seen* ballcap and a black windbreaker and jeans. He looked skinny. His eyes were wide behind his glasses. Our waiter, Jonah, took our orders without incident (Ty ordered a chicken-fried steak sandwich with an Iron City Light beer; I opted for smothered meatloaf and mashed potatoes and a Diet Coke).

"Wasn't sure you'd come," he said.

"You know I would," I replied. Tyler managed a smile that looked like it took some effort. I don't know if you've ever seen anyone who's haunted, but that's how Ty looked. He looked haunted.

"Saw your book," Tyler said. "Nicely done."

"Thanks," I said. I never know how to react when people compliment my work. Gratitude is all I can muster, which tangles up my tongue. Tyler slid an envelope to me across the table. "What's this?"

"All the unredacted data we have on what happened," Tyler said. "I think maybe they're keeping an eye out for me, but someone like you, maybe you can do something with it and they won't go after you the same way. Or maybe they will."

As a veteran Seenster, having access to this kind of scuttlebutt was golden. I was immensely flattered he'd even considered me.

"This is everything we uncovered," Tyler said, clamming up when Jonah brought our beverages. He waited until Jonah left before continuing. "Somebody fried our server and our workplace, but not before I'd gotten the files downloaded. I think they were waiting to see if anything could leak out before they took action."

"Holly really misses you," I said. "We all do."

"No way am I resurfacing," Tyler said. "Not with the stuff I've seen. And I'm not expecting you to do anything; I just wanted the information getting out there somehow. You do anything with it and you'll become as much of a target as the rest of us."

I didn't want to point out to Tyler that the others were all still alive and well. However, they also hadn't done more than tiptoe around the summerviolets. Tyler studied me with his war-weary eyes, and I really wanted to know what he'd been up to all of these months.

"You've been setting those fires, haven't you?" I asked. Tyler smiled at me without humor.

"Wherever I can, I burn out summerviolet patches," Tyler said. "I haven't yet figured out how to deal with the Fawcett plots. They're too big and well-protected. That's why I'm hoping getting some of this information out might help."

"You really should talk to Holly," I said. For sure, a reunion of Holly and Tyler would be epic Seenster fare.

"I'd love to, but they're watching her," Tyler said. "I watch them watching her, and they are constantly out there, tracking her."

Our food came, and we ate, while we saw some locals downing cans and bottles of Thirst, in festive orange and blue. They were doing shots of it and cheering uproariously, their eyes hard, their smiles tight.

"You know, Fawcett makes Thirst," Tyler said.

"For real?" I asked, although I already knew, as you know. Playing dumb often got people talking more than they otherwise would. He nodded.

"She gave them berries, and they brew it from them," Tyler said.

"Alien invader energy drink?" I asked. Tyler nodded again, while we saw the locals drinking it down and celebrating.

"She's always so accommodating," Tyler said. "We are being invaded, Lyle. Whether people understand this or not, it's happening. Do what you can with those files, if you feel up to it."

He fished something else from his jacket, and I wasn't sure what it could be, until he slid a set of car keys to me, as well as a business card.

"Ladygirl's keys," Tyler said. "Give those to Holly for me, would you? She's parked in a garage around here, the one marked on the card. It's paid up for the following month. Just get her the car. She'll know it was really me you talked to when you give her those keys."

"Yeah, okay," I said. My mind was awash with what was happening. I wanted to ask Tyler what he'd been doing after Summerville. I needed to know. But I also doubted that he'd tell me. He was willing to confide up to a point, but everything else would only get me or anybody else in trouble. "What are you going to do?"

Tyler looked at me with a beleaguered expression. "I'm going to stop Madame Summerville, naturally. She's got Fawcett in her pocket, but I'm not letting that hold me back."

His tired eyes went to the bar again, where the locals were gayly quaffing Thirst from shot glasses, cheering each other on mindlessly:

"Thirst! Thirst! Thirst! Thirst!"

"Don't drink that crap," Tyler said. "Not a drop."

He was so dead-serious, I held back from flippantly commenting that it was just an energy drink, and that I couldn't imagine a beverage having either portentous or apocalyptic consequences.

"Got it," I said.

"This is only the beginning," Tyler said. "Fight the good fight, Lyle. However you go about it. Just do *something*."

He set a twenty and a ten on the table and slipped out of there before I could stammer out a reply. Not wanting to make a scene, I watched him go, elbowing past the Thirst drinkers, who cavorted to pumping music like drunken dervishes, celebrating a holiday not remotely of their own invention.

THE
END

APPENDIX

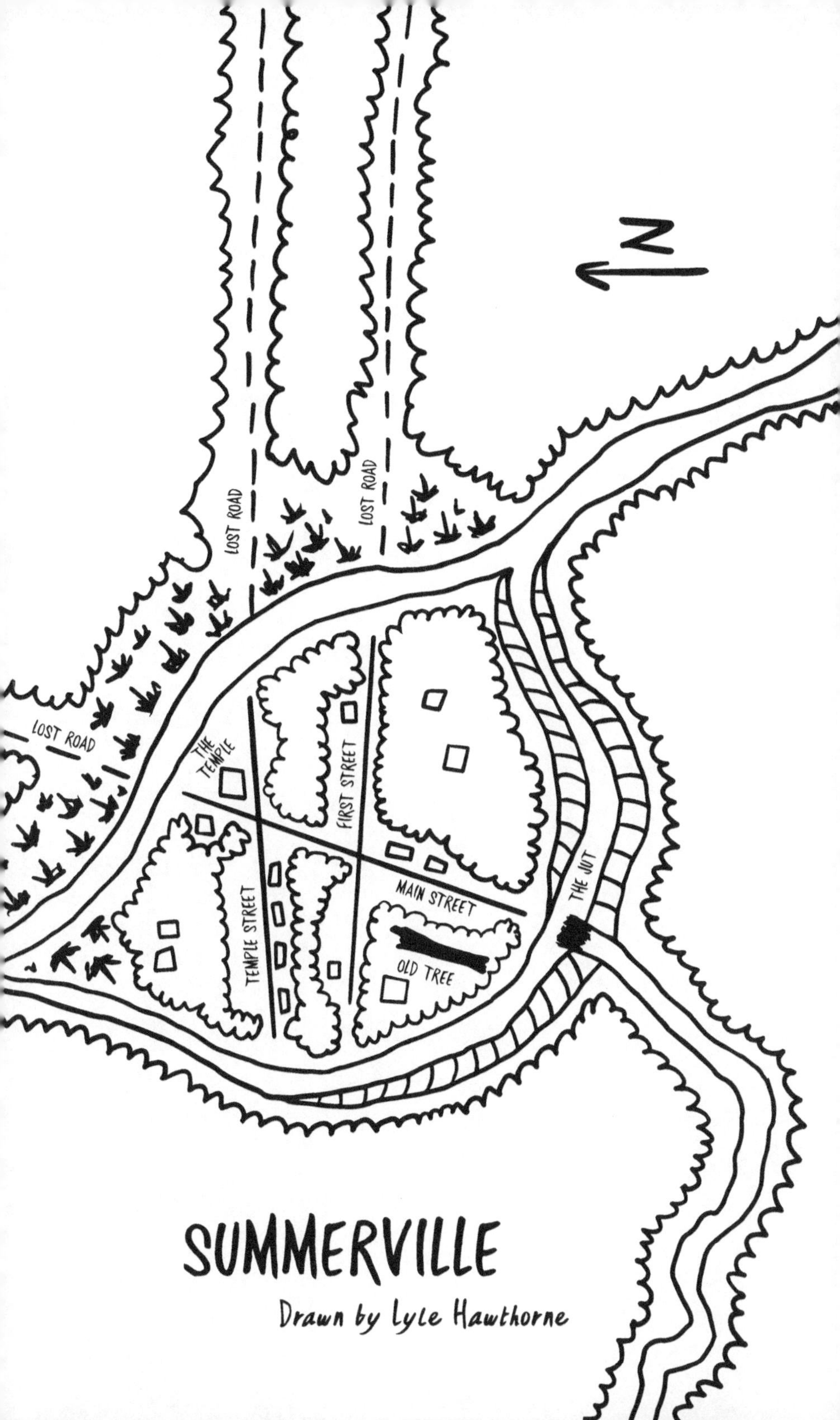

N
LOST ROAD
LOST ROAD
LOST ROAD
THE TEMPLE
FIRST STREET
TEMPLE STREET
MAIN STREET
OLD TREE
THE JUT
SUMMERVILLE
Drawn by Lyle Hawthorne

A NOTE ON THE TYPE

The text of this book is set in Minion Pro, an Adobe Original typeface designed by Robert Slimbach. The first version of Minion was released in 1990 and is inspired by classical, old style typefaces of the late Renaissance, a period of elegant, beautiful, and highly readable type designs. Minion Pro combines the aesthetic and functional qualities that make text type highly readable with the versatility of OpenType digital technology, yielding unprecedented flexibility and typographic control, whether for lengthy text or display settings.

Robert Slimbach, who joined Adobe in 1987, began working seriously on type and calligraphy four years earlier in the type drawing department of Autologic in Newbury Park, California. Since then, he has concentrated primarily on designing text faces for digital technology, drawing inspiration from classical sources. In 1991, he received the Prix Charles Peignot from Association Typographique Internationale for excellence in type design. Slimbach now directs Adobe's type design program.

Headings of this book are set in Rockwell, by Monotype. The original Rockwell was produced by the Inland typefoundry in 1910, which issued it as Litho Antique. American Type Founders revived the face in the 1920s, with Morris Fuller Benton cutting several new weights. The Monotype Corporation produced its version of Rockwell in 1934; unfortunately, some of the literature erroneously referred to it as Stymie Bold, thereby creating confusion that still exists today.

Composed by Clever Crow Consulting and Design
Pittsburgh Pennsylvania

ACKNOWLEDGMENTS

I would like to thank all of my readers, who offered their time, attention, and opinions to the writing and revision of this novel. I would also like to thank Christine Marie Scott of Clever Crow Consulting and Design in Pittsburgh for her wonderful cover art and her invaluable assistance with the layout of these pages.

ABOUT THE AUTHOR

Born in Missouri, growing up in Ohio, and settling in Chicago, Dave Neal has always written fiction, but only got really serious about it in the late 90s. He brings a strong Rust Belt perspective to his writing, a kind of "Northern Gothic" aesthetic reflective of his background.

Writing his first novel at 29, he then devoted time to his craft and worked on short stories, occupying a space between genre and literary fiction, with an emphasis on horror, science fiction, and fantasy. He has seen some of his short stories published in "Albedo 1," Ireland's premier magazine of speculative fiction, and he won second place in their Aeon Award in 2008 for his short story, "Aegis." He has lived in Chicago since 1993, and is a passionate fan of music, a student of pop culture, an avid photographer and bicycler, and enjoys cooking.

As D.T. Neal he has published seven novels, *Saamaanthaa*, *The Happening*, and *Norm*—collectively known as The Wolfshadow Trilogy—*Chosen, Suckage, Return to Summerville* and the cosmic folk horror-comedy thriller, *The Cursed Earth*. He has also published three novellas—*Relict, Summerville*, and *The Day of the Nightfish*, and two collections—*Singularities*, a collection of science fiction stories, and *The Thing in Yellow*, a collection of King in Yellow mythos-based stories.

He is also the co-editor of The Fiends in the Furrows folk horror anthologies: *The Fiends in the Furrows: An Anthology of Folk Horror*, *The Fiends in the Furrows II: More Tales of Folk Horror*, and *The Fiends in the Furrows III: Final Harvest*.

"**The king would be proud...**
Great collection of creepy, unsettled
stories. Well written, bleak, cruel
and unkind stories."
—Mr. E. C. Young, AMAZON review

"Survival & Ocean Horror combined,
this little novella certainly quenched my thirst.
This is the type of horror I love!
Being stranded somewhere, with some kind
of monstrosity hunting you down!
MORE, PLEASE!"
—Michelle {Book Hangovers}, GOODREADS review

N*P
NOSETOUCH PRESS

www.ingramcontent.com/pod-product-compliance
Lightning Source LLC
Chambersburg PA
CBHW061523210726
48287CB00006B/1804